LET'S DO LUNCH

BY
K.A. JORDAN

JAN 2 8 2015

F JOR
Let's do lunch / by K.A. Jordan.

33814001089692
ASHTABULA COUNTY DISTRICT LIBRARY

Published by K. A. Jordan, Create Space Edition

ISBN-10: 1-4637-0224-8

ISBN: 978-1-4637-0224-3

Copyright © 2010 by K. A. Jordan

All rights reserved.

This book may not be reproduced, scanned or distributed in any printed or electronic form without permission from the author. Digital copies are available from the author. Quotations for reviews are fine. Please do not contribute to piracy of copyrighted materials in violation of the author's rights.

Dedication

This book is dedicated to my husband, my parents and sister, my extended family and all my friends, near and far, past and present. So many people have helped me and given me encouragement, I am so grateful to all of you.

Special thanks to: Karen, Dale and Jeff, who read the rough draft for me and told the truth. To the people of Bard's Corner, Forward Motion, Authonomy and Romance Angels Network, may you all follow your dreams and make them come true.

Chapter 1

ELIZABETHTOWN, KENTUCKY – 2006

It was a misty May morning in Elizabethtown, Kentucky. Lindsey Bennett parked her truck in the lot beside the Civil War era bank that housed her restaurant. She juggled a coffee cup, new menus and her keys to get the door unlocked.

Once inside, the faint scent of cleaning products greeted her nose. She dumped everything on the nearest table. This was her favorite time, when the restaurant was so quiet she could hear the coolers hum, like sleepy bees.

She made coffee, looking around to see what she needed to do before she could start cooking. The answering machine light was blinking. She hit the button.

"Hi, Miz Lindsey." The voice was that of a young woman, the cook-in-training. "This isn't working out. I guess there is nothing else to say." That was the message from Sunday. There was a beep then she was back – giving Lindsey the address to send her last check.

Lindsey grimaced, feeling equal parts annoyance and relief. The girl couldn't cook pasta. Rose, her experienced cook, would be leaving soon. She needed a replacement.

Lindsey flipped open her cell phone to call the employment agency. She drummed her fingers on the table as she waited for the other side to pick up.

"Work Fair Employment, Roger speaking."

"Hello, this is Lindsey Bennett of 'Let's do Lunch' in E'town."

"Miss Bennett." His voice was deep with a southern accent. "How is that gal doing?"

"Fortunately for me, she quit," Lindsey said.

"Well, I'm sorry to hear that." Behind the country drawl was a note of contempt that always put her back up. "I've sent the most experienced people I've got."

"You're sending me stoners, bimbos and twits," Lindsey said between her teeth. "I could put an ad in the newspaper to get people from fast food. I need someone who can cook."

"Are you willing to pay for a chef to come from Louisville or Lexington?"

Lindsey was silent. He knew the limit of her salary range. He seemed to delight in playing dumb, making her look like a raving lunatic.

"Miss Bennett, experienced cooks don't grow on trees."

"Flipping burgers is not cooking."

"Why won't you give these young people a chance?"

"I need someone who can use a chef's knife without cutting themselves."

"Well, I've got one candidate that meets your criteria." His emphasis on 'criteria' gave it the connotation of 'unreasonable.' "He has one year experience as a nursing home cook, four years in the Army."

"Army cook," she sighed. The horror stories about Army food were part of her childhood. Still anyone with five years experience should know how to follow a recipe.

"Would you like to set up an appointment?"

"Get him in here today, around four."

"That's short notice."

"If he wants the job, he'll be here." Lindsey closed her cell phone with a snap. She wheeled a dolly to her truck. She stacked two coolers of just-picked produce on the dolly and wheeled it all inside.

Ah, well, her father had warned her that hiring would be the hardest part of owning a business. The best part was waiting for her. It was time to get chopping.

Lindsey surveyed the cramped kitchen with a critical eye to be sure everything was in place. The preparatory work was the key to good food. She peeled and chopped onions then ran carrots through the food processor, radishes and celery followed. She turned the radio to her favorite station, humming along as she worked. Just as she was taking the pot of potatoes off the stove, Lindsey heard a knock at the door. She looked over her shoulder. Rose had arrived. Lindsey wiped her hands as she hurried to the door.

"Morning," Lindsey sang out. "How are you?"

"The Lord has blessed me with a new day." Rose was Afro-American, heavy set and motherly, she wore her gray hair short and crisp. "Sometimes that's as good as it gets."

"That bad?"

"Oh, I swear, if it's not one of them children worrying me near to death, it is another one. This morning it was a ruckus between Kevin and his daddy. Kevin's Algebra teacher emailed that Kevin got an 'F' on a test. I should have known something was amiss. He's been too good."

"I'm sorry to hear that."

"I don't know what I'm going to do when school lets out." Rose's extended family kept her close to God. She attended church regularly, praying for her troubled family. "Even if I'm there, I can't lock him in his room. Teen-aged boys aren't house pets." She smiled at Lindsey. "Well, that's enough of my troubles."

"I was about to get started on the lettuce." Lindsey opened one of the coolers, lifted out plastic baskets of produce. She started rinsing; the lettuce was beautiful, spiky red, deep green romaine, sweet butter crunch still as fresh smelling, crisp and dewy as when they'd picked it, just hours ago.

"I'll get busy." Rose walked to the fridge, humming along to the radio. They tore spinach and lettuce into a bowl set in ice, peeled new potatoes and chopped them into potato salad. By ten o'clock they were ready, the meats sliced and salads chilling. Lindsey and Rose sat down in the dining room to have coffee.

"Here's Mom and Heather." Lindsey rose to let them in.

Lindsey's younger sister, Heather, followed Eleanor, their mother. The resemblance was strong. Heather was a taller and more slender, version of their mother, all three with dark hair, high cheekbones. Eleanor and Heather had green eyes while Lindsey's were hazel.

Heather held a harvest basket overflowing with white and lavender lilac blossoms. The heady scent wafted through the room.

"Good God what a morning," Heather greeted them. "Travis missed the bus again. School's almost over, why can't he keep it together for a couple weeks?"

"I shall refrain from saying 'boys will be boys' since you weren't much different at that age." Eleanor smiled.

"I was never like that," Heather denied. "Girls are easier to raise than boys."

"Raising children is harder now than ever." Rose shook her head. "Wait until he's a teenager like my grandson Kevin. The high schools are filled with gangs and drugs."

"If his father was alive, he would keep Travis in line." Heather grumbled walking to the sink in the back.

Lindsey exchanged a 'there-she-goes-again' look with Rose as she went back to cooking. Heather held on to her late husband the way a miser held onto gold. Lindsey suspected that the Richard Morgan enshrined in her sister's heart bore little resemblance to the man Heather married.

Eleanor got the vases for the flowers from the cast iron bank vault. It was the biggest storage area in the tiny restaurant. Heather emerged from the kitchen with a pitcher of water. Heather sat at the table with Eleanor to fill the vases with water and flowers.

The phone started to ring at around ten with carryout orders. Eleanor switched on the open sign. A couple of customers came in. The lunch rush was on. Sometime in the middle of the rush, Lindsey heard a bright, tinkling giggle. She turned to see her sister waiting on a bearded man.

"So what does a guy have to do to get a plate of fried chicken and French fries in this place?" His dark blond hair was pulled back, a reddish beard and mustache hid most of his face. He wore an Army T-shirt tucked into old jeans.

"Order from another restaurant and have it delivered. We don't serve fried food."

"You call this a menu?" he teased. "All I see is sissy food."

"This is not a greasy spoon," Heather chided. "Denny's is by the interstate."

"Health food in E'town? This is Kentucky, girl. Even steak is breaded and fried."

"Honey, if you don't like our pasta salad, I'll take you to McDonalds and buy you a Big Mac." Heather giggled.

"That's a deal!" He winked at Heather. "I'll take a club sandwich, too. Just don't serve me a little bitty sandwich, or you'll owe me that Big Mac."

"What was that about?" Lindsey asked as Heather came back behind the counter.

"He's giving me a hard time." Heather rolled her eyes. Waitress-baiting was a national pass-time; a good waitress took advantage of it.

"So what did he order?" Lindsey took the ticket with a grin.

"A super-club sandwich and pasta salad, make it good, or I'll owe him a Big Mac."

"Can't have that." Lindsey stacked the sandwich high, then squirted a smiley face on the top of a slice of tomato with mayonnaise. They giggled together before Lindsey started the next order.

A few minutes later, Lindsey saw him at the register, paying Heather for his meal.

"Well, do I owe you a Big Mac?" Heather grinned at him.

"No ma'am, it was very good." He looked over at Lindsey. "I take back everything I said about sissy food." He held Lindsey's gaze for a moment then tipped a finger towards one eyebrow in a mock salute. Lindsey smiled back and waved.

Lindsey made sandwiches and dished out various salads, sprinkled bacon bits or sunflower seeds, croutons or pretzel buttons. By the time the rush was over, shortly after two, Lindsey and Rose were dragging, the gallons of pasta salad were gone and they all were in dire need of a break.

Lindsey shooed Rose out of the kitchen then grabbed cups of coffee for both of them. Everyone was glad they didn't stay open for dinner. After the short break, they were on cleanup detail. Heather counted the little notebook pages, ninety-five meals served total, 40 take out orders, a typical Monday. They pooled the tips between them so everyone had some pocket money.

"Well ladies, another great day," Lindsey congratulated them. "We've got a heck of a team here."

"Did you ever hear from the agency about the cook?" Eleanor asked with a frown.

"I'm interviewing a cook today," Lindsey announced. Rose and Eleanor looked pleased.

"Tell me you found someone who knows how to cook," Heather said.

"Your father needs help in the garden, too," Eleanor said. "He was just talking about it this morning."

"Dad has to find someone. I hope he has an easier time of it. Help is hard to find."

"I hate to leave but I need to keep that grandson of mine on the straight and narrow. If I can just keep him out of trouble this summer, his daddy and I might make something of him yet." Rose sighed. "Wish I could have kept my daughters out of trouble. I was working two jobs just to keep the roof over our heads in those days." Rose was determined to save her grandson from the drug scene that had the boy's mother and two aunts in and out of jails and rehabs. "I'll see you all tomorrow, God willing."

Eleanor locked the door behind Rose then went to the old register, to cash out for the day. The machine printed in a monotonous whir, whir, whir, while Eleanor counted the drawer to make out the deposit. Lindsey went back to the kitchen to finish the last of the dishes while Heather cleaned the dining area. With just six tables, it was important to keep everything tidy.

After they left, Lindsey did some detailed clean up as she waited for the interview. The building was quiet, so quiet that she could hear the coolers humming. Lindsey looked around with a satisfied sigh. She never got tired of being here, never lost the thrill of having her own little Queendom.

A dark-haired man in kaki-colored Dockers and a green polo shirt knocked at the door. Lindsey opened the door for him.

"Hi, good to meet you, I'm Brandon Pendleton." He was handsome, with dark brown hair, faintly sun-streaked and curly. He looked to be twenty-something, with a narrow jaw, a straight nose and a mobile mouth. He gave her a high wattage smile.

"Lindsey Bennett." She was conscious of her disheveled state, as she shook his hand. "Please have a seat." The application and the pen were already on the table. "Could you fill out the application for me, please? Can I get you some ice tea?"

"Sure, sweet tea is fine." He sat down, turned to watch her with one arm draped over the back of the bench.

Lindsey retreated behind the counter to get glasses. She took a deep breath as she poured two glasses of sweet tea. She was grateful that her mother wasn't here to probe his prospects as a potential son-in-law.

What would her father do? The Colonel wouldn't allow a pretty face to distract him.

That thought steadied her. This wasn't a date. Pendleton was a prospective employee. She needed a cook, not a boy-toy. Still she couldn't help glancing at her reflection in the cooler's glass door.

"Get a grip," she mouthed silently at her ghostly reflection.

"Let me know when you are ready." She set his tea on the table, then went back to cleaning behind the counter.

"I'm set," he said a couple of minutes later. Lindsey slid into the seat across from him. She took the simple application from him, looking it over for a moment. He'd left the nursing home a month ago. He'd been in the Army two years before that. There was a year unaccounted for, but she'd seen worse.

"Let me tell you a little bit about the restaurant, because what I do here is different from most places." Lindsey hoped that she wasn't wasting her breath. "We keep to foods that are wholesome: nothing fried in fat or doused with gravy."

"Way cool." Brandon grinned. "Completely opposite most restaurants."

"I think of it as 'slow food' instead of 'fast food'. My family grows most of the produce on our farm. It isn't organic, but it is close." Lindsey took a sip of tea.

"Who wants poison sprayed on their food?"

"Exactly, with most food you never know what's in it, on it, or how old it is. This way we know the vegetables are fresh, because I bring them to work with me every morning."

"Grow it on the farm and sell it at the restaurant." Brandon nodded. "You must make a lot of money by cutting out the middle man." He saluted her with the glass of tea. "That's an impressive business plan."

His eyes said he admired more than just her business plan.

"Thank you." Lindsey was flattered, and a bit flustered.

"You have the perfect location for this type of restaurant. The County Government offices are right across the square." Brandon gave her a mischievous smile. "All the old fogies must love this place."

"Those *are* my best customers."

"You know, my experience in the nursing home ties in perfectly. I learned a lot about special diets and menus while I was there."

"How long were you there?"

"A year." He tipped his hand back and forth. "More or less." His mobile mouth made a sour expression.

"Why did you leave?"

"I had a difference of opinion with the manager." He shifted backwards, to lean against the seat. "Which looks like it was a good thing for me in the long run." Brandon raised one wing-shaped eyebrow at her, an outright come-on.

Taken by surprise; Lindsey cleared her throat, she'd never had a prospective employee flirt so blatantly with her. What had she been about to ask him? Her whole line of questioning was gone from her head. She looked at the application again.

"Where did you get your original training?"

"Fort Lee, Virginia." Brandon gave her a cocky grin. "They tossed me into the program like a football. Sink or swim, it was crazy. I cooked all morning, soldiered in the afternoon, and partied all night."

Army training wasn't like that. Lindsey raised an eyebrow, warning him to stop talking smack.

"Once basic training was over." He caught her disapproval, becoming business-like again. "I learned to follow recipes, how to adjust for the number of servings, I can do that math in my head in ounces or metric."

"Where were you stationed?"

"All over, I swear I hit every backwater post between here and Afghanistan." Brandon shook his head. "I was in 'Stan for two years. Now I'm going to make that training pay off." He sounded sincere. "So what kind of hours do you keep here?"

"I get in before eight to get everything ready. The rest of the crew comes in around nine. We open for business at ten, and generally everything is done by three." Lindsey played her trump card. "We have weekends off."

"No nights, no weekends?" Brandon sat back in his chair, looking very surprised. "No shit? I mean that's great! Sign me up!"

Lindsey smiled at his enthusiastic response.

"Why aren't you open for three meals?" He asked, drawing his eyebrows together. "Your menu is geared to an older crowd; you could be missing out on a lot of money."

"The last owner tried serving three traditional meals, but he went bankrupt." Lindsey shrugged. "Someday I may give breakfast a try. But now is not the time."

"Maybe what you need is a good waitress to bring in a crowd."

"My mother and sister wait tables for me." She gestured at the small space, six booths and six seats at the counter. "It doesn't take that many people to run this place."

She quizzed him about cooking. As she had expected, he knew the basics, nothing fancy, but enough to tell her that he was a trained cook, not an over-confident burger-boy.

She stood to indicate the interview was over. He stood too; they walked to the door.

"It was a pleasure to meet you," he said in a deep sexy voice.

Lindsey locked the door behind her. She watched him drive off in a glittering, blood red Pontiac Grand AM. He was the 'give them an inch and they'll take a mile' type. Her ex-boyfriend Tommy was cut from the same cloth.

Lindsey heaved a sigh.

Just out of college, Lindsey had landed the job at a big insurance company call center. She met Tommy her first day. He was the opposite of every military man she'd ever met: soft featured and disorganized. Casual flirtation escalated until they were living together, but they ended up on different shifts. The relationship floundered along, until 9/11 when Heather's husband was killed at the Pentagon. Tommy's outrageous behavior that day was the final straw.

She didn't want to think about the past, her day wasn't over yet.

When Lindsey got home, the family sat down at a big glass-topped table under the pergola where an ancient wisteria sent out tendrils of flower buds.

"So, tell us all about him," Eleanor quizzed her.

"The most important question: is he good looking?" Heather giggled.

"Oh, well enough, if you like 'em tall, dark and handsome." Lindsey teased her sister.

Heather sat back and fanned herself.

"He was trained by the Army."

"You don't want him." Jim snorted. "That's the worst food on the planet!"

There was laughter all around.

"I've got good news, too. I found someone to help in the garden. He's a veteran, back from Iraq, with lots of time on his hands."

"That's terrific." Lindsey smiled. "Maybe I'll get to sleep in until – oh six o'clock or so."

"Don't count on it." Heather joked. "Dad doesn't like slackers." They all laughed again.

The next day Lindsey called the nursing home to check Brandon's references. The Human Resources department would only verify the date of his employment. Frustrated, Lindsey looked at his application. Everything seemed in order.

Lindsey called Brandon to offer him the job.

"Hello?" Music and loud voices in the background drowned out Brandon's voice.

"Brandon, its Lindsey at 'Let's Do Lunch'."

"Hang on a second, I can't hear you." Brandon was silent a moment, then the noise faded. When he came back his voice dropped to a sexy growl. "Hey Lindsey. What's your pleasure?"

Lindsey rolled her eyes.

"I called to see if you would like to come to work for me?"

"Oh yeah, I sure would. When do I start?"

"Can you come in Monday morning at eight?"

"I'll be there." His voice dropped again. "I can hardly wait."

Lindsey hung up the phone before she allowed herself to laugh. This was going to be interesting.

Chapter 2

Monday, the family harvested produce then sat down to breakfast under a pergola. The sturdy structure supported an old wisteria that was just sending out shoots.

"I want to make some changes," Jim announced. "I want to experiment with something."

"What did you have in mind?" Lindsey paused between sips of coffee.

"Heirloom tomatoes," he said. "They have the most intriguing names: Mortgage Lifter, Cherokee Purple, all thought extinct until a few years ago. The problem is I can't find any."

"Have you looked them up over the Internet?" Lindsey asked.

"I wouldn't touch one of those infernal machines." Jim stabbed his eggs.

"It's dead easy, Papaw." Travis piped up. "I could do it."

"That's a great idea," Lindsey said to encourage them.

"Okay, sport." Jim smiled at Travis. "We'll give it a shot."

"I'll get on it." Travis bounced up from the table.

"Oh, that's a no go!" Heather stopped him. "The school bus comes in half an hour."

"Okay." Travis slanted a glance at his mother. "I'll look it up at school and email the sites here."

"Have you got all your homework done?" Heather frowned.

"I have plenty of library time." Travis turned back to Jim. "If you make me a list, I'll look up sources for all the vegetables you want."

"You get ready. I'll make the list," Jim promised.

Travis bounced away, a big smile on his face. Jim grinned as he wrote out the list. Lindsey bit her lip to stop from chuckling aloud.

Later Lindsey pulled up to her restaurant and parked her truck. As she was getting ready to unload coolers, Brandon arrived in his red Grand AM, the stereo blasting.

Lindsey wondered how he could afford the expensive car on a cook's wages.

After they hauled the coolers in, Lindsey showed him where to find everything. Brandon shelled peas while Lindsey explained the menu. When the other's started coming in, Lindsey made introductions.

"Brandon, this is my mother, Eleanor."

"I see where Lindsey inherited her beauty."

"Flattery will get you nowhere." Eleanor winked at him. "But keep talking."

Brandon smiled a little wider but his cell rang, distracting him. He gave Lindsey a sheepish smile as he pulled it out of his pocket.

"Excuse me," he said turning away.

Eleanor raised her eyebrows. Lindsey let it ride since he was off the phone in a moment.

Heather came in, dressed in Capri length jeans and a white shirt. She had her hair up in a clip; the style showed off her face. She wore just enough makeup to enhance her cheekbones. Lindsey wondered if Heather was ready to start dating again.

"I can't believe Travis missed the bus again!" Heather complained. "Honestly mother, I don't know what to do with that child. I shouldn't have to play father as well as mother."

"Heather, this is Brandon." Lindsey watched Brandon's face. When Heather smiled and shook his hand, Brandon looked thunderstruck. Lindsey's jealously of her sister flared up. Men fell for Heather like ripe apples fell off trees.

"Hello beautiful babe," he said in his sexy growl.

"Don't call me 'babe.'" Heather gave him a quelling look. "I have a name. It's Heather. Use it."

Lindsey winced, so much for that. Brandon's cheeks were red, his mouth twisted to one side as if he had bitten something sour.

"Is there any fresh coffee?" Heather looked at Lindsey, ignoring Brandon.

Lindsey waved towards the coffeepot, shooting a disapproving look at Heather. Why had Heather chosen today to cop an attitude? Heather rolled her eyes, mouthing her assessment of Brandon. "Gag me."

"She's in a bad mood," Lindsey said softly. "Sorry about that."

"Not your fault." His brown eyes were hooded. "You can't choose your relatives."

"Isn't that the truth?" Lindsey sighed. Heather was usually all too happy to banter and flirt.

Unlike Heather, Rose took to Brandon.

Brandon knew his way around a kitchen. The constant ringing of his cell phone annoyed everyone. Lindsey made him put it on silent. It was crowded behind the counter with five people, but they managed.

The rest of the week passed the same. Brandon flirted as he worked, never missing a beat. He smoked too much, and his cell phone buzzed constantly. However, he was willing and able to take on any task that Lindsey gave him.

Lindsey decided that she was right to hire him after all.

"Morning boss." Brandon greeted her as he walked in the door.

"Morning." Lindsey looked up from her prep work. "How are you?"

"Fine as frog hair." Brandon affected a country drawl. "What's on the menu today?"

"The usual."

"Nothing new?"

"We're getting ready to plant the basil tonight. The adventures begin when we harvest the basil."

"I can't wait." Brandon's sly smile was capped with a twitch of an eyebrow. He filled the big stockpot then lifted it with a flex of bulging biceps. Everything about Brandon attracted a woman's attention: the sexy growl, the 'come-on' smiles, the strategically placed barbed wire tattoo on his biceps, the car, and the hint of 5 o'clock shadow on his jaw. Even the way he kept a couple extra buttons on his shirt undone to show off a thick gold chain.

The first few days of the heavy-handed come-ons had left her blushing. After a week, Lindsey was able to take it all in stride. Brandon was an equal-opportunity flirt. Luckily, his cooking was better than his 'charm.'

To give him credit, Brandon was a hard worker. He picked up the pasta salad recipe and sautéed the vegetable medley to perfection, tender and crisp. Cooking was effortless for him – a trait Lindsey admired much more than his Don Juan attitude.

Everything was ready by the time Heather and Eleanor arrived. While Eleanor took phone orders, Brandon and Rose cooked orders. While

Heather worked the dining room, Lindsey bussed the tables. By 2 o'clock, everything wound down.

Lindsey arrived home, changed into garden clothes then went to the garden to transplant ten flats of basil seedlings. Jim was running the rototiller while Eleanor popped the little plants out of their plastic six packs. Lindsey made holes with a bulb-setting tool, inserting the plants under the string in long straight rows. Heather and Travis watered the little plants, setting the roots.

Basil was the main ingredient in pesto, a flavoring that Lindsey used by the quart all summer. The basic recipe was olive oil, garlic, basil, cilantro, pine nuts and hard Parmesan cheese. By planting all the main ingredients, basil, garlic and cilantro, she could make a gallon for a fraction of the purchase price and have an infinite number of variations by using pecans, walnuts, sage, flavored basil, different herbs or even different types of cheese.

Lindsey was mentally creating menus, when she heard her mother cry out behind her. "Mom, are you okay?"

Eleanor was on the ground, clutching her ankle, rocking and moaning.

"What happened?" Heather was there in an instant.

Jim cut the tiller motor then was beside the girls as they knelt by Eleanor's side.

"It popped." Eleanor's eyes were squeezed shut, with tears caught in the lashes.

"Can you stand?"

"No!" She shook her head, clutching her ankle.

Jim worked the shoe off, careful not to jar her ankle. The flesh was puffy and swelling.

"I'll get some ice." Heather bolted for the house, Travis jogging behind her.

"How bad is it?" Jim said. "Can you move it?" Experimentally flexing, Eleanor stiffened, shaking her head.

"No, I can't move it, it hurts too much."

"Lindsey, get the car," Jim ordered.

When Heather and Lindsey came back, the three of them helped Eleanor into the car. While Eleanor held ice wrapped in a towel to her ankle, Jim drove them to the hospital emergency room on Fort Knox. Hours later a gloomy doctor informed them that Eleanor had broken two bones in her ankle.

"You have to understand," the doctor said as he was applying the cast. "Someone in their teens or twenties would heal in four to six weeks." He turned to Eleanor. "If you have osteoporosis, it complicates everything."

"Osteoporosis?" Jim's face was grim. "How would we know?"

"It will show up in the healing process," the doctor explained. "You're looking at twelve to sixteen weeks. With osteoporosis, we could be looking at six months or more."

There was stunned silence.

"Six months?" Eleanor looked at the doctor, disbelief written on her face. "Nonsense."

Jim smiled at her, giving her a wink. Lindsey and Heather exchanged a nervous look.

The ride home was very quiet.

Lindsey fidgeted, never once had she considered how her parent's aging would affect their health. If her mother's bones were brittle – how could she stand being cooped up for months? How would they take care of her?

Next to her, Heather stared out the window, a million miles away. Would Heather be able to help, or would Lindsey have to worry about her, too?

The next morning, harvesting vegetables in the garden, Lindsey's father looked exhausted. He hadn't even shaved.

"How is Mom?"

"She fell on her way to the bathroom." Jim tossed a handful of peas into a basket. "She couldn't keep the pills down." He sighed, rubbing the back of his neck. "There has to be something else they can give her."

"You should get her back to the doctor."

"I don't want her left alone today." Jim looked at Lindsey. "Could you stay with her?"

There was a pregnant silence.

"Ask Heather, I can't leave the restaurant."

"Heather's too moody." He gave Lindsey a one-sided smile. "Don't worry; your mother will get better in no time."

"Six months is a long time."

"The doctor was pessimistic, in case there were problems later." Jim shrugged it off. "I'm worried about her reaction to the medication."

"All the more reason to get her to the doctor," Lindsey said.

"This needs to be planted." He waved his hand across the unplanted sections of garden. "Where am I going to get time to sit in a waiting room?"

"Hire someone to help you." Lindsey's shoulders knotted, the fate of the restaurant hinged on the garden. "What about that guy?"

"He's a disabled vet, with a lot of time on his hands." Jim picked up an empty basket. "He would have to put in a lot of hours."

"Feed him," Lindsey joked. "You'll have to shove him out the door."

"That's a good idea." Jim grinned at her.

When Lindsey pulled up to her restaurant, Brandon was there – the Grand AM was polished to a glittering shine from the sunroof to the chrome wheels. Rap music played, the bass beat blasted like tank fire, boom, boom, boom until Brandon cut the engine. He stepped out, looking tanned, polished and professional in his pressed pants and restaurant whites; his dark, curly hair tousled.

Lindsey's breath caught in her throat.

Then he ruined it by checking his reflection in the glass.

Lindsey rolled her eyes.

They hauled the coolers inside. Brandon shelled peas while Lindsey snapped asparagus. She ran down the menu for the special of the day, so he would know what they were going to cook. While they were working, she told him about her mother's injury.

"She seemed to be in such good health, too." Brandon's voice was low and sorrowful. "I'm really sorry, Lindsey."

"What?" Lindsey recoiled. "You make it sound like she's dying."

"You never know. I saw it happen all the time. It started with a fall, a bruise or a broken bone, next thing you know it's blood clots, stroke, dementia and then they're gone." His eyebrows were drawn together, his brown eyes were sad. "You know that you can count on me in case the worst happens, right?"

"She'll be fine." Lindsey's throat started to close. She fought it off.

"Sure." He patted her shoulder with a damp hand. "Sure, she'll be fine."

Lindsey pulled herself together then grabbed another basket of asparagus. Work was the answer for worry.

"We're going to braise this asparagus in broth, serve it with herbs and pasta." Snapping asparagus, she explained. "The flavors should sparkle."

"Do you have some meat to use as a garnish? Maybe some smoked turkey?"

"Hmm, that's a thought." Lindsey paused. "That would work with chicken stock." She gave Brandon a smile of approval; she'd been right to hire him.

The doorbells chimed, Heather came in, her dark hair back in a clip, long gold earrings framing her face. Her green eyes were stark; she looked worried.

"Mom fell out of bed last night. Her face is all bruised."

Brandon gave Lindsey an 'I-told-you-so' look. Heather caught the exchange.

"What?" Heather demanded looking from one to another. "What's wrong?"

"I was just telling Lindsey about the ladies at the nursing home."

Lindsey glared at him. How many times had her mother warned: 'don't upset your sister?' Maybe she should have told Brandon how her sister over-reacted to bad news.

"I guess I shouldn't say anything," Brandon mumbled.

"Lindsey?" Heather's eyes went wide with panic.

"I talked to Dad this morning." Lindsey soothed. "I'm sure he can handle it."

"He called the hospital. The appointment isn't for days." Heather's voice was thin and shrill. "Those doctors don't care. We were at the ER for hours before they looked at her."

"A lady in the nursing home broke her leg, laid in an emergency room for eight hours before she saw a doctor," Brandon said mournfully. "She never got over it."

Lindsey wanted to kick him.

"Dad has work to do; somebody should be there with her." As she had done since Rich died, Heather turned to Lindsey. "We can't leave her alone. Hire a nurse for her."

"We can't afford a nurse. Dad will be in and out of the house. Mom will be fine." Guilt gnawed at her. What if Heather was right?

"Did Dad tell you that she fell out of bed?"

"Yes. He asked me to stay with her, but I need to be here."

"Is this place all you care about?" Heather's eyes were shiny. "We have one mother you should care about *her*."

"I *care*." Lindsey's eyes started to sting. "But I can't be two places at once."

"You should be home with Mom."

"I can't leave!" Lindsey set the chef's knife down, controlling her temper with an effort.

"If you really loved Mom you would be home with her!" Tears ran down Heather's face.

"You can't run this restaurant!"

"Why not?" Heather sniffed, wiping her eyes. "Rose and Brandon will help."

"I've got orders to call in." Lindsey served up her excuses. "I've got to order food, beverages, cleaning supplies – I've got to do the books, the taxes and the payroll. You can't do all that."

"I can do the ordering." Brandon grinned. "I used to do it at the nursing home."

"See?" Heather turned from Brandon to Lindsey. "Please Lindsey; it's just for one day."

"Okay, I'll go." Lindsey swallowed a big chunk of her pride. The restaurant would be okay for one day.

"Thank you." Heather wiped her eyes. "I have to pick Travis up after school. Is it okay if Brandon locks up?"

"Fine. Give your key to Brandon." Lindsey was not sure she was doing the right thing for the restaurant, but she *was* positive that her mother needed her. They rushed through the rest of the prep work.

Lindsey made Heather swear that she would call it she couldn't handle it.

Chapter 3

When Lindsey arrived at her sister's house, she found her mother in the bathroom, violently ill. Lindsey managed to get her mother settled back in bed, with a bucket next to her. Eleanor lay back on the pillows with a sigh.

"Mom, I think we should get you back to the hospital."

"Absolutely not, my head is pounding. I'm not moving an inch."

"But Mom…"

"Lindsey." Eleanor opened her eyes to glare at her daughter. "No is a complete sentence. Let me be."

There was no arguing with that tone of voice.

Lindsey tried to get in touch with the doctor. She was on hold so long that all three cordless phones went dead. Her cell phone was low on power, too. She gave the nurse her cell number before the connection was broken. Swearing under her breath, she put all three phones on their chargers. Didn't anybody ever charge the phones in this house?

Her father came in around noon.

"You changed your mind." He gave her a light kiss on the cheek. "Good."

"I was just in the way," she quipped.

He gave her a measuring look.

"What do you want for lunch?" Lindsey hid in the refrigerator.

Lindsey spent the rest of the afternoon waiting for the phone to ring. She checked on her mother every few minutes. The stress put her on a cleaning jag. The house was spotless when Heather got home. Lindsey had a monster headache.

"How did it go?"

"It was a madhouse, I counted a hundred orders." Heather collapsed at the table. "Brandon knows a waitress. She's coming in tomorrow." She gave Lindsey the deposit slip and the register tape. "How is Mom?"

"She's out cold." Lindsey rubbed the back of her neck. "She wouldn't eat."

"Why didn't you take her to the hospital?"

"She refused to go."

"Did you call the doctor?"

"I called the doctor," Lindsey snorted. "Every stupid phone in the house went dead. Don't you ever charge them?"

"Travis runs off with them." Heather countered. "Did you leave a number?"

"Of course! Nobody called back."

"Well, I had a whole day of nursing home horror stories." Heather shuddered. "Is Brandon right? Is it that serious?"

The two sisters looked at each other, neither one spoke for a moment.

"She goes back in tomorrow; I'll talk to the doctor."

"I'll sit with her." Heather collapsed into the chair by Eleanor's bed.

Lindsey checked the cash receipts. It was short twenty dollars. She counted four times. There was no receipt. Lindsey peeked in on Heather and her mother again.

"Heather, the bag is short twenty dollars."

Heather looked so tired and sad Lindsey felt guilty for bringing it up.

"I needed gas money." Heather shrugged. "It's not a big deal."

"Put in a slip next time so I know where it went," Lindsey suggested. "Otherwise my deposit is off."

"Whatever."

Heather stayed in the bedroom with Eleanor while Lindsey made dinner. Jim dragged in late for the meal. Travis bounced in behind him, wearing stained and dirty school clothes.

"Travis, go change before your mother sees you like that," Lindsey scolded. The boy shot a glance toward the bedroom then scooted upstairs.

"I've got to get some help." Jim washed his hands in the kitchen sink. "I can't do this alone. I'm going to call McTaggart tonight." He paused, his voice dropped. "Thank you for staying with your Mother."

"No problem."

"I want you to take her in to the hospital tomorrow."

"I – I don't know." Lindsey glanced at the bedroom door. "What about Heather?"

"Heather, run the restaurant tomorrow." Jim stepped into the bedroom. "Lindsey is taking your mother to the doctor."

"Yes, Dad."

Lindsey gritted her teeth; their father was the least tactful person on earth.

Lindsey felt torn in two. She wanted to help her mother, but Heather didn't know anything about running the restaurant. She ate dinner with a heavy heart; it sat like lead in her stomach. She couldn't be in two places at once.

It wasn't fair!

Lindsey tossed and turned all night worrying first about her mother, then about her father. Jim was a Vietnam veteran who suffered with Post-Traumatic Stress Disorder. When under stress he wouldn't sleep for days but be edgy and irritable, often flying into uncontrollable fits of rage or drinking himself senseless.

Which would it be this time?

In the garden the next morning, he was unshaven and haggard. Lindsey tried to talk to him, but he would not be drawn out. How would she cope if he went off the deep end?

They finished the harvest. In the house they found Heather throwing a fit at Travis, holding up the stained school clothes he had worn the day before.

"Richard Travis Morgan," Heather scolded. "How many times have I told you to change your clothes when you come home from school?"

"Sorry." Travis hung his head.

"What am I going to do with you?" Heather threw up her hands. "Your father would have a fit if he were here, you know that don't you?"

"Well, he isn't here," Travis shot back. "Stop talking about him like he's coming back."

There was silence.

Lindsey winced, truth from the mouths of babes.

"Get ready for school, now." Heather walked upstairs, throwing a parting shot at Travis. "If you miss the bus you're going to walk!"

Travis had a mulish set to his mouth, but a stern glance from his grandfather sent him scurrying.

At the hospital, Lindsey and Eleanor spent the day waiting – for the doctor, tests, x-rays, results, the doctor then the hospital pharmacy. Eleanor's face was bruised from hairline to cheekbone. By the time they got the test results, she looked shriveled and frail.

"Your blood pressure is dangerously high. A clot could form in your legs, be carried to your lungs or your brain. If you feel any burning pain, in your legs, chest or head, come in immediately," the doctor said to Eleanor. "I'm putting you on blood pressure medication to get this under control."

"Will that make me sick, too?"

"What is making you sick?"

"The pain medication," Eleanor said.

The doctor checked the chart, but shook his head.

"Anything else would be less effective."

"I can't eat!"

"I'll give you another prescription to help with the nausea."

Eleanor just looked at him. Lindsey wanted to groan aloud. More pills? Another agonizing wait at the pharmacy? Great.

Back at the house, the day's receipts were on the table, so Heather must be somewhere. Lindsey started supper. While supper cooked, she did a quick count of the day's receipts. The cash was short one hundred sixty-four dollars and some change.

Good grief, what happened? Lindsey counted again then pushed herself away from the table. She got up to check the calendar. Beverage order – had to be the beverage order! Where was the invoice? Drat it! Why couldn't Heather keep track of the simplest things? It didn't take any effort to put the stupid invoice in the bag!

She banged around the kitchen, venting her frustration on pots and pans. Heather stuck her head out of the bedroom.

"What is wrong with you?"

"Oh, gee, let me think," Lindsey snarled. "Maybe having a hundred and sixty dollars missing?"

"The soda guy came in." Heather glanced back in the bedroom.

"Mom is out cold." Lindsey still dropped her voice. "So where is the invoice?"

"It's not in the bag?"

"No, it isn't."

"Then it's in the cash drawer." Heather crossed her arms over her chest. "I don't see what the big deal is."

"You wouldn't."

"I'm doing my best here."

"Well, try harder." Lindsey took a breath to really lay into her sister. However, her father walked in through the patio. The sisters glared at each other. Jim walked into the kitchen where he started to wash up.

"How did it go at the hospital?"

"Mom's blood pressure was way up today, the doctor put her on medication for it." Lindsey swallowed. "He's worried that Mom could have a stroke."

"Stroke?" Jim's face was lined and grave.

"Yeah." Lindsey wanted to reassure them, but she couldn't.

"Brandon wasn't lying," Heather noted bitterly. "Imagine that."

Sunday Lindsey was cleaning the restaurant when her cell phone rang.

"Mom fainted." Heather was crying. "We're on our way to Ireland hospital, now."

"I'll be right there."

Eleanor was rushed inside. Heather and Travis waited for Lindsey. Travis wouldn't sit still. He was up and down, fidgeting until Heather snapped at him. He then drummed his heels against the chair, sulking.

Lindsey went to the cubby where her father sat, his back stiff and his hands clenched. She knew hospitals brought back bad memories. She could spare him the stress of waiting.

"Travis is acting up. If you take them home, I'll stay with Mom."

"I'll be fine," said Eleanor who was hooked up to an IV. "Go ahead."

Jim nodded then kissed Eleanor.

Eleanor dozed while they waited for the test results. A doctor Lindsey hadn't met before came with the diagnosis in the late afternoon.

"You're dehydrated. You need fluids."

"I'm too nauseous to drink."

"You've got to keep your strength up."

"I can't keep anything down." Eleanor protested. "I can't even eat."

"Try liquid meal replacements." The slightest hint of a smile crossed his face as he turned to Lindsey. "You can get them anywhere."

"See to it that she gets plenty of electrolytes. I'll give you a list before you leave. Stay away from sports drinks. They contain too much sugar. She needs to drink at least four glasses a day. The meal replacement shakes will make three more. Make sure she gets a couple glasses of water too. Fluids will help bring her blood pressure down."

"Bring her back tomorrow. We need to check her blood pressure, make sure the medication is working." The doctor handed Lindsey some paper work.

After a stop at the store for meal replacements, Lindsey drove back to the house in better spirits. Surely she could go back to work in the morning!

Her hopes were dashed when she reported to her father.

"I can't take her; I have a meeting at the Extension office." Jim rubbed his face. "You'll have to go."

"But Dad…" Lindsey protested.

He gave her 'the look.' This wasn't a request, but an order.

"What about Travis?" Heather protested. "He can't be trusted to catch the school bus."

"Leave Travis to me," Jim said with a glint of humor in his eyes. "After thirty years in the Army, I can handle a ten-year-old."

Eleanor's blood pressure was still high. The doctor ordered more tests. Lindsey had the foresight to bring her laptop to work on her books and the payroll. However, a day at a makeshift desk in a waiting room wasn't enough. She needed the invoices to balance the books. Out of desperation, Lindsey called the restaurant.

"Hey, boss lady." Brandon answered, cheerfully. "How are you?"

"I'm at the hospital with my mother."

"Oh, no."

"No, she's fine."

"Oh." He sounded relieved and surprised. Couldn't he be optimistic just once?

"Is Heather there?"

"No. She said she had to pick up her son." He paused. "She's been – um – worried about your mom. She's not holding up very well."

Lindsey bit back a scathing comment about his nursing home stories. Better not, he was picking up Heather's slack.

"Heather didn't bring any receipts home. Do you know where she put them?"

"No. You want me to take a look?"

"Yes." Lindsey listened while he rummaged around. "I have to get the books balanced and frankly, I can't do it without them."

"Oh, yeah, I know how that goes." Brandon took a deep breath. "You know that Heather paid the invoices in cash?"

"I'm the only person on the check book."

"Even the –" his phone cut out.

"What did you say?"

"Nothing." His tone was uncertain. "It was nothing." His phone cut out again.

"How is the waitress doing?"

"Mychou is great. She had it all under control in no time." His phone cut out yet again. "Look, I've got another call coming in. I'll call back when I find the receipts."

"Okay."

"Later then."

Why was Brandon so pessimistic? He had her jumping every time her mother twitched. She went back to her books, but he didn't call back. She was going to choke Heather!

When they got back to the house, a red truck was parked in the driveway.

Help at last.

Lindsey's relief was short-lived. The deposit didn't balance again. Lindsey glanced over the register tape. It was a mess. How was she supposed to balance the books?

"Heather, did you bring the invoices home?" Lindsey did her best to be pleasant when she wanted to scream.

"I couldn't find them."

"What happened with the register?"

"The new girl couldn't get the hang of it. Every time I turned my back she made another mistake." Heather shook her head. "It was pitiful."

"What's she like?"

"I think she's Vietnamese or Korean. She flirts with every guy who walks in." Heather rolled her eyes. "It's disgusting."

"How is Brandon doing?"

"If he's not talking about the god-forsaken nursing home, he's acting like a clown. You sure know how to pick 'em."

"Well, this is only…" Lindsey's cell phone chirped. "Crap." She fished in her pocket for it.

Heather started clearing the dinner table.

"Hi, this is Lindsey."

"How are you?" Rose's voice was a welcome distraction.

"We are hanging in there." Lindsey walked outside. "How is everything going for you?"

Rose sighed; the sound put Lindsey on alert.

"What's wrong?"

"Things just aren't the same without you."

"I'll be back as soon as Mother is feeling better."

"How is Eleanor?"

"Not so good." Lindsey spilled it all in a rush, aching to get it off her chest. "Her blood pressure is sky high. We've had her on two different pain pills; both of them make her sick. I don't think she's had a solid meal in a week."

Rose made a sympathetic noise.

"I've never seen her like this, I'm terrified. She looks frail. I think we've been to the hospital every day this week."

"How is your father holding up?"

"Dad can't sleep. He's up at dawn, out in the garden working. I know he's worried, but he can't show it." Lindsey took a deep breath. "Oh, Rose, what if she doesn't get better?"

"Now Lindsey, don't you talk like that," Rose scolded gently. "The good Lord is watching over you and your Mama. You just hang in there."

"I'm sorry I can't get back in, you know that I'll be back as soon as I can."

"You just take care of your Mama, we'll be all right."

"Okay." Lindsey smiled. "I'll talk to you later."

"Take care."

The call from Rose galvanized Lindsey; she had to check on things. She went outside to speak to her father. She found him in the garden, talking to a tall, broad-shouldered man.

"Lindsey, come meet Kevin McTaggart. Tag, this is my daughter Lindsey."

"How do you do?" Lindsey shook his hand.

"Pleased to meet you," his voice was low with a pleasant touch of the south. He looked familiar, with long dark blonde hair, reddish beard and mustache. His blue eyes crinkled at the corners. "Call me Tag."

"I've seen you before." Lindsey racked her mind to place him.

"I stopped in for lunch last week."

This was the guy from the restaurant, the one who gave Heather such a hard time. He could have been any age from 30 to 40. His jeans were well worn, his shirt old and frayed, both showed the results of a hard day's work in the garden. But his smile was genuine, he reminded Lindsey of a friendly, shaggy, stray dog.

"Tag started this morning." Jim grinned. "We got a lot of work done today."

"That's great! Listen, Dad - Heather lost my invoices. I really have to go in tomorrow." As Lindsey spoke to her father, she looked at Tag. He was watching her, intently. There was something in his eyes, just for a second.

What was he thinking, looking at her like that?

Chapter 4

The restaurant was open when Lindsey arrived. The sandwich board proclaimed: "Breakfast your way - $5.95." Just her luck, Brandon was making changes.

A pretty, young Asian woman was chatting with two customers sitting at the front table. The girl was dressed in faded jeans and a nice, if worn, shirt. She wore her long hair braided back. Thin and petite, she was in her early twenties.

This must be Mychou.

Lindsey brushed passed her on her way to the kitchen. The smell of burning grease assaulted her nostrils. Brandon was cooking bacon, sausage and hash browns on the grill. Enough to feed far more than the two people seated.

"What are you doing?" Lindsey was dismayed by the mess. She didn't have time for this!

"Breakfast," Brandon replied with an engaging grin as he swirled a pan of frying eggs.

"Are you frying those in olive oil?" Part of her mind screamed to fire him on the spot. The more practical part wondered who would run the restaurant if she did?

"It was that or butter." Brandon gave the eggs a flip, spilling oil down the side of the pan. The gas burner flared, billowed a choking cloud of smoke. He left the eggs to check on the pasta for the daily special. "How's your Mom?"

"Much better," Lindsey lied to keep from hearing his nursing home stories. Stay focused on receipts, she thought as she rummaged through the cash drawer.

Nothing.

"I'm glad to hear that she's still – you know – doing okay." He swirled the eggs again.

Lindsey shuddered; extra virgin olive oil was too expensive to waste frying eggs!

"Your Mom is lucky to have you to look after her." He set the pan down to flip sausages. "So many ladies came to the home; their families never came see them. No wonder they died in a couple of weeks."

Lindsey deliberately changed the subject.

"Brandon, you can't change the menu."

"What menu? The price is on the board." Brandon finished flipping sausage and scraped the grease off the grill. His movements were quick and automatic; he was obviously used to cooking like this.

"How can you get the lunch prep completed before we open at ten o'clock?"

"Honey, now don't you worry," Brandon laid the accent on thick. He tipped his head to one side and batted his eyes at her. "Ah have every thang un-der con-trol."

Lindsey's cell phone rang.

"Oh, damn," Lindsey swore. It was Heather.

"Come home. Mom fell again."

"I can't! I need the receipts you lost! I have to get the books balanced. I've got taxes due in a week." Lindsey closed her eyes. "You're supposed to be running this place for me!"

"I'm doing the best I can. Between your damn restaurant and Travis I'm too busy to care about some damn piece of paper."

"Talk to Dad then."

"Yeah. Right." Heather hung up.

"Is everything all right?" Brandon asked.

"Everything is fubarred." Lindsey ground her teeth. Stay calm, she thought, stay focused on her missing paperwork. She could handle Brandon and the menu later.

"I got'cha covered, doll-face." He gave her a sexy smile and a wink. Leave it to Brandon to try to make her laugh. "Take care of your Mom. Take all the time you need."

"Okay, but if breakfast doesn't take off, we stop." Lindsey would humor him for one more day. "Agreed?" She stuffed her invoices in her back pocket before she forgot them.

"Don't worry, I can run this place with one hand tied behind my back." He winked at her as he plated his eggs. "Hey, Mychou, come meet the boss."

"Hello, Miss Lindsey." The girl came behind the counter, smiling. She had the dainty features common in Asian woman and a shy smile.

"Nice to meet you." Lindsey wondered why Heather didn't like her.

"I'm pleased to be here." Mychou picked up the plates.

"It's okay, Lindsey." Brandon took Lindsey's hand. "I've got this place under control." The compassion in his face, so sincere, could she leave him here one more day?

"Okay." She barely protested as he guided her from the kitchen, out the door and to the truck. He loaded the four coolers onto the dolly.

"Take good care of your mother," he advised.

Lindsey sat in the truck, feeling utterly torn in two, holding in frustrated tears. Her mother needed her, but her restaurant was being turned into a Greasy Spoon. She drove down 31W home to Sonora. When she arrived at the house, the red truck was back in the driveway. Heather was on her way out the door.

"You'd better take Mom back to the hospital." Heather told Lindsey as she crossed the porch. "She's not doing very well."

"Where is Dad?" Lindsey looked around.

"Dad and his helper are in the back field."

Lindsey walked to her parents' bedroom. Her mother was propped up on pillows, pale against the white sheets. Her eyes were closed; bruises bloomed, huge and dark across her face and arms. Her skin was as white as milk, her lips pressed together.

Her mother looked so frail. Brandon's nursing home stories flashed through her mind. She left the bedroom and walked to the patio. More tears stung her eyes and closed her throat. If she started crying, she'd never stop.

Wisteria shoots hung down from the pergola. Tiny lavender flower buds wafted her with sweet scent, cleansing the lingering odor of burnt grease from her nose. She ran her fingers through her hair, worry for her mother pushing all other thoughts away.

She watched as Jim held the gate, Tag drove the tractor through. It was time to plant sweet corn for summer relishes and a roast corn salsa to serve with pita bread. The restaurant depended on the garden to survive. Planting couldn't fall behind schedule.

Lindsey bowed her head, saying a silent prayer for strength before she returned to the house. Her mother's health was more important than the restaurant.

The next day was another frustrating round of waiting rooms and tests that found nothing wrong. Eleanor was sunk in silent misery, alternately groggy and sick. Lindsey and Eleanor were both exhausted when they got back home that evening.

Another day shot to hell.

Heather was home, storming around the house in a fury. Lindsey got her mother settled in bed before venturing out.

"What happened?"

"Rose quit today."

"Why?" Lindsey bit back a curse.

"She *said* it was because her grandson didn't come home last night." Heather tilted her head from side to side.

"We knew it was coming." Lindsey sighed. "Can Mychou pick up the slack?"

"Mychou is impossible. She ignores me. Brandon lets her do whatever she wants. I hate her!" In another of her abrupt changes of mood, Heather wilted into a chair, bursting into tears.

"What's wrong?" Lindsey knelt by her side.

"I've been so worried about Mom." Heather sobbed. "The dreams are back. I keep looking for her in that damn airplane."

"I'm so sorry." Lindsey took Heather's hand.

Heather drove them to DC to identify Rich's body. It had taken hours to get through traffic. The reality of the smoldering ruin was a thousand times worse than what they'd seen on TV. Heather frequently had nightmares about it - sometimes Lindsey did as well.

"I can't lose her, too!" Heather sobbed while Lindsey held her. Finally, she stopped crying and wiped her eyes.

"Mom is getting better." Lindsey refused to believe otherwise.

"I don't mean to be a pain in the butt."

"I love you anyway."

"I love you, too." Heather gave Lindsey a teary smile.

"Just hang in there for a few more days."

"I'll try."

As she walked home, Lindsey wanted to tear her hair out. She opened the chain-link gate. It grated on a concrete slab.

Lindsey looked down, jarred from her worry.

Someone had installed stepping-stones under the gate where rain tended to collect. They had also mowed her lawn and used a weed-eater on the fence between the two properties.

She was deeply touched. Had her father done this for her? He wasn't the kind of person who gave praise. Maybe this was his way of thanking her.

She should call Rose, just to check on her. Kevin, the grandson, was always in trouble, skipping school, fighting, failing classes. No wonder Rose felt she had to stay home with him.

The timing couldn't be worse!

Brandon was going to have to do all the cooking. Heather was no help. Lindsey had to get back to the restaurant, soon.

She called Rose, but got no answer or voice mail. Lindsey called Brandon. He answered but there was a lot of noise in the background. Was Brandon in a bar?

"Hello, Lindsey," he drawled in his deep voice. "What's your pleasure?"

"What's been going on?" Lindsey asked. "Did Rose quit today?"

"Yeah." Brandon's voice was casual, the sexy tone dropped for the moment. "I guess her grandson came home late last night. I thought she was over reacting, the kid probably got laid or something. Big deal."

"How are Heather and Mychou getting along?"

"Mychou gets along with everybody who pulls their weight." The implication hung in the air for a moment. "I guess Heather told you about their little tiff."

"What did they have a 'tiff' over?"

"Oh, you know how petty girls are."

Brandon's unconcern irritated her.

"Just tell me!"

"Okay, okay!" Brandon's tone changed to placating. "Mychou is working circles around Heather and making great tips. Heather tried to make Mychou split her tips."

"We always pool the tips and split them even."

"You can't treat a good waitress like that. It doesn't give them any incentive."

"I pay good wages. No one has to live on tips."

"Mychou has two kids, their father isn't around. She needs the money really bad." Brandon cleared his throat. "Look, I hate to say this, but Heather isn't pulling her weight."

"What?" Lindsey held her cell so tight her knuckles were white.

"Well, she comes in late. She leaves early. She goes on crying jags, just up and turns on the waterworks." He dropped his voice. "I'm starting to think she's a few french-fries short of a happy meal, if you get my drift."

"Brandon!" Lindsey sputtered, amused at the description and appalled that he would say such a thing. She'd seen for herself how emotional Heather was these days.

"Look, I know that she's your sister, but let's be real. You've got a business to run, you can't baby-sit somebody who can't keep it together."

"That's my sister you are talking about."

"Hey, you asked, I'm just trying to tell you what's going on." He was back to his 'aw-shucks' tone of voice. "Heather finds fault with everything Mychou does. It's obvious why: Mychou's younger, she's cuter, and she's got all the guys tipping big. Heather can't handle it. She's on Mychou's back every minute. Pick, pick, pick – you're gonna lose a good waitress if you don't get your sister in line."

"Heather is in charge when I'm not there."

"You've got the fox guarding the hen house. How many invoices do you have? I found one in the trash. What does that tell you?"

"We need to get back on track here. Mychou's the problem. She can't run a register. I don't need any friction between them right now. She's got to stop giving Heather a hard time. "

"Heather would say that, wouldn't she, to take the heat off herself?" Brandon's phone beeped, cutting him off. "Look, say the word and I turn a blind eye. She's your sister, if you say it didn't happen then it didn't happen."

"That's not what I meant."

His phone cut out again.

"I've got another call, I'll be right back."

Was Heather jealous of Mychou? Had a younger and prettier girl turned her sister into a shrew?

Heather's moods changed at the drop of a hat, angry one minute, crying the next.

Lindsey felt like her head was going to explode.

It wasn't right that she had to rely on Brandon to take up the slack for Heather. Until she got back to the restaurant, she had to give him more responsibility.

Chapter 5

Lindsey was determined to get back to her restaurant for at least two hours. Her father and McTaggart were in the garden. Lindsey washed the produce and loaded coolers.

Her mind elsewhere, she bumped into Tag. He grasped her shoulders for a moment then released her.

"Are you all right?" He looked at her with amusement.

"Sorry about that."

"You're up early." The sun was barely peeking over the horizon.

"I've got a lot of work to do." She smiled. "Do you like working for my father?"

"We get along pretty well. This is quite an operation your father has here." Tag gestured, taking in the huge garden.

"Have you ever worked – I guess this isn't really a farm, is it?" Lindsey finished stacking the baskets in the cooler in front of her.

"Sort of – it's either a little farm or a big market garden. Whatever." Tag shrugged. "It's interesting to see a restaurant from this point of view." Tag picked up the cooler, walked to the truck with it, still talking. "Jim gave me a stack of books." He waited while she packed a second cooler. "I've got the gist of it."

"My father grew up on a farm."

"He has some great ideas." Tag indicated the second cooler. "Is that ready?"

"Oh, I've got it." As Lindsey moved to take it off the bench; he laid a hand on top.

"I have it." Tag's voice was slightly sharp.

Lindsey raised her hands in surrender, as Tag loaded the cooler.

"I'll see you later." He tipped one finger at his eyebrow in a mock salute.

She got to the restaurant later than usual. Brandon and Mychou were inside at the counter, drinking coffee. Brandon came to the door when Lindsey tapped on the window and waved. He had the dolly waiting.

"Hey, good-looking," he said in a seductive tone as they walked to the back alley parking lot. "What's on the menu today?"

"Blarney, by the sound of it." Lindsey laughed.

"Nothing new?" At the truck, Brandon lifted a cooler out from one side. He wasn't a tall man, but he did have nice strong arms.

"Not yet, we're still planting."

They had all four coolers stacked on the dolly. He rolled them to the door, then to the back of the restaurant.

"Mychou, could you give us a hand?"

"Yes, Miss Lindsey." Mychou was dressed in Capri length jeans, and a pressed cotton blouse, her long hair was braided back. Both the jeans and the blouse looked well worn.

"This is beautiful lettuce." Mychou ran her fingers though the red lettuce before dumping it into the sink to wash, then tear into bit-sized pieces.

"Here it comes." Brandon made space ship noises as he stacked a steamer over boiling water. "Perfect landing!"

Lindsey giggled.

Brandon started clowning to keep her laughing. He turned shelling peas into machine gun fire, used green onions for a mustache while talking like Groucho Marx. They chopped vegetables, steamed potatoes, boiled pasta and mixed up the potato and pasta salads. All the while the girls giggled helplessly at his antics.

"Taste test!" Lindsey proclaimed as she dished out samples.

"This is good." Mychou nibbled daintily at the pasta salad.

"This is fabulous! Where did you get these recipes?"

"They are family recipes," Lindsey admitted. "Fresh food just tastes better."

"You're amazing." Brandon told her.

Lindsey glowed. It was nice to be appreciated, especially by a young, handsome cook.

Everything was ready at nine-thirty on the dot. Heather walked in the door as Lindsey was walking out.

"Dad's waiting for you," Heather said. "I'll pick Travis up on the way home."

"Okay," Lindsey said, then added. "Heather, I'm still missing a bunch of invoices. Can you look for them, please?"

Heather's eyes narrowed but she nodded, her lips pursed. Heather needed to suck it up. Lindsey wasn't happy about this either.

Eleanor was nauseous after taking her medication. Thanks to the doctor, Lindsey knew to give her Ensure instead of solid food. She got her mother settled in bed, waiting for a half hour to make sure Eleanor didn't get sick. Her mother fell asleep; the pain pills had done their job.

Lindsey cleaned the house, got Travis' clothes presoaking then started a big lunch for her father and Tag. She whipped up chicken sandwiches, braised the last of the asparagus, and had the food waiting when the men came in for lunch.

"I'm starving." Tag remarked as he washed up. "That smells really good." He was sunburned, and sweaty from the heat. Lindsey noticed that Tag had a second helping of everything. There weren't any leftovers when she cleared the table.

"How is your Mother?" Jim peeked into the bedroom. Eleanor was still asleep.

"She didn't throw up. I guess a diet of sports drinks and meal shakes is an improvement." At the edge of her vision she noted that Tag was listening, slouched against the doorway to the dining room.

"Dad, I have to get some book work done, can you stay with her?"

"Until Heather comes home?" Jim turned to Tag, switching tone of voice and posture from casual to – military crisp. "Can you handle it?" He sounded like he was assigning a mission to a squad leader.

Tag's reaction was to stand straight, in military 'at ease.'

"Yes, sir," Tag replied crisply in return.

The irony of the scruffy appearance and the military carriage set off Lindsey's sense of humor. She stifled the impulse to giggle.

"Good, carry on then." Jim turned from Tag to Lindsey. "We're set. I'll take care of supper." He made supper sound like a ground support mission. Her father saw the laughter she smothered and raised an eyebrow in stern disapproval. She held her breath until Tag walked out the door. Her father gave the 'get moving' look that meant no questions.

Lindsey wondered what her father was up to. Then as she walked home, she started worrying about the books. Heather had always been sloppy with money, but this – this was a new low for her sister.

To take her mind off her problems, Lindsey peered over the fence at the 40 by 20 plot of new garden. Her father preferred free organic fertilizer over expensive store-bought. They collected compost from a dozen farms in two counties for this area. There was never enough.

Tag drove up on the garden tractor, pulling a load of compost and tools. Lindsey watched him dump the load, spread it out then rake the soil into a long low hill, four by eight feet, and a couple of inches high.

"What you are doing?" That sounded harsher than she had intended.

"Making raised beds." Tag answered. She noted the hesitant way he moved on the rough ground, lame from some injury. "They use less water, fertilizer and grow more in less space. The point is to fertilize the plants, not the space between rows." He gestured at the garden on the other side of her sister's house. "We'll redo that side next year."

She couldn't imagine her father changing his planting methods in mid-season to something so – disorganized. Who had made the change?

"Was this your idea or his?"

"His. You heard him tell me to carry on." He looked at her with amusement. Didn't anyone respect her? "This is his project."

"Well, he never mentioned it to me." Lindsey couldn't help the frosty tone. She was out of the loop in a critical project.

"You've been busy."

"I've got to catch up on my book work." It was time to retreat.

"Later." Tag went back to his task.

Lindsey went into her house and fired up the computer. She looked outside while it booted up. She saw the flash of metal at Tag's left ankle, the lower part of his leg and his foot was missing. He worked slowly, taking short breaks.

Lindsey hit the books – and the data on her spreadsheet hit back. The business was sliding into the red. Jim bought irrigation equipment, repaired the barn, and done a hundred small improvements to double the size of the garden. Three new employees had taken the profit for the month.

She had to suck it up.

So far, Brandon's breakfast brainchild wasn't profitable. She needed to keep an eye on it and pull the plug as tactfully as possible. That thought made her smile. Keeping an eye on Brandon was easy; keeping her eyes off Brandon was a challenge.

She took a stab at cleaning up her house. She washed dishes, dusted and washed a load of clothes, trying to wear herself out so she could sleep. But her thoughts ran in circles like a hamster on a wheel. She made a mug of chamomile tea, drank it on the front porch. That put her front row for a symphony of animal sounds: spring peepers, crickets, coyotes singing nearby.

How long had it been since she had a vacation?

Not since the plane hit the Pentagon.

Heather had called in hysterics, Rich was at the Pentagon; not answering his cell. Lindsey left work early. She wanted to pack a bag, let Tommy know she was going to Heather's house. When she walked into the apartment, it reeked of crack. Tommy was having sex with a man.

For a bleak moment, she relived the shock, the shame and the burning anger.

The confrontation had been ugly. It had escalated into a full-blown fight that left the apartment wrecked. Her life changed that day. She left her childish wish for marriage and family in the apartment with the rest of the trash. She stayed with Heather, moved next door when her parents came back to Kentucky.

When Lindsey went back to work, it didn't occur to her that Tommy would be a problem. The first time her computer was sabotaged, she knew who did it. Her key files were erased several times, but she had backups. She started getting spam from porn sites. She'd complained to her boss. A company-wide virus infection was traced to her PC. That was the last straw. She sold her stock to pay for night classes at a culinary school.

The details of Tommy's infidelity were secret from her family, especially from her father. In hindsight, she should have known that Tommy was bisexual. How naïve was that?

Her parents lost their house in Arizona, and their retirement money, when the stock market went bad. Heather was struggling to survive on Rich's insurance money. They needed Lindsey to succeed. Everyone's future was tied up in her restaurant; she couldn't let them down.

Lindsey hung her head, prayed for help, guidance or a sign that things would be all right. She got no answer from God, just the singing of coyote, crickets, frogs and the feeling that if she went back to bed, she could sleep.

He was in the desert, on patrol, just outside Falluja. The sun burned his eyes, his skin; the heat was stifling, with the weight of his flak jacket, pack and ammunition dragging him down. He could taste the dust, sour and gritty. The sweat running down his face stung his eyes. He could hear small arms fire in the distance, coming closer.

He shifted his weight, but didn't feel his gun. Where was it? He looked at his empty hands and felt panic run through his gut. He started checking for a weapon, any weapon, stripping off the backpack, spilling the contents on the ground: Water, rations, ammunition, spent shells. No gun, not even a side arm. Where was his M-16?

He heard shots coming closer, a sharp burst of machine gun fire. He tore through his pockets, stripping off his flak jacket, panting with the force of his fear. He had no weapons. Not even a pocketknife. He was unarmed in the middle of freaking Falluja!

He shouted out loud, using every curse he could think of.

That woke him, he sat up in bed, in the dark, with pain shooting down his left leg. It felt like his foot was on fire! Groaning softly he rocked, clutching his knee. It was just a dream, he told himself over and over. He was not back in Falluja, it was just another bad dream.

When he could, he got up. He may as well get going. Thank God he had a place to go. There was nothing worse than sitting, reliving the nightmares, dreading the night to come. Pills hadn't stopped the dreams; bourbon hadn't stopped the dreams. The combination of the two had almost killed him.

Now that he had work to do, his life had purpose again. He felt he could hold on to his sanity a little longer.

Chapter 6

Thursday morning Lindsey found her father and Tag in the garden. By the look of the baskets waiting for her, they had been there for a couple of hours. Lindsey wondered how anyone could get up that early, as she rinsed produce then packed the coolers. Heather brought out coffee and breakfast wraps for them. They ate under the pergola. Lindsey listened to her father and Tag talking about the garden, while Heather sulked inside.

Lindsey watched Tag load the coolers in Heather's car. Then she watched Heather drive down the road. She sighed; then realized that Tag was watching her. He tipped a finger at his eyebrow in a mock salute. Lindsey gave him a little smile.

After days of being a zombie, Eleanor was alert and cranky. She refused the pain medication, and complained the whole trip to Ireland Hospital. When Eleanor was on a tear, everyone ducked for cover. Lindsey steeled herself for the ordeal to come.

This time the doctor was a middle-aged black woman.

"I need out of this cast," Eleanor said. "It's too heavy and too small. It is cutting the circulation off in my foot. Look at my toes! They're blue!"

"Hmm." The doctor touched Eleanor's toes. "You must still have some swelling."

"The damn thing is too small."

The doctor gave Eleanor a thoughtful look as she picked up the chart.

"You've been having a lot of problems. I see your blood pressure is better. Are you still getting nauseated?"

"Yes," Eleanor said. "What really bothers me is I can't take a shower." Eleanor was talking with her hands. "Have you ever gone two weeks without a shower? I feel like my skin is crawling! Please, get me out of this cast!"

"I don't know." The doctor shook her head.

"I can't spend six months in the damn thing!" Eleanor snapped. "It's ridiculous."

"Six months?" The woman cocked her head. "Who said you would have to spend six months in a cast?" She looked back through the chart, tsking under her breath.

"Every other doctor seemed to think it would take six months at the very least." Eleanor added with considerable bitterness. "They all said it was my age."

The doctor didn't answer. She flipped through the chart for the third time then sat at the computer to check the x-rays. After a few minutes, she turned around.

"I see nothing that would indicate a longer than normal healing time, even though you are past menopause." She shrugged. "Maybe I know more about women since I am one."

Eleanor cocked her head. Lindsey crossed her fingers.

"Beside the high blood pressure, I see no problems. If you keep drinking fluids and taking the medication even that should subside."

"So I can get out of this cast?" Eleanor asked again.

"Being inactive is not good." The doctor did not give a direct answer. "Let me see what we can do." She took the chart with her when she left.

"Finally, a doctor with some sense." Eleanor kicked the cast lightly with her other foot. She smiled at Lindsey for the first time in days.

Lindsey smiled back. She wanted to laugh out-loud. Finally! Something was going right. Once rid of the plaster cast Eleanor was fitted with a light walking cast. They drove home in triumph. Eleanor went back to bed, exhausted, but cheerful.

That afternoon, Lindsey worked on her books, while her father sat with her mother. Hunched over her laptop, she picked through the tangle of her finances. The end of the month was only a few days away. She wasn't sure what the sales had been, nor how much sales tax she owed. Her payroll taxes were due at the end of June. She wasn't sure what the new waitress was paid. Surely, Heather wasn't paying her cash? Where was the damn invoice for the beverage order?

She heard her father's steps on the porch.

"Lindsey?" He called.

"Come on in." Lindsey turned around.

"We need to talk." Jim's face was grim and set. The silver in his dark hair glinted in the afternoon light.

"Is Mom all right?" She squeaked, looking at his face.

"Yes, she's fine." He reassured her. "There is a problem at the restaurant."

"What is it?" Lindsey's heart skipped a beat.

"Heather called." Her father took her hand. "The assistant prosecutor was in today. Someone put a roach in his pasta salad."

"Oh, my God." Lindsey slumped in her chair. She bit her lips as her eyes filled with tears. How could that have happened? They sprayed four times a year; the restaurant was clean. She knew it was clean.

"Now, listen to me, all is not lost." He gave her a chuck under the chin, disapproving of her tears, telling her to pull herself together.

"How can you say that?" Lindsey felt like her whole world was caving in, but her father expected her to take this calmly. For a moment, she hated his military discipline.

"I did some damage control for you." Jim's face was lined and tired, he looked much older than his sixty-eight years. "He doesn't blame you. He thinks your new waitress did it. He said he put her husband in jail on drug charges."

"Oh my God." Lindsey could not imagine how any sane person could do something so awful to another. "How horrible."

"You can bet that word will get around. The Health Inspector will be there, looking to shut you down."

Lindsey nodded dumbly.

"What about Mom?" Lindsey was still on the edge of tears.

"I've talked it over with your Mother." He ran his fingers through his short silver hair. "She's getting around better without the cast." He pressed his lips together. "I've been selfish. It was a mistake to take you from your work. The restaurant can't run without you." He didn't often admit to making mistakes. "You need to get in there tomorrow, bright and early to get that woman out of your restaurant!"

"Chin up, girl, we'll get through this." He gave her a hug as he stood to leave.

Lindsey's eyes followed him as he walked out the door. Then she let herself break down in tears.

By morning Lindsey was a nervous wreck, she had never fired anyone before. Her previous employees had all quit before she'd had to fire them. She wanted to ask her father to come with her, but Tag was by himself.

They got everything picked together. Lindsey kept looking at her watch, wondering what was going on. When Heather came out with their breakfast and coffee, Tag wisely excused himself.

"I'm sorry." Heather said, blushing red. "I really don't know what else to say." The two women looked at one another. Heather's hair was back in a clip, except for two long tendrils. She tugged nervously at one, barely able to look Lindsey in the eye.

"What happened?" Lindsey was getting tired of playing things down for Heather's sake. When would her sister start acting like a grownup?

"It was really busy." Heather frowned, thinking hard, her eyebrows pulled together. "All I know is that he came in, ordered, then he called me back. It was awful. Humiliating to say the very least. I almost fell over myself apologizing to him."

"What did he say?" Lindsey was almost afraid to ask.

"He just pointed at it. It was dead. Then he asked to talk to the owner, to you. Everyone in the restaurant just kind of looked at their food and walked out. When I called the house, Dad answered. The two of them talked for a few minutes. Then he left. What could I say?" Heather rubbed her forehead.

"I don't know," Lindsey said. "We aren't careless, I can prove that. We don't have roaches; we spray regularly. I set out sticky traps that would catch any type of bug. If we were infested I would know."

"The place is a mess," Heather said critically. "Brandon isn't keeping up with it, not like you do. That girl isn't much help." Heather pulled at her hair. "Why would she do that?"

"The prosecutor thought that she put the bug in his food because he put her husband in jail for selling drugs." Lindsey tried to keep the criticism out of her voice. The effort left her words slightly clipped.

"I'm the one who hired her." Heather hung her head, her voice cracked. "I should have known better."

"It's hard to hire people these days, it's not like you can check up on them easily. You never know who's walking through the door. You can only hope for the best." Lindsey was trying to keep Heather from breaking down, while she felt shaky herself.

There is only one of me, she thought defiantly; I can't be everywhere at once. This was Heather's disaster, but I'm the one who has to clean it up.

"Where is Dad?" Lindsey asked.

"What do you need Dad for?" Heather looked up with a frown.

"I want him to come with me." Lindsey explained.

"Can't you handle it yourself?" Heather demanded, switching moods once again. "Are you planning on hiding behind Dad all your life?"

"He's the one who talked to the customer. I want him to be my witness."

"Don't be ridiculous." Heather snorted with contempt. "It's not that hard. She's fired. What is she going to do? Stay?"

Lindsey blushed and said nothing.

Lindsey went in to her restaurant feeling like she was stepping into a lion's den. The restaurant floors were filthy; something crunched underfoot. Brandon was working on the grill.

Mychou was drinking coffee at the counter. She was wearing new slacks and a short-sleeved shirt. Lindsey bit her lip, was this where her money had gone?

"We need to talk." Lindsey motioned Mychou to join her at a table.

How to do this with some dignity saved on both sides? Maybe it was possible. She hated confrontations, but this was unavoidable.

"I'm sorry." She tried to break the bad news gently. "After the incident with the bug, I have to let you go."

"What?" Mychou looked stunned, her eyes went wide and her face lost all color.

"I think you should find a job somewhere else."

"I need this job," Mychou said. "You can't just fire me. I've got two kids to take care of!" Then she dropped the 'sweet girl' act. Her eyes narrowed, her face went hard. "It's because I'm Vietnamese, isn't it?"

"No," Lindsey denied.

"Your father is a veteran of the Vietnam War, isn't he?"

"That has nothing to do with it." Lindsey never imagined that Mychou would play the race card after she'd tried to be nice about this.

"I think it does," Mychou said, drawing herself to her full height. "Those vets hate the Vietnamese. They always have."

"You are off topic." Lindsey smothered her anger. How could this silly girl talk about her father like that? "You put a roach in the assistant prosecutor's food yesterday. That's why I'm firing you."

"That's a lie!" the woman's dark eyes flashed. "I had nothing to do with that. He wasn't my customer, I never touched his food."

"That's not what Heather said."

"That doesn't mean I put a roach in his food."

Lindsey was floundering, not knowing what to say. She hadn't talked to the customer. That was a mistake. She'd made too many mistakes. There had to be a way to get control back.

"I have kids and a car payment! You can't just fire me. I have rights you know."

"Here are your wages." Lindsey opened her checkbook, wrote a check for a week's pay.

"Brandon, she's trying to fire me!" Mychou shouted.

"Hey, hey, what's going on?" Brandon said from the kitchen. Mychou turned to him.

"She thinks she can fire me, for NO REASON!" Mychou told him. "I've got kids to feed, I need this job!"

Brandon looked at Lindsey; his eyebrows drawn together. "You can't fire her without a reason. It's against the law."

"She put a roach in a customer's food!" Lindsey lost her temper. "Isn't that reason enough?"

"I did not! Your crazy sister did that!" Mychou snarled, standing up, grabbing her purse. "I'll sue you for every penny you have! When this is over, I'll own this restaurant!" She snatched the check from Lindsey's hand then stormed out of the restaurant.

"You shouldn't have done that." Brandon's eyes were concerned.

"It's my restaurant!" Lindsey snapped. "I can hire and fire as needed!"

"Now, wait just a minute," Brandon said to Lindsey. "You should have talked to me first. I would have warned you not to try something like that. She will sue you, she's dating a lawyer."

"Yesterday she put a roach in a customer's food. That's 'just cause' enough for anybody."

"I was here when it happened, Mychou didn't serve him." Brandon said, shaking his head. "You can't blame her for it."

Lindsey hesitated. She should have gotten her father to come with her!

"Heather served the guy." He gave Lindsey a pitying look. "You really have to do something about your sister. Get her to a shrink or something."

"What do you mean?" Lindsey was baffled. What on earth was he talking about?

"She's not right in the head. Always talking about her husband like she just left him at the breakfast table. It's downright creepy. Then there is her attitude. You've seen how rude Heather is to me. Well she's ten times worse to Mychou. I think it's clear why Heather is blaming Mychou. Heather's jealous of Mychou and wants her out of here. You're being manipulated."

Lindsey felt frustrated and helpless, more because she knew Heather didn't like Brandon. Heather did still talk about Rich a lot. She hadn't seen Heather with Mychou; maybe they didn't get along either? Lindsey bit her lip. Could Brandon be right? It sounded plausible, a classic case of 'he said, she said.'

No. Lindsey squared her shoulders. He wasn't right. Mychou had done it, not Heather. She had to stick to what she *knew* was right.

"My decision is final." Lindsey tried to end the subject.

"Come on, you need to get a grip." Brandon gestured around them. "We open in two hours. You don't have a single waitress. You'd better get Mychou back here, pronto."

"The restaurant is not going to open today." Lindsey informed him; nettled at his presumption. This was her business, not his. "We have to get the place cleaned up, or the inspectors are going to shut it down Monday." She couldn't resist adding. "Are you sure that the kitchen will pass inspection?" His expression changed from smug to unsure. Lindsey felt a surge of satisfaction, followed by fear. What DID her kitchen look like? She started walking that way.

"We've been so busy and so short handed." He explained. "Your sister left early every day this week, so it's just been me and Mychou closing up."

The kitchen looked okay from a distance, but a closer look told a different story. There was grease everywhere. The pans weren't clean; the dishes had been stacked in pots and stashed on the floor under the sinks. As Lindsey walked around the kitchen fury replaced helplessness as she ran her fingers over dull, greasy stainless steel.

Her spotless kitchen was a wreck.

"This is not acceptable." The glare she gave Brandon would have done her father proud. "We need to get this place cleaned up." Lindsey unconsciously adopted her father's military bearing and tone of voice. "No excuses, no breaks, no bullshit! Is that clear Brandon?"

"I'm sorry," Brandon said his boyishly handsome face contrite. "We've been so busy. It just got away from me."

"Then we had better get on it!" Lindsey replied, tossing him a broom. She put on an apron and gloves before she pulled dirty dishes from under the sink. They spent the entire day cleaning. Brandon was surprisingly thorough, once they got started. It was early evening before Lindsey pronounced the restaurant finished. She collapsed on a stool, dog-tired. Brandon came up behind her and started to massage her shoulders.

"You are *so* tense," his expert hands worked the knots out of her shoulders and neck; it felt wonderful, Lindsey melted with a sigh.

"How about we go out for a steak dinner and a drink? We'll go to the steak house down by the interstate." Brandon murmured in her ear. "I'll treat."

"No, I'll buy." She looked around with satisfaction. The place looked great. He had made up for the mess with all his hard work. Lindsey was ready to forgive him.

"Then let me drive," he said.

"No thanks. I can't leave my truck here."

They finished up and walked out. Lindsey locked the doors behind them. She followed him down Rt. 62 to the cluster of restaurants by I-65. The steak house was already packed. They waited at the bar. Lindsey sipped a glass of white wine. Brandon was gearing up to party.

"Hey, how about we knock back a couple of shots?" Brandon said as he motioned to the bartender. "Hey, Greg, give me a couple of Snakebites over here."

"Hey, Brandon." The blonde man looked up with a big smile. "Two Snakebites coming up," he said as he handed a couple of drinks to the waitress.

"No!" Lindsey held up her hand, shaking her head at the handsome blonde bartender. "White wine, only, thank you."

The bartender brought the shots along with wine for Lindsey and a beer for Brandon. Lindsey watched Brandon knock back the first shot. He shuddered after he swallowed it then licked his lips.

"Damn that was good." He gave her the 'come-on' smile that she thought of as his trademark. "Sure you don't want this one?"

"White wine is plenty." Lindsey was in no hurry to drink her wine.

"Here's looking at you." Brandon picked up the shot glass. He saluted her before he knocked it back.

"Come on, Lindsey, don't be so uptight." Brandon gave her a sly come-on smile, his brown eyes were filled with mischief. "You deserve one night to let your hair down." Brandon reached behind her head to take the clip from her hair. When her hair slid down her neck in soft dark waves, his expression changed from mischievous to smoldering. He reached out to smooth her hair from her face. His touch was so sensuous that Lindsey stopped breathing. Brandon gave her a knowing smile as he handed her the clip.

"That's more like it."

Lindsey looked away, conflicted. How long had it been since she'd let a man touch her? She'd been so busy. Her one romance had ended in a cluttered apartment turned crack house. The memory stirred in her mind like a snake, scaled and cold. Here she was with an attractive man who seemed to appreciate her but all her brain would do was nag.

While they waited for their steaks, Brandon kept her entertained with parodies of the country songs over the speakers. The evening was as good as the excellent steak. Between Brandon's jokes and the wine, Lindsey was very relaxed and giggly. Eventually the steak was gone. The day's work and the wine caught up with her; Lindsey stifled a yawn.

"We need to leave," Lindsey said with regret.

"We can go somewhere else," Brandon suggested with a wink.

Lindsey smiled and shook her head. She left a good-sized tip for the waitress then they walked out. Brandon walked her to her truck.

"Are you sure that you don't want to go somewhere else?" Brandon asked in a husky voice. "My apartment isn't far away. We could have a few drinks; get to know each other better. Friends with benefits, how about it?"

For a long moment, Lindsey was tempted. Brandon was handsome, broad-shouldered, with dark tousled hair, dark half-lidded eyes and his smile was as seductive as his honey-toned voice. He ran the tips of his fingers over her arm to her shoulder. When she didn't pull away he tried to raise the ante with a passionate kiss. Brandon kissed her like he was going to eat her, pinning her against the truck.

It was overwhelming, too much too fast. Lindsey couldn't breathe. Panic shot through her. She squirmed to get her hands between their bodies.

"Brandon stop." She broke away from his mouth. She pushed him away.

"You don't know what you are missing." He seemed very sure of that.

Lindsey was equally sure that she wanted to go home. Thank heaven she hadn't ridden here in his car. She would have no control over where he took her.

"Good night," Lindsey said climbing into her truck. She wiped the taste of him, whiskey and cigarettes, from her mouth. Two glasses of wine had taken all her common sense; now she was sober and scared. She started the truck, waved goodbye as if her heart wasn't racing with anxiety and her hands shook uncontrollably.

Was this Tommy's legacy?

No, Brandon just didn't turn her on. He wasn't her type, obviously.

Chapter 7

Saturday Lindsey assured her family that she had fired Mychou. She didn't mention the woman's threat to sue. It seemed like an empty threat. Why would anyone sue over a waitress' job?

In the afternoon, she finished her bookwork. She spent the evening researching recipes to try as the garden produce changed with the seasons. She designed new menus, lowering a few prices on the spreadsheet and running some numbers.

She had just enough time on her hands to feel lonely. Just enough time to get angry at herself, instead of Brandon. She had gone out to eat with co-workers before but always in a group. She knew he was a flirt. Being alone with him had been a mistake.

She never wanted to see him again, but she couldn't very well fire him for kissing her. That was over kill. Should she talk to him about it, or just try to forget it had happened? Would she be safe alone with him in the restaurant?

What was her problem with men anyway? She'd dated in high school; there had been boyfriends in college. Until Tommy, she had never been in love, look how that had turned out. When Brandon had kissed her, she'd all but freaked out on him.

With a sigh she stopped denying the truth. She knew what had happened. During her confrontation with Tommy and his lover, the two men had gotten violent. In the tussle, she'd put Tommy's lover through a glass coffee table and broken Tommy's nose. She'd gotten away, bruised and scared.

She was a horrible judge of character when it came to men. Look how Brandon treated her; he didn't respect her. She possessed none of her father's natural leadership. The trickle of self-doubt became an avalanche.

Would she be able to pull her family through this crisis? Would she lose the restaurant? What if her mother DID have some type of side effect or blood clot, have a stroke and die? What would become of her father? He depended on her mother for so much; would they lose him too?

She went to bed, feeling cold, small and alone. Doubt and fear nagged at her. It stalked her sleep, sending uneasy dreams of burning buildings and the overwhelming smell of jet fuel.

Sunday morning, Lindsey dressed in shorts and a tank top before she reported for duty in the garden. The garden work would keep her skin a sun-kissed golden tan. She had lunch with her family. Later, she went to her restaurant to polish the stainless steel, fuss about putting everything in perfect order. By the time she went back home, Sunday evening, her restaurant sparkled. She was ready for the inspector. There were new menus, more fresh vegetables from the garden, lower prices to entice the clientele back.

She prayed with all her heart that the worst was over; there would be better times ahead. Finally, she fell into a deep dreamless sleep.

The morning started out great. She joined her father and Tag in the garden to pick produce. From the look of the baskets, the two compulsive early risers had been at it since long before dawn.

"I've got to get caught up," Lindsey said aloud as she started rinsing. This time she left the coolers in place, knowing that Tag would be along in a moment. She was about half-finished when Jim and Tag came to the benches, the last of the produce in their hands. Jim was grinning.

"We have already gotten twice as much as last year," he said to Lindsey. "All that compost has made a world of difference."

Lindsey gave him the thumbs up. All that shoveling had been worth it.

"Which ones are ready?" Tag asked.

Lindsey pointed to the full coolers. He loaded them into the back of the truck. It was silly. She could load them herself. But he was offended if she did it herself.

"How are the salad greens selling?" Jim asked.

"As fast as I make salads, they go out the door," Lindsey said. "There isn't much left at the end of the day. Everyone loves the butter-crunch lettuce."

"By July all this will bolt," Jim mused. "We need to find a heat-resistance strain of loose leaf lettuce pretty soon."

"Where would you find a heat-resistance lettuce?" Tag asked.

"Travis found the heirloom tomatoes on the Internet," Jim said. "Maybe he can find lettuce."

"What kind of Internet connection have you got out here?" Tag was leaning against the truck with his arms folded. His sleeveless shirt was dark with sweat. There were a few small scars, and a particularly deep one across his forearm, white against his tan.

"I haven't a clue." Jim shook his head. "Lindsey, do you know what Tag is talking about?"

"Yes." Lindsey smiled at Tag. "It's dialup. You know how slow that is."

"I've got a high speed connection at my place," Tag said. "I couldn't go back to dial up."

"What do you need Internet for?" Jim raised an eyebrow at him. "Or shouldn't I ask?"

Tag and Lindsey exchanged a look of amusement. It was clear that Jim knew only the worst parts of the Internet.

"I couldn't live without Internet." Tag eyes danced with mischief, but he held Jim's gaze without flinching. "I keep in touch with my friends overseas with e-mail. I use web-cam to talk to my younger brother in San Diego. He's the real geek in the family. My father e-mails me at least once a month." He chuckled. "I get *way* too much spam from my sisters."

"That's all Greek to me." Jim shook his head, unconvinced.

How interesting, Lindsey thought watching them. Not many men could look her father in the eye like that. Her brother-in-law had never been able to, but Tag was completely at ease.

As Lindsey drove into town, she wondered about Tag. He seemed to be pleasant company and a hard worker. How old was he? How long had he been in the military? Where had he gotten the scars on his arms, how had he lost his leg? She was in the restaurant, occupied with her curiosity, when the phone rang.

"Lindsey Bennett," she answered automatically, not recognizing the number.

"Are you the owner of a restaurant called 'Let's Do Lunch?'" The voice was male, very smug, bordering on sneering.

"I am." Lindsey sat up; alarm bells went off in her head. What now?

"I'm Davis Burns of Burns and Simon." Davis Burns had a smooth voice that was low pitched and menacing. "I represent an employee of yours, Mychou Snyder."

"Former employee," Lindsey replied.

"Ah, you need to reconsider your rash actions, Miss Bennett. Are you aware that a law suit is about to be filed against you?"

"That's ridiculous."

"I have the papers right here in my hand." He sounded smug. "All I need to do is file them at the County Courthouse. From that point you can kiss your restaurant goodbye."

"I can hire a lawyer of my own. We can play this out in court."

"For how long?" he asked. "My client has an excellent case, termination without just cause, discrimination and racism. We can draw this out as long as you like." He made a sound that could have been a chuckle. "How deep are your pockets?"

Was he a lawyer or an extortionist?

All Lindsey's financial worries came crashing in on her. She started to panic. It wasn't just her money at stake. The whole family had invested in the restaurant. They had trusted her enough that there was no sheltering corporation.

"It doesn't have to go that far," he said into the silence. "All my client wants is her job."

"Her job?" Lindsey exhaled.

"Her job," he affirmed. "She comes back to work this morning. All is – well – not forgotten, of course, but forgiven. A misunderstanding resolved – as long as there are no further – issues."

Issues? Lindsey ground her teeth, caught between a rock and a very hard place. How long could she play this game? Until her mother was back on her feet, she decided. It was going to be humiliating, but she could put up with Mychou for a few weeks.

"All right," Lindsey said. "She can come back to work."

"Today," he said firmly.

"Today," Lindsey agreed. "But she had better be on time."

"No problem." He hung up.

Lindsey was left glaring at her cell phone.

"Bastard!" Lindsey snarled then snapped the cell phone closed. This was such bull! But she didn't have much choice right now, did she? She paced and chewed her fingernails until Brandon came in whistling and snapping his fingers.

"Hey, good lookin', what you got cookin'?" he said, chucking her under the chin. "Are we ready for the big bad inspectors or what?" He danced a few steps. "I got knocked out, but I got up again. Nobody gonna keep me down."

He bounced to the kitchen where he danced around, flipping open the coolers, clowning until Lindsey was laughing aloud. It was as if the evening at the steak house had never happened. Lindsey decided to forget it, that phone call made a kiss seem so trivial.

They quickly ran through the morning routine of getting the daily specials ready. The Health Inspectors came in as predicted an hour before the regular opening time. They went through the restaurant with a fine toothed comb. They made half-dozen notes, but didn't have a thing to complain about. Lindsey was able to breathe easier when they were gone.

When Mychou showed up, she looked more like a model than a waitress. Her hair was cut short and streaked. She wore gold jewelry, new Capri length pants, a top that looked like silk and low-heeled sandals. Lindsey felt like a fat frumpy matron just looking at her. Where was Mychou getting all this money?

They got the restaurant open on time, with everything exactly the way it should be. But business had fallen off terribly; word of the bug had spread. The carry out lunch orders fell to a mere dozen. They served only 20 inside customers, most of that was coffee sales.

Yet even with the reduced business, Mychou couldn't work the register. She would ring; void and re-ring, swearing under her breath as she struggled to ring up her customers. The register tape was going to be a horrible mess. When Lindsey tried to correct Mychou, the woman was defensive.

"It doesn't work right," Mychou insisted. "I know how to use a register!" The threat "I'll sue" lay like a foul smell between them. Lindsey gritted her teeth wondering what she could do. Brandon looked up from his work when she came into the kitchen.

"You know, I admire the way you can handle all this," he said. "You have such a knack for multi-tasking. Not very many people can do that."

"Thanks." The compliment distracted her for a moment.

"Most people would be overwhelmed."

"I am overwhelmed," Lindsey admitted. "I don't feel I can handle any more."

"Why don't you let me take on some of this for you? Feel free to delegate, whatever. I could run this place, you know." Brandon sounded sincere.

Lindsey studied him for a moment. Should she trust him? It was so tempting to give over some of the responsibility. Brandon pressed her when she hesitated.

"I know this guy who works as a register repairman. I can get him to look at the cash register. I can run this place until you get your mother back on her feet. You don't even need to be here."

"There's nothing wrong with the register." Lindsey sighed. "You can do the ordering. That would be a big help."

How could he screw it up?

"What about beverages?" Brandon asked. "We are running low on soda."

"Okay, take inventory. See what we need." She dug in her desk, handing him the little notebook where she kept all her account numbers. "Call it in. Have them deliver it later this week. I want invoices." Lindsey gave him a hard look.

"I can pick up the order for you." Brandon offered. "It's no big deal."

"Okay." Lindsey agreed. By the time she was done with the deposit, he had the orders written out and called in. He gave her the notebook and the orders.

She drove home awash in emotions, horrified from the conversation with that lawyer; elated to have passed the inspection; angry that she had been forced to take Mychou back. Afraid of what her family would say when they found out that she hadn't fired that awful woman after all. By the time she pulled into her driveway, it had all congealed like scorched gravy into depression.

She changed clothes, dumping her stuff from the restaurant on the table. There was more work to do. Somehow, she had to face her family without letting on how disastrously wrong the firing of Mychou had turned out.

Heather was zipping around in 'up' mode. Her dark side had vanished like storm clouds. The kitchen smelled heavenly, the grill was heating up. Her house was spotless and tidy. Eleanor was in the living room, in the recliner, a walker at her side. Lindsey was grateful not to have to deal with Heather's darker side on top of all the day's disappointments. She sat next to Travis at dinner, watching her nephew clown with Tag. Travis had taken to Tag like a duckling to a puddle. Hadn't Tag said he had a younger brother? Yes, he had, so he knew how to deal with a rowdy kid.

Tag was at ease with the family, eating dinner with them, teasing Travis, talking to Jim as if he were one of the family. A week of hard work had tanned him and toughened him up. Her father was cheerful; it seemed that he and Tag had gotten a lot of work done that morning.

"I've got those heirloom tomatoes I've been itching to try. Travis found a source for them and some old style pole beans that will probably sell pretty well." Her father reached over to rub Travis' head with his knuckles. The boy beamed back at his grandfather.

"These tomato plants need to have heavy duty support." He turned to Tag. "I've tried all those tomato supports – they are worthless – a total waste of money. We need something that won't break under the weight of the vines."

"Something re-usable," Tag agreed.

"Save some money that way." Jim got up to get paper.

The two of them sketched out something that Lindsey didn't see. She was sunk in her own misery.

"Lindsey can you give us a hand? We have to get the squash transplanted tonight," her father asked bringing her back to the present. There were yellow crookneck and a new small zucchini squash in the greenhouse that the restaurant would need for stir-fries in July. "If you'll help transplant, I can run the irrigation hoses to water the plants."

"Sure, Dad." Lindsey forced herself to sound cheerful. Maybe a few hours in the garden would help lift her spirits. She followed them to the new section. The squash beds were laid out, the compost dug in, the soil mounded into a raised bed about four inches high. Jim instructed them to plant a double row of plants, staggered diagonally, two feet apart. They offloaded flats of plants from the trailer. Then her father and Travis went back to the barn to load up the irrigation hoses.

It was just Lindsey and Tag. They knelt a few feet apart; the little squash plants by Lindsey's knee. The soil was freshly tilled, soft and crumbly. Lindsey handed Tag the first plant. His free hand gently caught her fingers, startling her into looking into his eyes. His eyes were blue and much older than his face.

"Hey, what's eating you?" His voice was very soft, kind; his level gaze seemed to look deep into her heart. "You haven't smiled since you came home. Why are you so down?"

Lindsey was worn thin by worry and lack of sleep, caught like a bug in a spider web by the events of the last couple of weeks. Even her hand was caught in his. He gave her no reason to pull away, but she felt frozen, his touch was so – intimate. He waited for her to speak, waited while she searched his eyes, waited while she discarded a dozen lies. Waited until she looked away; there was safety in silence.

"Don't give me that 'deer-in-the-headlights' look. I know stress when I see it," Tag said after a long moment. "You might hide it from your family.

But you can't hide it from somebody who's been there. Something is wrong. You might as well tell me about it."

Part of her wanted to tell him to mind his own damn business. The rest of her was captured in his grasp, pinned by his gaze like a rabbit. She felt exposed under his scrutiny: all her worry and her shame for letting her family down. She looked at their hands, her hand looked so small. He didn't take the hint to release her.

"You really should talk to somebody."

There wasn't anyone; she had left all her friends behind when she had come back to Elizabethtown. Maybe all this was showing on her face. She hoped not.

He rubbed his thumb across her knuckles – a gesture of encouragement? She looked up at him, finding her voice but not courage enough to tell him the whole truth.

"I am stressed." She made a vast understatement sound like a confession. Even that was painful. "What isn't wrong? I don't think anything has gone right in weeks."

"Jim told me about the roach." His eyes and his voice were compassionate.

Lindsey admitted to the tip of the iceberg, tried to make a joke of it.

"Two weeks without me and the place has gone to hell." She quipped, but there was no smile to lighten her words. Her heart was racing; this intimacy had knocked a hole in her defenses. Lindsey looked away, unable to continue. She waved him away with her free hand, refusing to speak again.

"Okay, whenever you're willing to talk, I'm willing to listen." He released her hand as gently as he had captured it.

"Tell me what Dad has planned for the tomatoes." She took in a shaky breath, changing the subject. Was she disappointed that he backed off or was she relieved?

"It will be a double row, like this one with four by sixteen foot panels in the center."

"What's with the double rows? We've never used them before." She pulled another plant out of the flat, handed it to him. Quizzing him on the changes he and her father were making would take her mind off her problems. There had to be something going right somewhere in this mess!

"Double rows save space and resources."

"We have plenty of room." Less than a quarter of the fifteen acres was cultivated.

"This layout conserves water and fertilizer. Put two rows close together, in blocks." He gestured with spread hands. "We will have ample walking space between blocks. We can even drive the garden tractor right up to the plants, either to water, feed or harvest."

He went from soft spoken to animate, as he continued to work. "We're going to use 16-foot welded wire fence panels with four plants per side. We'll have eight feet to the next block of tomatoes. Instead of running soaker hoses, we will run a drip emitter to each plant, conserving gallons of water. Newspapers covered in wood chip mulch will keep weeds down and moisture in the soil."

"Last year we tried tomato cages and sprinklers during the drought. The tomato cages didn't hold up, the sprinklers made everything mold and rot. It was an awful mess."

"If this wire can hold a 600 pound pig, it can hold eight tomato plants." Tag grinned. "It's going to save us a hell of a lot of resources and work in the end."

It was therapeutic to hear him talk about the safer topic. However, now that he'd gotten past her defenses, Lindsey found she wanted to talk to him. He seemed kind.

Tag was watching her, his head cocked ever so slightly to one side, inquiring.

"There's money unaccounted for." She looked down, ashamed that she'd allowed things to get so totally out of hand. "I can't find invoice for the pay outs. Heather doesn't know where they went. She knows better than to throw them away."

She left out the lawyer, the threatened lawsuit, how she was blackmailed into taking Mychou back. That failure was too painful to mention.

"How bad is it?" Tag's voice was concerned, not accusing or contemptuous. It was a relief to have someone who listened.

"I've got a small reserve. Not enough to carry the business for more than a month or two. This is such a small town, everybody has heard about the bug. You can imagine how business has fallen off." Lindsey shrugged. "Heather says that Mychou did it, Mychou says Heather did it." She waved a hand in frustration. "Who knows? It's going to destroy business, maybe for months. I may lose everything, we might all lose everything."

"Good thing I'm not here for the money," he quipped.

Oh, he had a sense of humor but lousy timing. Lindsey wrinkled her nose at him.

"I know nothing about you." She handed him another plant. "Here you are asking me to confide in you, when I don't know the first thing about you."

"Are we going to trade information?" He raised an eyebrow at her. "Like 'truth or dare?'" The mischief in his expression said that he enjoyed playing games.

Lindsey decided to play. It was a kid's game.

"You asked first." Lindsey gave him a little smile. "Cough up some information."

"Sergeant Kevin McTaggart." He dug the hole as he answered her. "Army infantry for ten years, two tours of Iraq, distinguished duty, yada, yada, yada." He shrugged, placed the plant in the hole and covered it up. "Medically retired thanks to an IED. I lost three of my soldiers and my left foot in the blast. I've been home for two years; technically I'm still in the Army.

"My caseworker told me to get off my ass, find something to do. I met your father at the hospital about a month ago. He kept talking about this place, until he got me down here last week to take a look for myself. So here I am."

"Oh." She had known about his leg. But to hear it from him, to see the gray hair, the lines on his face and the shadows in his eyes, that saddened her. She struggled for something light to say, settled on, "we can sure use the help."

"You need help all right." He gave her a deadpan verbal poke. "An exterminator at the very least, your life has been taken over by rats."

"Are you applying for the job?" She enjoyed sparring with him.

"I'm out of the extermination business," he reminded her. "I'm available for consultation, but that's about it." He shifted on his knees to the next spot. He slanted her a measuring glance. "So have you ever been married?"

"What?" She handed him a plant. "What does that have to do with it?"

"Truth or dare, remember?" Tag snickered. "Are you going to take a dare already?"

"No." Lindsey gave him a sidelong glance. "I've never been married. I lived with a guy a few years ago." Lindsey had his full attention. "He was a network technician. He loved his computers, his games and his drugs. There wasn't a whole lot left for me. We were both working for the same company, long insane hours on different shifts." She shrugged.

"What do you think about all this?" She waved at the garden.

"I think it's great." Tag looked around. "Cut out the middle man, go straight to the restaurant. The books Jim loaned me are interesting. It's a new view of the world for me. I never paid any attention to food. I just ate whatever was put in front of me." He grinned. "How did you end up with the restaurant?"

"You've seen how the family cooks? I've always wanted a restaurant. Long before the company closed the call center. I cashed out my stock options. I enrolled in Culinary College and started looking for a place to open a restaurant." She opened her hands, palm up. "Here I am."

"You had stock options?" He raised an eyebrow at her.

"I had an IPO, stock options, double shifts, pissed off customers, not enough employees, high blood pressure, anxiety attacks *and* a hostile takeover." Lindsey made it sound like an order off a menu.

"Gee, I just got shot and blown up." They both chuckled. "Why did you break up with your boyfriend?"

"September 11th, 2001 I came home early, I walked into a crack house." Lindsey shook her head at the memory of the towers falling; Heather's frantic call. "I'd gotten a call from Heather that Rich was missing. When I got home Tommy was smoking crack, and screwing somebody else." She snorted with disgust, leaving out the shameful parts. "I don't understand why I stayed for so long." She thought of her question. "So are you married?"

"Divorced, after my first tour in Iraq." He dug another hole. "When I came back to the states, she came to see me in Walter Reed hospital. She didn't last the day." He covered up the plant.

Lindsey could see the memory was bitter.

"Why did you get divorced?"

"The first time I came home from Iraq, I realized that some other man had been living in my house." There was a feral look in his eyes. "It was uncanny, but it was like I could smell him on her skin."

"Ouch," Lindsey said. "That sounds like something out of 'the Jerry Springer show'."

"Oh yeah, high drama, lots of chaos." He gave a snort, dismissed the past. "So what would a guy have to do to get you out for a movie?"

"You mean like a date?" Lindsey asked, surprised and a little flustered.

"No, not a date," Tag teased. "Just a movie with a guy."

"I don't have time to date." Lindsey sounded defensive even to herself. "My restaurant takes up all my time." Lindsey sat back. How long had it been since she had a real date? The night she stooped so low as to go out for dinner and drinks with Brandon didn't count.

"All work and no play," there was a 'come-on' in Tag's voice. "You need to get out, have some fun."

"Why gardening?" she asked. "I mean it seems like an extreme career change." Lindsey heard the lawn tractor fire up; her father and Travis were on the way.

He gave a quirk of the eyebrow at the change of subject.

"I need an extreme change," he replied. "Iraq's a dusty hell hole."

She could see the pain, emotional and physical in his face.

"I go stir-crazy when I have nothing to do. The hard work suits me just fine. It's outside and most importantly nobody shoots at me." For a moment his eyes were bleak and haunted. He quickly shook it off, then asked his question.

"Tell me about Heather's husband."

"Lieutenant Colonel Richard Morgan," Lindsey answered with her late brother-in-law's full name. "He was in the Pentagon on 9/11 when the plane struck, not a dozen feet from where he was standing." Lindsey sighed. "It was horrible but they said he never knew what hit him. I don't think she will ever get over him."

"Has she tried?" Tag asked. "I mean, she talks about him all the time."

"You got that right," she said. "It really isn't fair to Travis that she carries on that way."

The tractor was coming closer. Soon, they wouldn't be able to talk like this. Talking to him had taken the edge off her stress. He was both kind and playful; some girl should have snapped him up by now.

"So why haven't you re-married?" She wondered aloud. When she looked into his face, she saw something raw and wounded. Oops! She'd accidentally struck a nerve.

"Dare." He looked down, his face blank, ending the game.

She felt sorry for him for just a moment.

"I'll have to think of something."

"Do that." He quirked his lips in a smile that did not reach his eyes.

Not only did he have a sense of humor, she thought, he had secrets.

Chapter 8

Tuesday, Lindsey turned into the alley behind the restaurant, wishing with all her heart that she'd never given Brandon a key. What's done is done, she told herself as she walked to the front door.

"Good morning, good looking boss lady." Brandon left the kitchen to meet her as she crossed the dining room. "What have we got fresh from the farm this morning?"

"More of the same." Lindsey ignored the tone of the greeting. Her nose itched at the smell of burning grease.

"What happened to your sister?" Brandon asked, spinning a finger by his temple. "Did you finally get her some help?"

"She's taking care of our mother."

"Traumatized minds snap, you know." There was a glint of malice in his eyes. "It's not like you have to lock her in the basement – like they did in the olden days."

"My sister is a widow, not a schizophrenic!" Lindsey corrected with exasperation.

"There was this one woman…" Brandon was already on another of his 'little old ladies at the nursing home' stories.

Lindsey tuned him out while she shelled peas. Mychou turned up a few minutes later, beautifully made up. She yawned covering her crimson-painted mouth with matching nails.

Lindsey wondered, was that where her missing money had gone? Or did Mychou have that lawyer boyfriend paying for her trips to the beauty parlor? She fumed for a moment, careful to hide her expression.

Lindsey was about to assign the lettuce washing to Mychou, but the bell on the door sounded. Two rough-looking men came to sit at the table by the door. They had coffee with lots and lots of sugar, chatted with her and left. Lindsey noticed the sugar packets scattered all over the table. Wasn't Mychou going to clean up after them?

Two more men came in, sat at the same table and ordered one breakfast to go. Mychou hovered over them, talking and giggling as if they were the best of friends. Brandon stopped his prep work to cook eggs then piled the Styrofoam clamshell with food. He slapped some on the plate for himself and offered a plate to Lindsey. She eyed the greasy mess with distaste.

"You've wasted half a package of bacon, six sausages and a bag of hash browns." Her voice sounded shrewish to her own ears. Well, too bad. It was her money being wasted.

"I wanted to be ready for the rush." He said, chewing his food. He'd already finished the sausage, and the bacon was vanishing fast. "You know, like you do for lunch." His cell phone rang; Brandon gave her that 'ah-shucks' smirk before turning away to answer it.

Lindsey shot him a disapproving look. "When did two customers become a rush?" Lindsey grumbled as she cleaned off the grill.

"Four guys," Mychou piped up. "In for breakfast." She put cups in the sink.

"I saw three men drinking coffee, they didn't order." Lindsey corrected.

Mychou walked out of the kitchen with a sniff.

"You better be nice to her," Brandon said softly, putting the phone in his pocket.

"I'm going to take care of the counter today." Lindsey informed him. Her plan was to keep Mychou away from her cash register.

However, the tables didn't get cleaned correctly. Mychou took the dirty dishes, but merely swept the tables off with her hand. There was a growing amount of crumbs and bits of paper on the floor.

"You need to wipe the table clean." Lindsey took the dishes from Mychou handing her a cloth. "Don't put the stuff on the floor."

"I'm just so busy." Mychou looked contrite. "Can't you help me?"

"I guess."

Lindsey regretted the words a moment later. As soon as Lindsey left the register, Mychou was ringing up tickets, voiding and re-ringing. She muttered that the register was broken when Lindsey tried to shoo her back to the tables. Lindsey couldn't be two places at once. When the rush was over the amount of money in the register did not reconcile to the tape.

Could she get some help? Lindsey stepped outside with her cell phone to call Rose. If Rose would come back, Lindsey would bus the tables herself. She just needed one person she could trust!

"Hi Rose, its Lindsey," Lindsey said a silent prayer.

"How are you?" Rose sounded genuinely glad to hear from her. "How's Eleanor?"

"She's doing much better!"

"I'm so glad."

"Rose," Lindsey hesitated. "Rose, I really need some help."

"Now, Lindsey...."

"Wait Rose, please! I can't do it all by myself." Lindsey pleaded. "I've got to keep an eye on that girl. If you would come back for a week or two I'm sure I could get enough proof to fire her."

"Good God! Um, um, um." Rose made sympathetic noises. "Where's Heather?"

"Taking care of Mom." Lindsey explained. "Mom's still having problems with medication so we don't dare leave her for too long."

"Well, it's good that Heather is home with Eleanor." Rose's voice had a 'no nonsense' tone. "You are needed right where you are and so am I. That Kevin of mine has *got* to settle down. I don't dare cut him loose, he'd be down at the park with the other no-good boys."

Lindsey was tired of begging. She felt depressed and defeated again, she sighed.

"But one of my boys needs a job."

Lindsey wondered which of the infamous male relatives he was. Some of Rose's "boys" were in and out of courts and jails. Lindsey had a very difficult time discerning which were sons, nephews, cousins or grandchildren. Rose had a very large extended family that included boys from church as well as neighbors.

"He's out of school for awhile."

"Your grandson?" Lindsey asked.

"Lord no!" Rose laughed. "My son Shawn, he's my college boy. I have great plans for my Shawn!"

"I'd love to have him," Lindsey said, silently praying that this would work out. She desperately needed a good worker.

"I'll call him," Rose promised. "He'll be there tomorrow."

"Thank you!"

"And honey," Rose's voice was compassionate but firm. "Get rid of those two!"

"I will! I swear!"

"Take care of your mama!"

"You know that I will." Lindsey sighed, Rose had two sons; one was a cop. Shawn must be the younger son. When she went back into the restaurant, Brandon was locking the door, from the outside. He gave her a little finger wave before he walked away.

There was no sign of Mychou.

"Where are you going?"

Lindsey looked around the kitchen in utter horror, at the stacks of dishes, pots and pans, glasses and silverware, dirt, food and paper on the floors. Lindsey stared after them, furious. She'd turned her back for two minutes and they'd left the entire clean up job to her!

She called her sister to let her know that she wouldn't be home for dinner. Fuming Lindsey went back into the kitchen to get started, attacking the job of cleaning with all her pent up anger. This was the last straw! She may end up stuck running this place by herself; but she was done letting people walk all over her!

It was nearly eight o'clock when she finished cleaning up. She stopped at a store on the way home, picking up a small, coiled plastic key ring. She would put the cash register key on it. She would lock the drawer taking the key everywhere with her. If the Princess wanted her job, all her cleanup work had better be finished before she left at night!

Lindsey was barely able to stay awake on the way home. Still she had some hope, Rose's young man would help clean up and bus tables so she could keep an eye on that dratted waitress.

Her father and Tag were behind her house, tilling the beds for the tomatoes. She waved at them. That meant she was going to be transplanting tomatoes tomorrow. She attacked her bookwork, getting everything finished before she went to sleep that night.

Rose's son Shawn turned out to be a mature and muscular man, not the youth she expected. He agreed to work for the wage she offered him. They agreed he could start the next day. Then Lindsey gave Mychou a list of side work; silently praying the woman would quit on the spot.

"I expect these to be completed before you go." Lindsey said as politely as she could.

Mychou sniffed, but she kept the list.

"Friday is the last day we are open for breakfast," she told them.

"Wait, we are just starting to get in a crowd." Brandon protested.

It was time to remind Brandon who was boss. She adopted a posture and tone of voice she had seen her father use a thousand times.

"Brandon, I agreed to a trial period. This week it ends. I haven't made any money on breakfast. I make money by serving lunch. We have to stay focused. Four customers who drink coffee do not constitute a crowd. I pay you to come in at eight o'clock to do prep work for *lunch*."

"Sorry." Brandon looked down like a contrite child. "I was just trying to help. Business being so slow and all, I thought you would make more money with a breakfast crowd." He looked at her with sad brown eyes.

Lindsey was tired of being manipulated. She stifled the impulse to apologize to him by remembering how he'd walked out last night, leaving her a mess.

"Furthermore, I expect this kitchen to be spotless before you leave." She said holding her ground, handing him a list of work to be completed. "Another trick like yesterday, you'll be back at the employment office."

She got him busy chopping while she was making salads. Instead of sneaking out back to smoke, or talking on his cell phone, he was right beside her.

Everything was ready when the phone started to ring. Lindsey felt she was getting her business back on track. Mychou waited the tables. Brandon filled orders, and Lindsey rang up the tickets.

"This wasn't what I ordered," a woman said handing her the bill. "It was good, but I asked for the pasta salad, I got potato salad."

Lindsey apologized to the woman. The next customer said pretty much the same thing. Lindsey apologized again. She told Brandon about the complaints.

"The orders are getting mixed up." Lindsey told Brandon. "You need to be more careful."

"Sorry." Brandon gave her puppy-dog eyes. "I'm really busy back here. I could use some help."

If he thought he could weasel her into helping him, he was sadly mistaken. She was not about to give Mychou free access to her cash register. His cell phone rang. Lindsey looked at him, pointedly. He looked at the number then silenced the ringer.

"Women, they just won't leave me alone." He shrugged giving her the 'ah-shucks' country-boy look.

Lindsey made a non-committal noise. To further her frustration, the day ended with the ticket count off. She'd counted thirty-six customers, ten take-out orders. There were thirty tickets. Lindsey's frustration broke out again. Had she miscounted, or were orders missing? With her mother and her sister working with her, it had never been an issue. Lindsey needed a better way to track orders.

The remainder of the day Lindsey spent in the garden with her father and Tag, setting up the tomato beds. There were four huge fence panels, four feet high and 16 feet in length strapped to the back of the trailer. Lindsey was on the trailer working the tie downs off. Her foot slipped, something gave, the heavy panels slid sideways, trapping her foot against the side of the trailer in a painful pinch.

"I'm stuck!" Panicked, Lindsey teetered, unable to right herself. If she went down with her foot caught, she'd break her leg for sure.

"I got you." Tag's strong hands caught her, holding her steady. She recovered her balance, keeping one hand on his broad shoulder. He took in the problem at a glance. He pushed the panel towards Jim, freeing Lindsey's foot.

"Jim, hold that."

"Come here, little girl." Tag scooped her up, setting her on the wheel casing.

Lindsey was utterly unnerved by her near fall. She huddled on the wheel casing, her face white, while Tag carefully removed her shoe and sock.

"Can you move your foot?" He looked over the red welt, rubbed her ankle with warm hands.

"Yes." Lindsey blushed as he ran his hands over her foot.

"You've got tiny little feet." Mischievously, he ran one finger across the arch of her foot, tickling her.

"Be nice." Lindsey protested twitching.

Tag tickled her again. Lindsey's mood broke; she giggled. The pain was going away, and her ankle didn't swell.

"Give my foot back."

Mischief danced in his blue eyes, almost as if he might refuse.

"I'm okay." Lindsey felt acutely self-conscious. Her father was watching them.

"You're good to go." Tag smiled at her. "Be more careful, okay?"

"Thank you." She quickly put her shoe back on then stood up to show them that she really was okay.

They wrestled the panels off the trailer, carried them to the new beds. Jim and Tag took turns driving posts. When they got the posts up, Jim and Tag held the panels while Lindsey set the zip ties. Once the panels were in place, they transplanted the heirloom tomatoes, set the drip irrigation lines. It was nearly dark, so they called it a night, elated at having the huge job behind them. To celebrate, they had apple pie with ice cream under the pergola.

As Lindsey rubbed her bruised ankle, she caught Tag watching her. Lindsey smiled at him with warmth. She liked Tag even if he looked like a shaggy dog. He was so – watchful – that he missed nothing.

Had his time in Iraq made him that way or was it an aspect of his personality that predated his time in service?

Chapter 9

The next morning, Lindsey woke up early to work in the garden. She had an idea while sleeping. It was so simple! She could keep track of both of her problems at one time, for very little cash.

Her father and Tag were already in the gardens, the produce picked: lettuce, spinach, the late peas, radishes and the second year parsley. Lindsey gave everything a quick rinse off then packed it up.

Lindsey took a quick trip to Wal-Mart. She was pleased to make it to the restaurant before Brandon. Lindsey pulled the pack of restaurant tickets out of the bag. She would get a handle on Mychou and put an end to Brandon's excuses. She threw away all the old ticket books, recording the numbers of the new tickets. She could match the tickets from the orders, tracking both Brandon and Mychou.

She was making coffee when there was a knock on the door. It was a deliveryman. Who was Ray Rick Supply? She peeked out the window, she'd never heard of these people.

"What have you got there?"

"Cleaning supplies." He had a couple of cases on a dolly. She let him in, and he made his way to the vault, where he stacked the cases. She scanned the invoice, yes, cleaning supplies and a case of drain cleaner. She walked to the little desk where they kept the orders. There was her note to order supplies and the list. Drain cleaner wasn't on that list.

"Hey." She caught the man at the door. "I didn't order the drain cleaner."

"So?" The look he gave her was unfriendly.

"Please, take it back." She fought the desire to scratch her nose; some vaguely familiar chemical smell irritated her sinuses. "I didn't order it," she said politely, trying not to sneeze.

"There will be a re-stocking fee." He made it sound expensive.

She stood her ground, imitating her father's stern no-nonsense look that always sent his soldiers scrambling. The man did as she asked, but the look he gave her was cold and hostile. There were alarm bells going off in her head. She stuffed the invoice in her back pocket.

Lindsey was turning to walk back to the kitchen, intending to call Ray Rick Supply. At that moment Brandon came bouncing into the restaurant, singing a hip-hop song. He grabbed her hand and swung her around so that she joined him in his dance. By the time she'd stopped laughing, she'd forgotten all about the delivery.

Lindsey waited until Mychou and Shawn came in to go over the ticket system. Lindsey felt she was being diplomatic, the mistakes needed to stop.

"I bought some real restaurant order tickets," Lindsey said sitting down with them. "I can tell that these are going to make everybody's job easier." She handled one book to Mychou. "Standard stuff, so Brandon will have a copy too. That way we will eliminate confusion with orders." Lindsey looked at Brandon and Mychou who looked blandly back at her. "Any questions?"

Today the lunch rush ran smoother. Brandon stopped making mistakes on the orders. Mychou was the picture of efficiency. Lindsey made the effort to compliment her on how well she handled the rush. Shawn had proved himself; the tables were clean as soon as the customer got up. He'd found time to do the pans and the dishes. Lindsey hadn't needed to leave the register. Things were getting better. It wasn't just Lindsey's wishful thinking.

That afternoon, while Jim and Eleanor were at the doctors, Lindsey and Tag were alone in the garden, weeding the rows of beans. Lindsey was grubbing out weeds for all she was worth, trying to work out worries that had re-surfaced on the way home. If she couldn't be rid of the weeds in her mind, she would get every one of the weeds out of the garden.

"Are you weeding or killing somebody over there?" Tag asked in a teasing tone, from the next row over. He had stopped weeding and was watching her.

"A bit of both." Lindsey stopped chopping the ground. How did he zero in on her feelings like that?

"You know, I can hear you worry all the way over here." He was looking right through her with those piercing blue eyes. "It's like a squeaky fan belt on an old pickup truck, squeak, squeak, squeak."

Lindsey laughed and blushed at the same time.

"Every night you come home just wound up and squeaking." He cocked his head slightly, still observing. "But you never talk to your family about it."

"I'm fine, really!" The lie sounded feeble to her ears.

"Get real." His tone was sharp; he gave a rueful smile then his voice dropped. "I have a councilor who would kick my butt from here to Chicago for a bald faced lie like: 'I'm fine'. Talking about it does help, you know."

Lindsey shook her head.

"You could talk to your father." He gave her a lazy smile. "Hell, I talk to your father."

Lindsey looked down.

"You should talk to somebody." His voice dropped in tone and timbre, coaxing. "You can talk to me."

Lindsey looked at him. Tag was leaning on the hand cultivator, relaxed but watching her with that level gaze. She recalled the game of 'truth or dare' days ago. She knew him better now.

"I can't tell my father that the restaurant is losing money. It's added stress he doesn't need. Between Mom's ankle and Heather's attitude, I don't know how he copes." She rubbed her forehead, worry was giving her a permanent tension headache. If things didn't get better she'd start having migraines again.

"My head hurts all the time," she confessed. "I can't sleep. If my life stays this screwed up much longer I'm going to end up in a rubber room."

"Rubber rooms are overrated."

Lindsey smiled briefly.

"I've got to get that woman out of my restaurant." She shook her head. "I've managed people before, but never like this woman. She is up to something, but I can't catch her at it."

He stepped closer. The more animated she became, the more he smiled at her. So he found her amusing? Fine, Lindsey let herself vent.

"I'll tell you how bad it is: I fired her Friday, because she put the roach in that poor guy's food." All wound up, she was talking with her hands, the hoe tucked under her arm.

"Monday morning, I got a call from her lawyer. She convinced him that I'm a racist, that I fired her without just cause. He said they would sue me if I didn't take her back. I – I didn't know what else to do." Lindsey shook her head. "Now I think she's stealing. Damn it, I know she's stealing, but I can't catch her at it. It's like some kind of a sick cat and mouse game. I'm trying to figure out the game, and I'm losing."

"Sounds like a war I visited once or twice," he said with grim humor. "You against them, only they aren't playing by the rules." His eyes were sad. "Honey, there aren't any rules."

"I have to win," she said waving one hand to encompass the house, the garden and her family. "All this depends on me."

"Does it really?" He asked, leaning on the cultivator over the row of bean plants. "Or are you taking on things that don't belong to you?"

"My parents lost most of their retirement savings when the market crashed after nine-eleven. That's why they are here living with Heather. They need the restaurant to succeed as badly as I do." She stamped a foot in frustration. "If only I knew how to beat her at her own game!"

"What have you tried?"

"I told the Princess that she has to do her side work. I've hired Shawn to bus tables and do the dishes. All the meal tickets are numbered. I run the cash register, *and* I take the key out when I'm not standing by it."

"Hey, sounds like you got it covered." He gave her shoulder a gentle tap with his fist. "You're on the right track." The smile had spread to his eyes, the corners crinkled as she continued.

"Brandon keeps telling me how women at the nursing home died of blood clots, or other horrible complications of minor injuries." Lindsey ground her teeth. "I get really frustrated with him."

"I've heard Heather talk about him. He sounds like one manipulative S.O.B."

"It worked on us once. Heather was nearly hysterical until I agreed to come home to stay with Mom." Lindsey sighed. "I was worried sick myself."

"I think we all over-reacted." Lindsey inhaled, sucking back bad memories. "I should have sent Heather home. Things would have turned out differently."

"Don't 'should' on yourself," Tag advised. "It will drive you crazy."

"Brandon keeps telling me that he can run the place for me."

"Sounds like the restaurant would go down the drain." Tag was grinning at her.

"With him in charge it would." She remembered the case of drain cleaner. "Speaking of drains, something else is weird. Brandon ordered from this company that I never use. Some guy delivered a case of industrial drain cleaner."

Tag gave her a puzzled look.

"Our pipes are plastic. We can't use drain cleaner."

"What did you do?"

"I sent it back."

"What else is he ordering?" There was no trace of humor now.

Lindsey cocked her head at him, until what he meant dawned on her. "You think he's stealing from me?"

"Why not? The girl is."

Lindsey shook her head, Brandon had a lot of faults, but he wasn't a thief.

"I let him order supplies." Lindsey thought about it. "He never asked me which companies I used. Maybe he called the wrong one. I can't blame him for making a mistake if I didn't give him the right information."

"Don't blow that off," Tag warned. "Have you checked the invoices?"

"I don't have any invoices." Lindsey shook her head. "Heather lost them all while I was gone."

"How long were you gone?"

"Not even two weeks." Lindsey thought about the dates. "There would have been a food order, a beverage order and a supply order."

"He's had lots of opportunity."

"No motive."

"Why not? There are a lot of reasons to steal. He could be selling stuff to his friends to make drugs or to get drugs."

"Brandon is not into drugs!" Lindsey scoffed at his suspicion. "You don't know him. He's clean cut, clean-shaven, even his jeans are pressed. Addicts are…"

Her voice trailed off as she took a good look at Tag.

Today Tag was wearing a faded brown T-shirt with the collar and sleeves cut off, tattered BTUs and a bandana to keep the hair and the sweat out of his eyes. His hair was shaggy and his beard untrimmed.

If anybody looked like an addict down on his luck, it was Tag.

"That bad, huh?" His eyebrows drew together thoughtfully.

Lindsey's blushing cheeks gave her away.

"Can't be that bad." Tag brought a hand to his beard, raising an eyebrow at her.

"I'm sorry." Lindsey's cheeks were flaming hot; she was sincerely contrite. "I was just trying to explain…" She stopped before she put her foot any deeper into her mouth.

"That your buddy doesn't look like an addict. So what does an addict look like?" The mischief in his eyes said Tag was needling her now, enjoying her discomfort.

"You're impossible." Lindsey went back to her weed chopping.

Tag didn't know Brandon, but she did. For a few minutes, she wrestled with the idea. Brandon was a lot of things, funny, vain, manipulative, and a good cook. Could he also be a thief? There was the car, the gold chain, the things he hinted about, parties on the weekends, women who chased him down, calling him all hours of the day.

She flicked a glance at Tag. He'd been around, obviously, while she had been relatively sheltered. He seemed sincerely concerned about this. She could check, make some calls just to be sure. No harm done.

"Tag?"

He looked up, serious for the moment.

"I'll call my vendors." Lindsey thought he was pleased at her promise. She'd vented all she could vent. She wanted to talk about safer subjects. "Are you sure that the new beds are less work?"

"Absolutely," he said, returning to the task at hand. "I hate weeding." He flicked a glance at her. "Unless I have someone to talk to while I'm at it."

Chapter 10

When Lindsey got to the garden, Tag and her father were already finished. They drank coffee and chatted about planting and watering schedules while Lindsey did the rinsing and packing. Lindsey was grateful to have the two of them handling the garden side of the business.

The family sat down to breakfast. She even had time for an extra cup of coffee before she drove into E'town.

The prep work went fast, Brandon clowned around, using a spatula as a microphone as he made up silly songs that kept them all in stitches.

Brandon's endless energy seemed unnatural, enviable, but unnatural. If Brandon did take drugs, it would be a stimulant. Like cocaine or … crystal meth. Lindsey sighed, almost hating herself for the thought. She didn't need another complication!

There were other customers drinking coffee. Most of them sat at one table, the one closest to the door. They came and went quickly. Lindsey found it annoying that Mychou spent more time with those customers than with the ones who ordered food. They all seemed to be friends of hers. Couldn't she visit with her friends *after* work?

Or was she being unreasonable? Well, money was money.

As she had promised, Lindsey called Ray Rick Supply before she went home that afternoon. She waited until she was alone in the restaurant before she picked up the phone. It felt like she was sneaking around behind Brandon's back. If this was only a simple mistake, she was going to feel like a complete fool.

"Hello, I'm Lindsey Bennett. I have a restaurant called 'Let's Do Lunch' in Elizabethtown."

"How can I help you?" The young woman's voice was bored.

"I have a problem with my account."

"Let me look up your account." The girl put Lindsey on hold, and didn't come back. Lindsey finally hung up and called in again.

"Hello, I'm Lindsey Bennett. I have a restaurant in Elizabethtown."

"How can I help you?" This was a different voice, older and less bored.

"I have a problem with my account." Lindsey was aggravated, but fought to keep it out of her voice. "I've had supplies delivered to my restaurant that I didn't order. I'm concerned that someone has stolen my account information."

"That's not likely," the woman said. "We don't have ordering over the Internet."

"It has nothing to do with the Internet." Lindsey ground her teeth together. "I need to know if someone has used my account information to order without my permission."

"Why?" The woman asked.

"I got a case of drain cleaner. I never order drain cleaner."

"Drain cleaner?" By the tone in her voice, the woman must think that Lindsey was crazy.

"I'm not going to pay for anything that I didn't order." Lindsey took a deep breath to keep herself calm. "I need to know if there are any charges outstanding on my account."

There was silence on the phone.

"Let me check your account information." Mercifully she did not put Lindsey on hold. "I don't see anything charged to the account."

"Can you send me an itemized copy of all the invoices for the last month?" Lindsey thought she could hear the woman groan under her breath.

"That's going to take time."

"Can't you just print it out?"

"I can't drop everything to look up delivery orders." The woman's voice was frosty. "It will take at least 10 days, it may take longer."

"You've got to be kidding." Lindsey suppressed a sigh. "Okay, in the meantime, we need to have some kind of security on this account so it doesn't happen again."

"I can't do that," the woman said. "You'd have to talk to the Manager."

"Can you transfer me?"

"Hold on."

Fortunately, Lindsey was only on hold a short time. The manager was able to lock the account to Lindsey's name and added a password for phone orders. The process was the same with the other supply-company, the food vendor and the beverage vendor. They reluctantly agreed to find all the invoices from her company for the last month and send her copies in seven to ten days.

Lindsey hoped that she wasn't wasting everyone's time with a wild goose chase. If Tag hadn't been so serious, she might have blown it off. Now she had something else to worry about.

That evening, Lindsey reluctantly joined the family for dinner. She knew Tag wanted her to spill it about the problems she was facing. It was hard enough for her to carry on without him sitting across from her, like a wolf waiting for the rabbit to jump.

"How is the restaurant doing?" Her father asked.

"All right." Lindsey ignored Tag's raised eyebrows.

"How is the garden?" She wanted to kick Tag under the table, but she couldn't remember which leg was which. She might break her toes. She rubbed the back of her neck, wanting nothing more than to get the hell out of the house. Heather was still bustling around the kitchen. Travis was busy eating with one hand, a hand-held game in the other.

"It's good to see you up and around." Lindsey turned to her mother.

"I'm glad to get out of bed." Eleanor tugged at the scarf she was wearing over her hair. "My head itches. I can't wash my hair."

"Go to the hair salon," Lindsey suggested. "They always wash your hair while you're in a chair. It should be easy enough."

"I haven't seen the girls in a month! That would certainly be a treat, wouldn't it?" Eleanor brightened up. "Heather, we'll have to do that!"

Lindsey nearly choked on her dinner: Heather? Didn't Lindsey deserve a treat too? Her resentment towards her sister was a hard knot in her throat. Lindsey closed her eyes, swallowed hard, and shut her mouth. She needed to pretend everything was fine, shouting her frustration at the table wasn't going to do it.

Her food stuck in her throat. Lindsey made an excuse to leave the table. She thought that two pairs of eyes followed her out of the room, but she wasn't sure. If Tag and her father ever compared notes, she was going to be in for it.

She worked on her books the rest of the evening, watching her father and Tag work in the garden without her.

Saturday, it was raining; no garden work this morning. Lindsey went back to bed, exhausted from the chaos at the restaurant, her sister's temper, her mother's favoritism, and her father's expectations. She just wanted one day to get some rest. She soaked in a tub of hot water, drank tea instead of coffee, going back to bed. That afternoon she finished the payroll, the quarterly taxes, and never changed out of her pajamas.

Why bother?

She was losing money hand over fist. At this rate she couldn't get a bank loan. Depressed and miserable, she shut off her cell phone and pulled the curtains shut.

Sunday, she awoke to a rainy day. Today she lay in bed, unwilling to face the morning. When she finally staggered into the shower, it was after ten. If only there was someplace she could hide. She felt like a failure.

Instead, she went to the restaurant where she spent the afternoon cleaning. Once everything was clean, she looked around with satisfaction. This was her place in the world as tiny as it was.

She would find a way to make it work out.

She drove home, careful on the wet roads. The rain was still coming down in intermittent showers. She splashed through puddles as she walked to her front door. She half expected the phone to ring, for her father or someone to knock or something. But that night the only sounds were crickets and rain on the roof.

Brandon and Mychou came in together, early. Lindsey looked them over as they entered the door. Brandon was clean and shaved; his uniform whites clean and pressed. Mychou was dressed in Capri pants, her freshly styled hair and makeup perfect. Brandon started out by sharpening his knives. Mychou cleaned the lettuce and made salads. Lindsey set up water to boil pasta and steam potatoes and carrots. When Shawn came in at nine on the dot, she put him to work sweeping the floors.

The doorbell chimed, two rough-looking guys came in. Mychou was quick to come out and wait on them. Mychou told them there would be no more breakfast. She tossed a sour look at Lindsey, most likely laying the blame on thick and heavy.

Lindsey sighed, wanting to defend herself, but she had prep work to do. She watched Mychou serve the customers coffee, with packet after packet of sugar.

Lindsey found herself watching Shawn. Dressed in jeans and a polo shirt, he was a handsome young black man. Lindsey wondered how old he really was; he didn't look like a teenager. Maybe he had gone back to college after a couple of years in the service? Rose had so many troubled young men under her wing it was hard to remember all the stories and the names that went together.

He was flirting outrageously with Mychou, showing off his biceps and posing. He was well-built but his posing wasn't acceptable. Lindsey waited until he came back in the kitchen to confront him.

"Shawn." Lindsey reprimanded him quietly. "You just started here, and I think that you are a great addition to the team. But – I'd be more comfortable if you didn't – if you would act a little more professionally towards Mychou."

The young man gave her a grin, embarrassed at being caught, or at being confronted?

"Yes, ma'am." He wiped the grin off his face quickly.

Lindsey pulled him towards the back of the room, by the sinks.

"Mychou's husband is in jail for a drug charge." Lindsey told him very softly,

Shawn gave her a startled look.

"Didn't she tell you that she was married?" Lindsey was biting her tongue to keep from giving him a lecture. He seemed like such a nice young man to be chasing after a married woman of questionable character.

"Look, Lindsey." He took a deep breath. "I work for you, but my personal life is my own business."

Lindsey drew back, stung. Well she'd put her nose where it didn't belong, didn't she? Fortunately, the early lunch crowd from the courthouse came in. Saved by the bell, Lindsey thought cynically, as she turned back to waiting on her customers.

Shawn alternately bused tables and did dishes. Mychou did all her side work before she left. Brandon had his station and the grill clean. Shawn washed dishes, while Lindsey helped dry them. They all left the restaurant at four o'clock.

Today, with Lindsey the only one on the register, the money count was exactly right.

It felt so good to be on top for once. She was sick of being the loser in this damn game.

Chapter 11

When Lindsey stepped inside her sister's house, Eleanor was sitting in the living room; her hair freshly touched up. Lindsey was about to compliment her, when she caught the angry vibe.

"What's going on?"

"The girls at the beauty shop were very surprised to see me today." Eleanor's face was set in angry lines. "It seems half the town thinks I'm at death's door."

"The shop has always been Gossip Central."

"What they are saying about your sister is much worse."

"Mom, you know I don't gossip." Lindsey looked around for help, but there was no sign of her father. Damn!

"Who's been saying that Heather had a nervous breakdown? That she put a roach in that man's food?" Eleanor stayed seated, but her erect posture shouted her indignation as loudly as if she were standing. "What a pack of lies! I have never felt so humiliated in my entire life!"

Lindsey gritted her teeth, Mychou must be starting rumors, who else?

"That woman is still working for you! Isn't she?" Heather put in her two cents worth from the doorway to the dining room.

"Unfortunately, yes." Lindsey turned to confront her sister.

"You told us that you fired her!" The fury in Heather's eyes and the set to her face made Lindsey cringe.

"I *did* fire her!" Lindsey choked out. "But her lawyer told me that they would sue if I didn't take her back."

"Why would anybody sue over a waitress job?" Eleanor snorted.

"Ask Heather, *she* hired the girl." Lindsey turned on her heel, walked out the door, closing it firmly behind her.

She saw her father and Tag in the back garden, putting up trellis for the cucumbers. She was so angry she didn't want to talk to anybody. Damn it, how could her mother treat her like that! Her thoughts were headed straight for self pity until she got up to her house.

Someone had set slabs of concrete in front of the stairs. Now a path of stepping-stones went from gate to stairs. She wouldn't have to worry about slipping in mud again. They had put in a lot of work. The concrete slabs were a foot and half square or better. The gesture touched her heart.

Had her father taken the time to do this? She smiled, genuinely pleased that he'd cared so much. Her mother and sister might judge her guilty, but her father still loved her. She sat on the top step allowing herself the luxury of frustrated tears. If she ever got her hands on Mychou, she was going to choke that woman!

When she was done crying, she made herself dinner, ignoring the bell when it rang. She didn't have to put up with this crap. Let her mother and Heather explain this quarrel to her father!

Lindsey woke up with all her stress settled in the pit of her stomach, she felt snarky and unrepentant about it. To spite her mood the morning was gorgeous, the breeze was sweet scented, the air was cool. Travis, out of school for the summer, worked beside Jim.

There was no sign of Tag.

"I see you have another helper," Lindsey said. "What happened to Tag?"

"Tag had an appointment at the hospital."

Lindsey missed the way Tag always waved to her, that silly almost-salute. She always felt that he knew that she was going into battle. Right now, he was the only person who understood what she was going through. She finished packing the coolers and went to work, feeling a little disappointed.

Brandon and Mychou arrived at the restaurant shortly after Lindsey, as usual. Everything was going smoothly until, as the lunch rush was building, Mychou and Shawn both vanished. Lindsey found them out back, smoking. Shawn was seductively toying with Mychou's dangling earrings. Lindsey cleared her throat. They jumped apart.

"Get back to work," Lindsey snarled. "We have a full dining room. I don't pay you to socialize."

Shawn shrugged and walked away.

Mychou flipped her cigarette in the parking lot, like she was flipping Lindsey the bird.

At three thirty, there was a knock at the door, an elderly Asian woman stood outside holding a baby. She waved to Mychou. Lindsey unlocked the door. There was a little girl clinging to the woman's leg. The woman glanced at Lindsey then spoke rapidly to Mychou. The little girl ran to Mychou, speaking in a mix of English and Vietnamese. Mychou hushed her daughter then looked at Lindsey.

"My grandmother wants me to take the children now."

"You're good to go," Lindsey said. She watched Mychou collect her purse and walk out holding her daughter's little hand. Lindsey felt a stab of envy. The little girl was so darling.

Once she had wanted children and a normal life. Since 9/11, so much had changed. Lindsey sighed, if there was such a thing as a normal life, she didn't qualify.

"Hey," Brandon said from behind her. "You want to go out and have a drink?" He was giving her the 'ah-shucks-ain't-I-cute' come on. He was cute, his curly hair was tousled, a hint of stubble framed his jaw, and his mouth curved in that sexy come-on smile. Was he actually flexing his biceps a bit?

Lindsey wanted to snicker. He was trying too hard, all of Brandon's careful posing didn't do a thing for her. Whatever 'it' was, Brandon didn't have it.

"No thanks," Lindsey said, politely. "Some other time."

"You don't know what you are missing." Brandon came a couple of steps closer, invading her space. "Come on, let's have a few drinks, a few laughs." He winked at her. "You know what I mean."

"Go home, Brandon." Lindsey wanted to roll her eyes.

Shawn snickered behind them.

"Everybody has to play a little." Brandon gave her puppy-dog eyes.

"Man, do not waste your time on the Ice Maiden." Shawn adopted a limp-wrist pose and lisped. "I'll have that drink. But you keep your hands to yourself, big boy."

"The company I'm forced to keep." Brandon grinned.

The two of them went towards the door Shawn, still clowning, sashayed with swinging hips. Brandon goosed Shawn as they walked out. Lindsey locked the door behind them. What a pair!

On the way home, she mentally ran through the garden produce that would be harvested in the morning. The early beans were ready. She could offer three-bean salad next week, with a green bean casserole as a menu option.

Tag's truck was parked in her driveway. Two freshly planted beds of flowers flanked her porch. It looked like someone had raided Heather's daylilies.

Her father and Tag were in the back garden planting the new beds. She waved and they waved back. She walked up the stairs. For once, the stairs were rock solid under her feet. The rotten boards on the deck had been replaced. How had her father found time for this? She would have to thank him. Her spirits lifted as she fought with the screen door latch. Finally springing it open, she entered her small trailer house.

The living room opened to the dining area, then to the kitchen. She bypassed the dining table, strewn with papers, old menus and recipes, going straight to her room. She tossed her purse and the moneybag on her antique waterfall vanity; then changed her work clothes for garden clothes. She slipped out the back door to join her father and Tag.

They'd cut a gap in the fence near her place for easier access. There was no gate up yet. Lindsey strolled through the gap. Tag and her father were planting cucumbers in one of the raised beds. She noticed there were wood-chips spread on the ground between the beds. Tag had his back to her, bent over one of the raised beds.

"We are planting the late beans," Jim said as she came up to them. "We're trying an heirloom pole bean. They are supposed to have the best flavor of any pole bean around." He seemed amused about something. "I never would have thought to look for seeds on the Internet."

"I wanted to thank you for fixing my stairs and the deck." She smiled at her father.

He slanted a glance at Tag.

"Oh? Tag, you didn't have to do that for me."

When Tag turned she was looking at a clean-cut stranger. Tag had shaved his beard and mustache. He had transformed from scruffy and disreputable to – utterly gorgeous. The beard had hidden a sharply defined jaw and a generous mouth. A thin scar ran on the right side of his chiseled face from chin to ear. His hair was just a bit longer than military style and it looked good on him.

Now she could visualize him in a uniform. My – my, she thought, that fine specimen hidden under all that shaggy hair. There was a shyness about him that caught her attention. He didn't quite meet her eyes.

"Well, hello there," she said in her lowest 'come on' voice. "Thank you for fixing my stairs and the deck."

"You're welcome." What Tag saw in her face pleased him. He lost his shyness; his mouth turned up in a one-sided smile that crinkled the corners of his eyes.

Her father was smirking; he caught her eye and mouthed the word 'flowers.'

"Did you plant the flowers too?" She asked as she looked back at Tag.

"Heather's needed thinning," Tag said with mischief in his eyes.

Lindsey wondered if he'd asked Heather before he'd taken her flowers.

"She won't miss them."

"She counts them every morning. They all have names." Lindsey snickered, positive he hadn't asked. They grinned at each other, co-conspirators.

Her father cleared his throat.

"Well now," her father cut the silence. "Since you are here, you'd better grab a packet of radishes." He had a twinkle in his eye. "These go around the foot of the cucumbers in a square of four. Then put five bib lettuce next to them, and go back to radishes."

"Why aren't we just planting cucumbers in nice straight rows, like we always do?" Lindsey asked.

"If we put three different crops in one bed, we get three harvests from the same space." Her father was enthused about this project, Lindsey could tell. "The radishes and the lettuce will be long gone before the cukes are tall enough to shade them out." He held out his hand, motioning at the bed itself. "We grow three times as much in the same space, fertilizing once, using the same amount of water. It is three times more efficient than gardening in rows."

So, her father and Tag were a team in this agricultural experiment. The thought of them as a team was comforting. Lindsey smiled at them both.

"It's a great way to run a market garden, more vegetables from the same space with less work, water and fertilizer." Jim said with a pleased smile.

Tag wagged his eyebrows at her. "Think what that will do for your bottom line."

"I guess it's going to take some getting used to." Her bottom line was all red ink. If the restaurant closed, they could open a roadside stand. "So hand me a packet of seeds."

They planted blocks until Heather rang the bell calling them for dinner. Lindsey planned to avoid dinner with the family. When her father and Tag set the tools aside, she started back towards her trailer.

"Lindsey," her father's voice was gentle. "Come to supper."

"I've got too much bookwork to do." Lindsey made her excuse. "I'll catch a sandwich."

"I heard about yesterday." He didn't usually get between his daughters and his wife. "I got an ear full." He flicked a glance at Tag, who kept a straight face. "We both got an ear full." The set to his jaw expressed his displeasure of having the family laundry aired at the dinner table.

"Then you know why I won't come to supper." Lindsey straightened her shoulders, squaring up for a battle of wills. "I don't deserve to be treated like that."

"I see." Her father took in her stance, the set to her jaw. He studied her for a moment. She stood straight; did not wilt under the appraisal that brought many a Staff Sargent to heel like a puppy. He shook his head.

"Carry on," he said, in automatic dismissal. He continued to her sister's house.

Tag caught her eye, without his beard and mustache his face was easy to read. The raised eyebrow said he found the exchange amusing.

She stifled the impulse to make him swear to keep her secrets. Then he winked. He would keep confidences, the wink said, but she was being stubborn.

Lindsey retreated to her home and her bookwork. When she caught up, she started researching recipes. The variations were endless and soothing. She printed several then ran them through her spreadsheets to expand them to restaurant-sized batches.

It was close to dark when someone knocked on her door. When Lindsey opened the door to see Tag, she was struck again by the change in his appearance. The phrase "friendly shaggy dog" didn't apply anymore. He even seemed to carry himself differently. Had he been hiding behind the beard? At least his voice and eyes were the same.

She waved him in, backing into her living room.

"Hi, I want to give you my cell number. In case you feel the need to talk." Framed in the doorway he seemed to loom over her, taller and broader of shoulder, more masculine. He must be over six feet tall.

Why hadn't she noticed this before?

"Thanks." Lindsey shook it off. He was the same person she'd been talking to all along. "If this keeps up, I won't have anybody to talk to." Lindsey reached for the phone in her purse.

"Your father had his say at dinner tonight. I've had my share of dressing down, but the one Jim gave Eleanor and Heather was a master piece."

Lindsey winced in sympathy as she rummaged through her purse.

"He never raised his voice, but he let them know he thought they were acting like children. The family is supposed to stick together."

"Mom and Heather have always stuck together," Lindsey said. She found her purse and pulled her cell phone out. "I'm glad somebody is sticking up for me."

"Hey, what am I, chopped liver?" He was messing with her now, giving her a hangdog expression that didn't make it to his laughing eyes.

"Pate`," Lindsey joked. "Fancy chopped liver."

"Day old chopped liver." He winked at her.

Lindsey giggled at him.

"You can call me anytime," he said. "I'm a light sleeper."

"What is sleep?" She quipped in false cheer. As she programmed her cell phone, he leaned over her shoulder, his number on the display. As she did the same for him, she felt his breath on her cheek. It was disconcerting.

"You all right?" Tag asked, his voice low. He laid a hand on her shoulder. "Did something happen at work?"

She looked at him sidelong, not about to admit the change in his appearance was having a profound effect on her. She was so used to seeing him scruffy; it almost felt like she had lost a friend. That was crazy!

"Everything was fine, for once."

"I don't like seeing you depressed."

"I'm tired, not depressed."

"Right." The tone in his voice said 'liar' but his face had only compassion.

She wasn't used to having his face so easy to read. He was worried about her. " I will call you. I promise." She meant it. He was a good listener, and she desperately needed someone she could talk to.

"That's better." Tag chucked her under the chin, much as her father had a few days before. "I'll see you tomorrow." He went out the door. "Good night."

"Good night," she replied. She sighed, exhaling tension and worry, finally feeling just how hard she'd pushed herself that day. As she watched him walk away she wondered, who was Tag, really?

Ex-military, wounded horribly in Iraq, yet he was unfailing in his kindness to her. His work with her father had taken a huge load off her shoulders. He worked for her father; the thought made her pause. Tag was another person she should keep from becoming attached to, because he worked for the family.

Her mind stopped there, she couldn't put Tag in the same category as Brandon.

The thought of Brandon raised all kinds of red flags in her mind; he seemed sincere, he seemed honest – but – those awful stories, the way he had kissed her. Brandon made her feel uncomfortable, like she was a step behind, trying to catch up.

Tag was different; from the first he had seemed to fit right in. She thought about the deck, and the flowers, she wasn't used to that kind of attention. Maybe she could get used to having this new, improved, Tag around.

Late that night, he was driving on a winding road, the Mustang GT engine roared as he downshifted for the turn. He shouted at the top of his lungs for the sheer joy of it. Another curve, a switchback, he was going too fast. The Mustang didn't make the turn. It soared off the road, changing into a Hummer as it hit desert sand.

He was back in Falluja! He could hear the guys behind him singing off key rap songs. He could taste the dust. Then he saw the car, with the driver chanting in a shrill voice. The concussion slammed into him.

Panic gripped him as the Hummer flipped! His left foot caught on fire. He could smell his own flesh burning as the flaming Hummer rolled. He heard the screams of the men dying around him.

He sat up in bed, panting. It felt like someone had peeled the nail off his big toe. He looked at the clock, three o'clock. There would be no more sleep tonight. There was nothing else to do but get up, as soon as the pain subsided. He clutched the remains of his left leg, pushing against his hands, breathing deep and slow.

What idiot had named this 'phantom pain?'

The pain was real. The damn leg was gone.

Damn the dreams!

What made him think he could have a normal life? He couldn't drag anyone into this ... nightmare world he lived in.

The guys in his therapy group had dogged him about the hair cut, got it in one that a woman was involved. They congratulated him for moving on with his life.

But they were wrong. He couldn't get involved, not even with her.

Yet, her tawny eyes haunted him, so shadowed, even when she smiled. He had seen that look before. Someone, something was pushing her to her limits.

Chapter 12

The next morning Lindsey and Tag looked out across the garden, where rows of wilting early peas climbed up bamboo poles.

"These won't last much longer. The late ones are still doing okay." They walked two rows down, where the late peas were still sending out little flowers. "We should get a couple more weeks out of these."

"I've got peas in the green salad, the pasta salad, and steamed with diced carrots. I need something else." Lindsey pointed down a few rows to the yellow beans. "I could take some of those beans to make up a stir fry."

"They need another week." He peered over the beans to the rows of basil. "We could pinch the basil."

"Pesto season begins." Lindsey grinned. "That changes everything. I'll sauté the vegetables, and toss some pasta with the pesto." She was getting excited. They walked through the bean rows to where the basil was growing quick and fragrant. Lindsey pinched a bit between her fingers, tasting it. The sweet basil tasted as good as it smelled. Tag seemed amused at her sampling.

"We'll just pinch the tips." Tag bent down to touch the plants. "They aren't really large, but a good pinch off the top will make them bush out."

"Have we got any cilantro?" They walked three rows down to the herbs. The cilantro was pungent, large enough to take a good snipping. Lindsey pinched a bit, inhaled, then passed the pinch to Tag. "Here, smell it."

"It smells good." Tag inhaled the sharp scent. "How much will you need?"

"I need a pint basket of cilantro and a peck basket of basil." They walked passed rows of herbs, the plants a foot high, brilliant green against the wood chip mulch.

"What else?" He asked.

"In pesto?" Lindsey counted the ingredients off on her fingers. "There's basil, garlic, cilantro, Parmesan cheese, olive oil and pine nuts or pecans."

"Pine nuts?" Tag quirked an eyebrow at her. "You're kidding."

"Yes, pine nuts." Lindsey smiled. "It doesn't have to be pine nuts. I could use walnuts or almonds." She liked explaining. "Pesto is very good, savory and fragrant with herbs and garlic."

"I see you pinching and smelling all the time," Tag remarked. "Why does it matter how it smells?"

"The smell is half the taste." Lindsey could see that he was amused. "Have you ever noticed the way that steak smells, compared to say, barbecued pork? The smoky flavors are enhanced by the spices, which changes the smell as well as the taste?"

"No. It all smells like food to me." He shrugged. "So what's this peso stuff?"

Lindsey giggled at his mispronunciation. "Pesto, like presto without the 'r'. It's an old traditional Italian flavoring that goes with a whole lot of food; I put it on pasta, on bread, on meat, on chicken, I even make a white barbecue sauce out of it."

"Never heard of it."

"I have to fix that. I'll make you vegetable sauté with pasta and pesto for dinner one night, how does that sound?" It was meant as a casual offer, to give her time to talk to him, without her father or Travis around.

"I don't know." Tag moved backwards slightly in an almost instinctive recoil. The amusement was gone. He looked … wary.

What was wrong with him? He sat down to supper with the family almost every night. Besides, he owed her. He'd lost his silly little game of truth or dare.

"Dare you," she said with a giddy smirk. She caught the startled look he shot at her, he had forgotten? "You owe me a dare. Or did you think that I forgot?"

She breathlessly waited for him to either stand up or back down. If he backed out she'd never let him live it down.

"What's the matter? Chicken?" Lindsey made chicken noises.

That did it, his tan took a red tint, he laughed.

"Where and when?"

"Saturday works for me," she said. "My place of course."

"Okay, that's a dare." The mischief was back in his eyes again.

"Good, that's settled." She rubbed her hands together. "We've got a lot to do."

Tag looked at the long rows of beans and herbs.

"Got that in one."

When she arrived in E'town, Lindsey was annoyed to find Brandon and Mychou already in the restaurant eating breakfast. The counter was littered with papers, plates, and packets of sugar and assorted junk. When Lindsey walked in, Mychou scrambled to clean up the mess, giving Lindsey a guilty look. Brandon waved, got up and walked towards her.

"Hey, there you are. Is everything okay at home?" Brandon had the dolly waiting by the door. "You are running late today."

"Everything is fine." Lindsey stifled the impulse to check her watch. She was *never* late. He was just manipulating her again, damn it.

"Your Mom all right?" He was blocking her way to the back.

"Yes, she's doing great." Lindsey let him turn her around so they could go back to the truck. She was inwardly fuming, but not sure how to handle this. Why did Brandon always make her feel like she was one step behind?

"That's good." Brandon opened the door for her with a little flourish. "I'm amazed at how well she's doing."

"I really don't like your being in the restaurant when I'm not here." Lindsey took charge of the conversation before he got her sidetracked.

"Well, we got an early start this morning." Brandon gave her the innocent country-boy smile as he reached for the coolers. "We were talking. Mychou's got problems. She's not getting any child support from her husband. The state is giving her a hard time about assistance."

It couldn't be easy to raise two little kids, even with help. Lindsey pressed her lips together. It sounded plausible, but Brandon always sounded plausible.

Should she let it go? She hated confrontations. No, she was tired of feeling a step behind. *She* owned the restaurant.

"I want the key back."

"Now Lindsey, I'm surprised at you." Brandon's 'ah-shucks' expression changed to one of bafflement. "I'm hurt that you would say that, after all I've done for you."

Surprised, maybe. Hurt? Not a chance, Lindsey thought.

"I'm here on time every morning." Lindsey held out her hand. "There is no reason for you to have a key."

"What if your mother takes a turn? It could happen."

"Mother is fine."

"I'm glad to hear that, but just in case – you know that things can happen suddenly."

"Just give me the key." Her voice betrayed her anger; for once she didn't care. Lindsey held out her hand, all but holding her breath. She was prepared for an argument, she wasn't sure what form it would take.

"You don't trust me?" Brandon sounded hurt. "Lindsey, what have I done to deserve this?" He put his hand on her shoulder. He looked puzzled, hurt, and … expectant.

Was he expecting her to apologize and forget the whole thing?

"Did I give you any reason to doubt my honesty?"

Not exactly, was it an order of drain cleaner or the crawly feeling when she walked in this morning? Neither one was much of an argument. Lindsey lost her certainty, but she kept her hand out. She wouldn't apologize, or take it back, not this time.

Brandon recoiled. There was a flash of fury in his eyes.

"I don't believe this. This is so unfair. Is there anyone you trust, Lindsey? Do you treat all your friends like this?" Brandon reached into his pocket for his keys.

Lindsey held her ground with Brandon, just as she had held her ground with her father yesterday. It was a struggle to stay silent, hold eye contact and not waver until he laid the key in her hand.

"Paranoia is how it starts, you know. Pretty soon you will be as crazy as your sister!" Brandon turned away, taking the dolly stacked with coolers inside.

Lindsey leaned against her truck, trembling. She had no proof and very little basis for her suspicion. Lindsey was more concerned about Mychou's inability to ring up an order. But her gut instinct was to protect herself, her business and her family.

She would call the locksmith, tonight.

In the garden that night Lindsey half-expected another 'come to supper' order from her father. When it didn't come, she wasn't sure if she liked it or not.

"Something sure smells good." Tag lounged against the tractor.

Lindsey sniffed. Someone was grilling beef, most likely hamburgers. Lindsey had brought her supper home. She was determined to hold out another day or two to get her point across.

"It smells burnt to me."

"Somebody had a bad day at work."

"What makes you say that?"

"Your hackles are up."

"Are not!" She bristled then laughed. "I guess I am a little snarky. Brandon and Mychou made a mess in the restaurant this morning, before I got there.

"They just walked in?" Tag's eyebrows rose.

"Brandon had a key." Lindsey shrugged then gave him a narrow glance. "Mind you I said 'had.' I got the key back from Brandon this morning."

"I take it that he wasn't happy about it."

"No, but I've got the key." Lindsey remembered the flash of fury in Brandon's eyes, and frowned. "He was pretty ticked off."

"What if we are wrong?" She asked. "What if Brandon isn't doing anything shady? I've all but accused him."

"What if we're right?" Tag countered. "If he is up to something, what are you going to do about it? Fire him, or have him arrested?"

"Arrested?" Lindsey drew back. "I don't want him arrested. I just don't want him stealing from me." Lindsey bit her lip. "I have to be sure."

"Have you gotten those invoices yet?"

"No," she sighed. "Seven to ten days, so any day now."

"You'll let me know when they get here?" He was looking at her from under his eyebrows; the sardonic look made her smile.

"Yes."

"I'll give you 'moron' support." Tag promised with a wink.

That evening around nine o'clock, her cell phone chirped with a brief text message: "rup? Tag." Lindsey looked at the cryptic message for a moment before the meaning dawned on her. She dialed his number.

"Hey."

"Hey, you're up," his voice was relaxed. There was music in the background. "I wasn't sure if you were the 'early to bed, early to rise' type or not."

"I'm up half the night anymore." Lindsey moved to the kitchen where she had a mug of tea heating in the microwave. "I'd do almost anything for a good night sleep."

"I sleep better now that I'm working," he told her. "Last year I didn't get much sleep."

"Bad dreams?" She winced at the blunt question.

"You would not believe," he admitted. "There isn't much anybody can do about it. I hear they fade in time." He gave a skeptical snort. "Not fast enough to suit me."

Yes, she thought, remind me that you've been through worse than my petty problems. I need to have a better perspective so I don't feel sorry for myself.

"My mind is like a hamster on a wheel," Lindsey said. "Racing the same ground over and over." She sighed. "It doesn't matter how hard I work, it never shuts off."

"I think you need to get away for a while." His voice dropped, deep and seductive. "How about a few hours of R&R some weekend?"

"I'm going to have to catch up on my work before I commit to anything." A smile spread across her face, to think he'd tried to turn down her offer of dinner.

"Why the switch?"

Tag was silent for a moment.

"I got my butt chewed out at group." There was a breath of humor in his voice. "I was told to get out and have some fun."

"Oh?" Lindsey wasn't sure what to say.

"Yeah, so I'll think of something fun for us to do."

"Okay." Lindsey stifled a yawn. "I need to turn in."

"Sure," Tag said. "I'll see you in the morning."

After she closed her cell, Lindsey looked at it for a moment. Just like that, she'd agreed to go somewhere with him. She didn't have a clue where they would go or what they would do. If that had been Brandon, she'd have turned him down flat.

Tag wasn't Brandon, comparing the two of them was absurd. Even before he was shaved and sheared, Tag had – what was it? The intangible quality remained nameless for a long moment before it came to her: honor. Tag had honor, Brandon did not. For a satisfying moment she was sure, absolutely sure that she was right. She finished her tea, lay down, and fell asleep with a smile.

Another rainy morning, Lindsey gathered up her boots and a slicker to go out to pick. Her father and Tag were already busy. They got the job done as quickly as possible. There was no chitchat: they all wanted to get back to dry clothes.

Lindsey made it to the restaurant before eight. She got the produce in before Brandon and Mychou arrived. Once they were inside, she set everyone to a task. Since it was raining they didn't sneak outside to smoke.

Mychou was cleaning under the counter, she let out a dainty shriek, recoiled and landed on her rump. "A bug!"

"Where?" Lindsey turned around.

Seeing Mychou sprawled gracelessly on the floor made Lindsey giggle. Shawn came over to see what the fuss was about. Brandon stopped his prep work to watch Mychou. He grinned widely, crossing his arms across his chest. There was a malicious gleam in his eyes.

"On the shelf." Mychou scrambled to her knees.

She grabbed an empty paper towel roll, using it to poke the miscellaneous items on the shelf. She gingerly picked up some papers, shook them out before laying them on the floor. Then she started emptying the shelf, including extra cups and glasses.

"Not on the floor!" Lindsey protested, snatching up cups.

Mychou made an exasperated noise, but started stacking things on the counter. "This is nasty. When did you clean here last?" She asked sweeping dust bunnies onto the floor. "Get me some spray cleaner." She ordered Shawn.

"She's off on a cleaning jag." Brandon snorted, idly scratching his elbow. "This could take all day."

"Ha! There it is!" Mychou swept something small and brown onto the floor with her paper towel roll. "I got it!" She stamped the 'bug' several times.

"Yep, you got it." Lindsey peered at a scrap of brown paper. She exchanged an amused look with Brandon and Shawn. They all laughed while Mychou pouted. Lindsey went to get the broom and dustpan, still chuckling.

"You need glasses," Brandon laughed. "You about stamped that scrap into the floor."

"Shut up, Brandon." Mychou folded her arms across her chest. She was so small that she barely came to his shoulder. "I saw a bug."

"Well, where is it?" he shook his head. "You're a hoot, girl."

"Here's the spray cleaner." Shawn handed over the spray cleaner and a fresh roll of paper towels. "You may as well finish cleaning." He was grinning too.

"Somebody's got to do it," Mychou snapped. She proceeded to clean the shelves with a frantic energy that Lindsey found repellant. Every time that Mychou found a scrap she would sweep it to the floor and stamp on it.

Brandon surveyed the stuff she had stepped on.

"Two scraps of paper, a packet of sweetener, a Cheeto and three pieces of popcorn." Brandon hooted. "What's next? Dust bunnies and grains of salt?"

"You think you're so funny!" Mychou snapped.

"No, I think you're funny," he retorted.

Lindsey hid a grin behind her hand. They sounded like little kids.

"You're freaking out."

"I am *not*." Mychou stood up, dusted off her hands. "I need a cigarette." She stalked past him with her dainty nose in the air.

"She's going to knock you out one of these days." Shawn shook his head at Brandon.

"Not," Brandon retorted. He turned back to his cooking.

What was the relationship between Mychou and Brandon? Lindsey wondered as she swept up the floor. They seemed to know each other really well. Maybe they had dated at one time? She could see Brandon with Mychou on his arm. They would be a perfectly dressed pair of dolls. She emptied the dustpan into the trash.

The carryout orders were up as more people pooled resources to keep from going out in the wet. Shawn and Mychou helped Brandon box up lunches while Lindsey took phone orders.

Brandon was in one of his playful moods. He and Shawn got going on a rap song made out of the sandwich menu. Lindsey actually wrote a few of the names down, she might as well take advantage of Brandon's creativity.

As the afternoon wore down Brandon caught the cleaning bug; he scrubbed his area, sharpened his knives and straightened up the storeroom before he left. Mychou helped Shawn with the dishes. Lindsey was grateful that things were running so smoothly.

It was still raining when Lindsey got home that night. The garden needed the water, but she missed talking to Tag. She could unwind, vent a bit, knowing he understood without judging. She picked up her cell around eight to call him.

"Hi, it's Lindsey."

"Hey there," he sounded pleased. "Everything all right?"

"Okay." She sat down on the couch. "I didn't see you this afternoon. I thought I'd call to check on you for a change."

"We got rained out," his voice was low and lazy. "This is the first week day I've had off in a while. All last year this place felt like a prison cell, now I kind of like it."

"I hope you got some rest?" Lindsey could feel the tension melt out of her muscles.

"I got this place cleaned up, the dust was pretty thick. I actually worked up a sweat." Tag chuckled. "How was business?"

"We sold a lot of carry-outs today," Lindsey said. "Otherwise it was pretty slow."

"Have finances improved?"

"I'm not bleeding money anymore," Lindsey was glad to say. "But I still may need the loan. It depends on how the summer goes. If the garden continues to produce like this, I should catch up by September. If we get another drought, I'll need a loan to get through the winter."

"How does it work? Do you pay your father market prices for the produce?"

"No, usually half, which is more than he would make selling to a wholesaler." Lindsey paused, thinking ahead a few months. "The longer the garden produces the more money I save. Last year the August drought killed the tomatoes and peppers just as they hit their peak." She sighed. "I can't take a hit like that this year."

"Don't worry. We have drip irrigation set up. When it gets dry, we will be ready." He paused for a minute. "Does the water come from a well, or is county water?"

"It's county water," Lindsey said. "The garden is the biggest part of Heather's water bill."

"That isn't good."

"Now do you see what we are up against? There are more variables than just food sales. I don't want Dad worried about my part of the business. He's got enough troubles."

There was a moment of silence.

"He's worried about you."

"Oh no." Lindsey closed her eyes.

"Well, I think you should tell him about the problems at the restaurant."

"I can't, I have no proof." Lindsey bit her lip. "It is easier to handle this crap myself."

"Truth or dare: Is it easier to handle or to hide?"

"That's low," Lindsey complained then she sighed. "I don't know. That's the truth."

"Lindsey, please don't shut everybody out." Tag's voice dropped in tone and timber. "It's not good for you."

Suddenly Lindsey's nose stung with tears. She needed – what? Her family to give her some respect, or acknowledgement or a pat on the back for all her work? That wasn't going to happen as long as she was keeping things from them.

"I talk to you," she said softly so she wouldn't choke on unshed tears.

"I'm here for you," Tag affirmed. "But I'm not the only person who cares. You are under a lot of stress. Personal experience talking: you need the support of people who care about you. Being stubborn is great, just be stubborn about the right things." There was a breath of humor in his voice. "I never thought I would be handing out that particular lecture. I heard it daily for months."

Lindsey fidgeted for a moment; maybe she was being stubborn. Maybe she would feel better sharing some or all of this mess with her family.

"Okay," she said. "You're right."

"That's more like it." His voice was teasing, not triumphant.

Lindsey rolled her eyes.

Another drizzly morning, the grass was wet and slick, the sky promised more rain. The forecast was for spotty showers all weekend. They got everything picked and packed quickly. Lindsey lingered to have coffee with Tag and her father in the shelter of the barn. They discussed irrigation, debating their best course of action.

Lindsey drove to work in a drizzling mist. She was the first to arrive. Shawn was early arriving a moment later. Where was Brandon? Lindsey put Shawn to work in the kitchen.

"Are you going to college?" Lindsey wondered why he was working for her when he could have a better job?

"Yes. I'm in my first year at Western."

"What is your major?" Had Rose ever mentioned it? Lindsey didn't recall.

"Ah, well," he hesitated. "I haven't declared one yet."

"Don't tell me you're wasting money on a General Studies degree."

"No." He looked uncomfortable. "There are a whole lot of classes that you have to take, no matter what your major is. Didn't you go to college?"

"Twice," Lindsey said with a smile. "University of Louisville for a B.S. in Business and then an Associates in Culinary from a private college."

"A Business degree?" Shawn shook his head. "I figured you for a school teacher."

"What does that mean?" Lindsey frowned. Was that mockery in his voice?

"I can't see you in a power suit." A faint smile crossed his face. "But you'd make a good elementary school teacher."

"What?" That was an insult, or she'd never heard one. Lindsey set her chef's knife down before she threatened him with it.

"I'm a pretty good judge of character."

Lindsey frowned at him. She was about to retort when Mychou knocked on the door. Shawn hurried over to let her in out of the rain. While Mychou folded her umbrella, Brandon came in behind her. Mychou was immaculate, her shirt and pants freshly pressed, but she had no welcoming smile, not even for Shawn. Her lips were pressed together and her eyes were stormy. Brandon was behind her, equally tense. It looked like they had been quarreling.

"You're late," Lindsey said with a glance at the clock.

"My car broke down," Mychou said softly. "Brandon had to get me."

"You need a better car," Shawn said.

"I need more money." Mychou shot a look at Brandon.

Lindsey secretly crossed her fingers. Please, God let her find work somewhere else. The sooner Mychou was gone, the happier Lindsey would be. Brandon took Shawn's place at the prep table, wielding the knife savagely. From time to time his shoulders would twitch.

Mychou tackled cleaning under the counter as if she hadn't done it once already this week. She removed everything from under the counter, cleaning every nook and cranny. This time there was no joking about bugs.

Lindsey watched both of them from the corner of her eye, careful to not get in the way. If only she could wave a magic wand and make them disappear!

When the customers started coming in, Mychou left off her cleaning. There were several people in and out, they drank coffee and didn't order food. Lindsey noted with some annoyance that most of them took several packets of sugar in their coffee. Mychou had a pocket full of packets to keep the holders full.

As Lindsey was ringing up tickets her nose started to itch, an acrid odor hung in the air, sharp and chemical. She had to hold her breath to keep from sneezing. The people in front of her had only ordered coffee. She noted how drawn and lined their faces were. The odor seemed to be coming from them.

She caught another big whiff of the odor later that afternoon while she was putting gas in her car. She traced the odor to its source, a pump labeled 'Kerosene.'

The smell made her hair stand on end. Where had she smelled it before? Kerosene smelled just like jet fuel. Her mind flashed back to That Day in Washington. The air at the Pentagon had been thick with the smell of death and jet fuel.

Why would she smell kerosene in the restaurant? No one used kerosene to heat in the summer. What was going on? Was this just a coincidence?

The feeling of being two steps behind came back, with a vengeance.

When she parked her truck, she looked over at Heather's house. She had promised Tag that she would make up with her family so her father wouldn't be worried enough to ask questions. It was time to make good on her promise to make 'face'.

Her father was watching CNN. He gave her a hug and a kiss on the cheek.

Her mother was in the kitchen helping Travis with his homework. She also gave Lindsey a hug and a kiss on the cheek. So Lindsey felt she had been forgiven, even though the gossip had nothing to do with her.

Heather was cooking spaghetti and meatballs. She waved. "Are you going to stay for supper? I've made plenty."

"Sure." Lindsey smiled. "How is everyone doing?"

"I've got a test tomorrow," Travis said. "Are you good with math?"

"Some things," Lindsey said. "What do you need help with?" She sat down to look it over. The problems were fairly straight forward. Dinner was pleasant, she left feeling that things had been smoothed over.

Tag called around nine that night.

"Hey, you want to go to a movie tomorrow night?"

"After dinner?" Lindsey asked. "Sure, what's playing?"

"Does it matter? We'll find something."

"Nothing too bloody, I hope." Lindsey said, thinking how for most guys the more blood the better they liked the movie.

"I prefer comedies myself," Tag replied, dryly. "I think I've seen enough blood."

Lindsey winced; she was being insensitive, again!

"That was thoughtless of me," she said. "I'm sorry."

"I'm *so* sensitive," he teased. "Really."

Chapter 13

How was she going to serve dinner tonight? Lindsey surveyed her kitchen with dismay. Her table was awash in a sea of paper that lapped over the side and dripped to the floor. Her laptop was under there, somewhere.

She needed to do books.

No, she could afford to carve a few hours from her weekend to cook for a friend.

Lindsey made short work of the table by tossing all the old envelopes, then sorting it into three piles. The piles went into baskets, which went into the spare room, with all the rest of the junk.

That helped make the place presentable.

Once the house was clean, Lindsey paused for a moment. She was already feeling a prickle of unease. There was so much she *should* be doing – it didn't feel right to be planning dinner with Tag.

What was wrong with having a friend?

Nothing, Lindsey told herself firmly. Tag's friendship was a precious gift that she cherished. If it never came to more than friendship, then so what? Lindsey had ruined one friendship trying to make it more than it was meant to be. Look how that had turned out?

She didn't have to make that mistake again.

There was one consolation, no matter what happened between her and Tag, she would never catch *him* in bed with another man.

Of that she was certain.

When Tag arrived, Lindsey was chopping the tomatoes. The pasta water simmered, almost ready. Everything for the pesto sat next to the blender. She asked Tag to blend the pesto. She chopped yellow and green squash, onions, garlic and celery. Then she put a sauté pan on to heat. While that heated, she cut marinated sirloin into cubes. By then Tag was done with the pesto, so she directed him to put a slice of mozzarella cheese on each piece of bread.

"Watch this." She started with the garlic and onions then added from there. In just minutes she had the majority of the dish completed.

Tag leaned against the counter, watching.

"How do you get all this to happen at the same time?" Tag asked when she popped the brochette into the oven. The fettuccini was draining, the vegetables and beef ready. It was a matter of tossing the fettuccini with pesto in a big serving dish, pouring the beef and vegetables over that, then getting the brochette out of the oven, topping them with a mix of tomato and pesto.

"Practice." Lindsey shooed him out of the way. "Take a seat, it's ready." She did the final touches then laid the meal out on the table. She opened a bottle of good red wine then slid into her chair.

"I can't get over how your whole family cooks," Tag said. "I've watched Jim and Heather set out an impressive spread in less than an hour. It's just amazing."

"My Grandmother was Italian," Lindsey told him. "She loved to cook and would teach anybody who would venture into the kitchen. She taught my father everything he knows." She grinned at him. "I've heard mother joke that she married him because he could cook better than she could."

She tasted her pasta dish. The pasta was firm, the vegetables were a bit crisp, the beef just a touch spicy. She inhaled the fragrance of the dish; everything was just the way she liked it.

Tag watched her with that amused look in his eyes.

"Smell it," Lindsey urged him. "It's fragrant."

"It does smell good." Tag grinned at her, inhaling deeply. "What is your obsession with the way things smell?"

"Good food should be a feast for the senses, smell as well as taste."

"What is the white stuff?" He looked at his salad, three kinds of lettuce, tomato, peppers, radishes, and crumbled feta cheese.

"It's feta, a sharp cheese." She speared a bit then offered it to him. "Taste it."

Tag gave her a level look before he let her feed him the cheese. Lindsey felt her cheeks get a little warm. It's *food*, she told herself, not a flirtation.

"It's tart." He wrinkled his nose.

"It's supposed to be." Lindsey served him the brochette. "Here, this is brochette."

"Is that basil?" Tag asked, just before he took a bite.

"You should recognize it. The garden is full of it."

"This is good, really good," he said as he savored it. "There is a lot of garlic in this."

"I like garlic." Lindsey shrugged. "It's healthy, lowers the blood pressure and acts as a tonic." Then she grinned. "We're both eating the same thing." She took a bite of the warm crusty bread herself. "I love this stuff."

"Now, red wine to wash it down." Lindsey poured two glasses of the full-bodied red wine.

"I've never liked wine." Tag gave her a sly look. "I think the only wine I've had was Mad Dog."

"This is not Mad Dog." Lindsey giggled, shaking her head. She took another sip of wine. "It's not an expensive red wine, but it's a good one."

Tag took a sip. "It tastes a lot better than Mad Dog."

"I should hope so."

"I may not be able to handle wine. I'm a mere beer drinker." His blue eyes lit up with the opportunity to rib her. "Are you trying to get me drunk and take advantage of me?"

Okay, *he* wanted to flirt.

"Does beer go with Italian food?" Lindsey blushed as she turned back to her food. "I'll let you figure the rest out on your own."

"This is great," Tag said after a few bites.

"I was starting to wonder about you." Lindsey's face lit up in a smile.

"I love to eat." Tag saluted her with his glass of wine. "Here's to a great cook."

"I told my father if we started feeding you, you wouldn't mind working all these long hours." Lindsey chuckled, remembering. "I guess I got that right."

"It gives me a reason to get up in the morning. I was losing my mind cooped up in that apartment." He was silent a moment. His expression changed as he remembered. "Those were some of the worst months of my life."

"How did you meet my father?"

"I'd run into him down at the hospital. We talked about the Army." He looked happier at the memory. "It's funny how things work out sometimes. I never thought I'd enjoy being a farmer so much."

"It has got its perks." Lindsey lifted her fork of pasta at him in salute. "We may live on top of each other, but we eat like kings."

"My family gets together one Sunday a month at my mother's house. We have a big pot roast dinner. I hardly see my sisters otherwise."

"Sometimes I wish I stayed in Louisville," Lindsey confessed. "It's a lot harder to have your own life when your family lives next door."

"Not to mention being in business with them," Tag smiled. "Though it's working out pretty well, as far as I can tell."

"Yeah," Lindsey smiled. "We worked well together until Mom broke her ankle. I guess she was the glue that held us together." She stabbed a cube of sirloin. "It was anxiety about Mom that set Heather off, I know it was. But that's enough about my family. Tell me about yours."

"I have two older sisters, both married with kids, they live here in E'town. My father is still in the military. He's out in Colorado. My parents divorced when I was about nine. Mom stayed here and married a local guy. I think she was tired of moving around. It wasn't like she and my father fought a lot, he was always gone." He took a drink of wine. "This isn't bad. I think I could get used to it."

"Red wine is traditional with Italian food." Lindsey decided to keep him talking. "How did you get in the Army?"

"I was in ROTC, went to college for engineering. I had my heart set on a military career. I wanted to see the world. My father said I should wait to go in as an officer. I didn't want to wait."

"Will you go back to work in engineering?" Lindsey asked, thinking he was wasting his talents here as a farm hand.

"I'm not thinking that far ahead." Tag looked down. "Someday, maybe. But this is fine for now." He looked back at Lindsey. "There are plenty of problems to solve here. Like setting up the tomato supports, designing the irrigation system. Jim and I are looking into harvesting rainwater, to see what it would take to get off county water."

"How are you going to harvest rainwater?"

"Well, the house has gutters that collect the runoff from the roof. If I calculate the square footage of the roof, multiply that by the inches of rainfall, we have an idea of how much water we can get in an average rain."

"That sounds complicated," Lindsey said.

"That's the easy part," Tag said. "Where it gets tricky is figuring out how much water the garden will need to keep producing throughout the summer, factoring in the different ways we can get the water to the plants. I've a spreadsheet where I'm working it out. It has to be practical and cost effective, which is a whole different ball game." He grinned. "If I can solve this problem, I can do anything."

"I had no idea." Lindsey shook her head. "Frankly it sounds like a huge investment. We don't have the money for a project of this size."

"Ah." Tag grinned. "That's where your father has the contacts. He has been in touch with the Extension office. There may be grant money available."

"Seriously?" Lindsey asked. "We are so small."

"It never hurts to ask."

They finished eating; Lindsey cleared the table, Tag helped her with the dishes.

"Now that's done," Tag grinned. "Come on Lynn, we are going for a ride." They walked out to the driveway. Lindsey was surprised to see that he'd come in a different vehicle, a white Mustang with wide blue racing stripes down the center of the roof and hood. The car was immaculate.

"What did you think, that the old beater truck was the best I could do?" Tag teased her as he opened the door. "What kind of music do you like?"

"What have you got?" Lindsey settled into the white leather seat.

"The mp3 player is right there. Take a look."

Lindsey picked up the mp3 player, fiddled with it until she figured it out. There was an extensive music library. She scrolled through the list, until she found something she liked.

Tag was a careful driver. They discussed music as they drove up to Louisville. Tag could quote lyrics from songs that Lindsey barely remembered from her childhood. They made a game of it. She would find a song, play a few notes and he would identify the title and artist.

They never discussed the restaurant. Lindsey was able to give her brain a break. The movie was a comedy that they enjoyed. The ride home was very relaxing. She was able to enjoy talking 'getting-to-know-you' trivia. He spoke a little of his career in the Army, and mentioned some of the places he'd been stationed. She'd been to some of the same places when her father was on active duty. They compared notes on Germany and various bases.

They pulled into her driveway.

"Come on, I'll walk you to the door just to prove that I'm civilized."

She said all the polite things as they walked. He paused at the bottom of the stairs.

"Chivalry has been satisfied." Tag grinned. "You owe me a hug." Lindsey gingerly hugged him, aware of the difference in height and the scent of his cologne.

"You're a mess," he murmured. "Not a word about your problems all night." He pulled her closer. "How are you going to learn to share the burden if you don't talk?"

"I thought I was supposed to relax," she replied. "You know, have dinner and a movie with a friend."

He released her so she was looking up at him.

"I want to be more than a friend," he said softly. "Someday."

"You say I'm a mess," she snorted. "But you want to be more than friends?"

"It's a vote of confidence," he quipped. "I'm betting that you get it worked out."

"That's sweet of you," she teased.

"I can be sweet." He brushed his lips to hers, a sweet gentle kiss that sent shock waves through her. "Blame it on the wine. I've been wanting to do that all evening."

"Really?" Lindsey moved closer in invitation. The second time he kissed her, the press of his lips was gentle, but there was an underlying tension. She had the impression of a deep hunger, held back by force of will. When he broke the kiss, Lindsey clung to him for a moment to get her breath back.

"You need your beauty sleep, princess." He brushed her cheek with his fingertips. "I'll see you Monday."

She went obediently into the house, but after he left, she sat on her mended porch steps, drinking a cup of hot chamomile tea. The thick scent of honeysuckle wafted to her on a cool breeze.

Tonight she was sleepless for a different reason.

Chapter 14

Sunday morning, Lindsey walked into her sister's house. Her mother was sitting at the kitchen table, peeling apples.

"Hey, look who's up and at 'em." Lindsey gave her mother a hug before she got herself a cup of coffee.

"I got tired of sitting in bed." Eleanor smiled. "We're working on an apple pie for supper." She lowered her voice. "Did I see a white car in your driveway last night?"

"Yes, I made dinner for Tag yesterday." Lindsey gave her mother a shy smile. "After that, he drove us up to Louisville for a movie."

"Wonderful." Eleanor beamed. "Did you have a good time?"

Lindsey nodded; she was about to say more when Heather came into the room. Lindsey could tell by the frown on her sister's face that Heather was in a bad mood.

"Morning," Lindsey said.

"Morning," Heather said stiffly. "How are you coming with the apples, Mom?"

"I'm about done," Eleanor said. "I was just talking to Lindsey about her date last night."

"I saw a strange car over there." Heather scowled. "My God, Lindsey don't you have any pride?"

Lindsey's jaw dropped.

"I don't see how it concerns you." Lindsey bristled, shocked and hurt.

"You're my sister, of course it concerns me."

"What?" Lindsey snapped. "Since when? You can't tell me who to date."

"Well it's my property," Heather snapped. "I have some say about what goes on over there."

"What are you implying?"

"I don't think you should have men over there."

"It's called dating, Heather." Lindsey's temper slipped its leash. "People date all the time. It's not a big deal."

"Aren't there laws against dating employees?" Heather's tone was haughty. She put her hands on her hips, spoiling for a fight. "I thought you learned your lesson last time."

"How dare you! Just because you dress in sack cloth and ashes doesn't mean that I have to live like a damn nun."

"Better that, than dragging that creep home!"

"Geeze, Heather!" Lindsey shouted. "Where the hell did you get that from?"

"Brandon is the most disgusting man I've ever laid eyes on!"

"What does Brandon have to do with this?" Lindsey sputtered.

"Wasn't that his car over there?"

"I wouldn't go out with Brandon if he were the last man alive!"

"Well, who did you go out with?" Heather dropped her voice.

"It's none of your business!"

"Lindsey, please, don't fight with your sister!"

"Goodbye." Lindsey stalked out the door. How could Heather say things like that to her? She heard her mother's voice, but not the words, and then she heard her sister burst into sobs.

Just like Heather, first she's a raving witch then she turns on the water works. Maybe Brandon was right. Heather was crazy. Whatever was wrong with Heather, Lindsey wasn't putting up with it.

"Lindsey wait!" Heather called after her.

Lindsey ignored the summons.

Later that evening, she was working in the garden with her father, watering the tomatoes, testing hoses and drip irrigation emitters.

"Lindsey." Jim stopped for a break after they'd checked all the hoses. "I heard about this morning."

Lindsey winced, she was no longer angry with her sister. How could Heather think she was with Brandon? "Your mother laid into Heather and the fur flew, let me tell you!" He paused. "I don't know what's gotten into Heather lately. She's been so touchy."

"She's not the same person," Lindsey agreed. "I'm worried about her."

"Your mother had a long talk with Heather. I'm hoping it will do some good." Jim smiled sadly. "Don't let her stop you from living your life. Just be careful."

Lindsey smiled at him.

"Lindsey?" it was Heather. Lindsey set her jaw before she turned around. Of course, Heather would apologize in front of their father.

"I'm so sorry." Heather held out her hand. "I don't have any right to be so critical."

"You've got that right." Lindsey wanted to get this over with. "You can't choose my friends for me." She crossed her arms over her chest.

"I thought that you were with Brandon," Heather confessed. "He seemed determined to win you over."

"He's a good cook." Lindsey dared Heather to contradict her. "I need him at the restaurant. So what if he's a flirt? He just needs a firm hand."

"I still think you are in for trouble," Heather blurted. "Tag is hardly your type."

"What does that mean?" Lindsey demanded, her temper flaring.

"You know what I mean." Heather shook her head. "You are out of your league."

"Just say it!"

"That man is a soldier. I'll bet he bleeds red, white and blue."

"Tag *was* a soldier," Lindsey corrected. "He's not one anymore."

"Bet me and *lose*."

"You are just saying that because you were miserable with Rich."

"We were very happy!"

"Like hell you were!" Lindsey lashed out at Heather, then turned and walked away before she said anything else.

Heather didn't follow her.

What was that all about? Had Heather decided that she wanted Tag? What went on while Lindsey was working? Did he tease and flirt with Heather, the way he did with her? All her certainties shattered. Lindsey shivered, suddenly cold and scared.

Lindsey got to the restaurant with Brandon's car right behind her. His handsome features were drawn, his eyes sunken in his head. His shoulder's twitched every few seconds.

"Are you okay?" Lindsey was unable to ignore his jerky movements any longer.

"Tired, real tired." He rubbed his neck. "I haven't had much sleep."

"He gives 'burning the candle at both ends' a new meaning." Mychou snickered as she walked by.

Brandon glared at her back. "You've got no room to talk."

"Eat something," Lindsey urged. "It will make you feel better."

"Food, now there's a concept." Brandon stretched his neck from side to side. Lindsey could hear the bones popping.

"Whip up a couple omelets," Lindsey suggested. "I'll keep the prep work going."

Brandon whipped up four omelets, loaded with bacon, cheese, green pepper, mushrooms and onions. The four of them sat down to eat. Brandon and Shawn ate like they were starving. Mychou polished off half her omelet in short order.

Brandon ate the rest.

A few minutes later, Brandon started to yawn, he seemed asleep on his feet. Lindsey decided to let him go home, before he chopped off one of his fingers. She hoped he would make it without getting into a wreck.

"Go home, get some sleep," Lindsey told him. "We can manage for one day without you." Which was how she ended up the only cook on the busiest day they'd had in weeks. She finally gave up control of the cash register. There was no surprise when the register came up twenty-seven dollars short.

Lindsey was so tired she didn't care.

That evening, when she got home, it was time to tear out the dead pea vines and get that area ready for the fall crops. It was hot and messy work. Lindsey was stumbling with exhaustion after only a few minutes.

I need something to keep me going, she thought. No wonder people took speed.

"Are you all right?" Her father motioned her to sit on the trailer. "Take a break."

"Tired," Lindsey admitted. "It was a rough day." Her head was pounding.

"You seem to be having a lot of those." Jim looked very concerned.

"Yeah, things aren't running as smoothly as they used to," Lindsey admitted.

"We can handle this," her father said. "Go get some rest."

Lindsey smiled, gave her father a hug then waved goodbye to Travis and Tag.

Once in the house, she fell into bed, just lying down helped her headache. She dozed on and off until nine, when her cell phone chirped with a text message: "rup?" Lindsey smiled at her phone then called him.

"Yo." Tag's voice was deep and lazy. "I'm surprised that you're still up."

"I'm awake," Lindsey said. "Barely."

"I just wanted to check on you," he said. "What happened today?"

"Brandon came in, looking like death warmed over," Lindsey said. "I got him to eat, then he sort of passed out on his feet. I sent him home. Then I had my busiest day all month."

She thought about the endless energy that Brandon usually had.

"On days like this, I could use something to keep me going. Maybe Brandon would give me some."

"Tell me you're joking." His voice was curt and flat.

"Of – of course," Lindsey stuttered. "I was kidding."

"You have no idea what that crap does to your mind." Tag sounded angry. "You can only take so much, then you tweak and crash out. It's not a pretty sight." There was disapproval in his voice. "Give it a few days and see what a wreck he becomes, you'll see."

"I was kidding." Lindsey was surprised at the venom in his voice. "Really."

"It's too easy to get on that crap and too hard to get off it."

"Is this personal experience talking?" Lindsey wondered aloud.

"In Falluja we went for days on very little sleep. A lot of the guys thought crystal was the answer. When they started tweaking, they screwed up royally. A couple of civilians got killed because they were paranoid as hell. They shot first and never bothered to see what they were shooting at."

"Wow, that's sad," Lindsey said. "I mean, you hear things about the effects of meth, but I've never really known anybody who used it."

"Tweakers are crazy and dangerous," Tag said. "Hopefully your buddy will run out of the stuff before he gets too freaked out."

Tuesday morning Lindsey got up with more energy. They got the produce, salad greens and beans picked in good time. The tomatoes and squash were coming along, but it would be July before she could start serving either.

They got the fall planting schedule worked out over breakfast. They would have until the end of July to lay out the beds for broccoli, pakchoi, fall spinach, carrots and salad greens.

At the restaurant, Brandon and Shawn came in first. Lindsey and Brandon made up all the cold salads while Shawn washed the produce. Mychou was late; she offered no explanation but got right to work wiping down tables.

"Mychou," Lindsey asked finally. "Why were you late?"

Mychou looked up frowning. "My car wouldn't start," she said in a clipped voice. "It took forever to find someone to help me." She shot a glare at Brandon. "Some people can't be depended upon."

Brandon looked up from his chopping.

"I'm not your freaking taxi service," he snapped. "You should junk that old wreck and get something that runs."

"I can't afford it." Mychou put her hands on her hips. "I'm not getting any child support."

"So what does that have to do with me?" Brandon asked. "It's not my fault that your husband is a dead beat."

"He is not!"

"No, that's right, he's in prison." Brandon thunked himself in the forehead. "I keep forgetting that little detail."

"At least he's good to me, not like *some* people I know."

"Oh, yeah." Brandon rolled his eyes. "You sure know how to pick 'em."

"Screw you, Brandon." She tossed the towel onto a table. "I need a smoke." Mychou stalked out. Shawn left the sink to follow her outside.

Lindsey watched them go, wondering what it all meant.

"There's another worthless dog sniffing after her," Brandon snarled under his breath, then shot a look at Lindsey. "She never learns, just hooks up with whatever is handy."

Some things were better left alone. That combination of familiarity and contempt was hard to come by, unless there had been a serious relationship at one time. Lindsey would admit to morbid curiosity about the two of them. Apparently neither of Mychou's children were Brandon's.

It wasn't long before Mychou and Shawn came back. Lindsey sighed; they wasted more time smoking. At least talking with Shawn had calmed Mychou down. She didn't look at Brandon, she just returned to her work.

As the orders were called in, Lindsey and Brandon packed the take-out boxes. When the customers started coming in, Lindsey left that to Brandon and Shawn.

It was a busy day. There were lots of people at the counter and tables. A surprising number just had coffee. It was irritating. She couldn't refuse to serve people who didn't order food; that would be stupid.

Later in the day, Lindsey caught a glimpse of a wad of cash in Mychou's apron as the waitress came back and forth. The coffee drinkers were terrific tippers.

Lindsey watched Mychou as closely as she could. But business had picked up and she was hard pressed to keep up. Whatever Mychou was up to, Lindsey never saw any sign of it.

Just after closing, Mychou's grandmother brought the little girl and her baby brother. Mychou was in the middle of her side work; she slanted a glance at Lindsey before putting her daughter at a table near the door. Mychou set the baby carrier on the floor.

"Mommy has work to do," she said. "Stay here and watch your brother." Mychou hurried through the last of her work before she went back to her children.

Lindsey noticed that the little girl was wearing a frilly new dress. When Mychou left, Lindsey watched the small woman balance the baby carrier as she shut the door behind them.

It couldn't be easy to be a single parent of two small children. Lindsey sighed then turned back to her work.

Was she being unfair to Mychou? The girl was just trying to get by with two kids and an old car that broke down all the time. Good jobs were hard to come by in a small town. It made sense that Mychou would do anything to keep a good paying job.

Still, having her lawyer threaten Lindsey's family was a low blow.

Lindsey bit her thumbnail, wondering what she would do if she were in Mychou's shoes.

"Hey, Lindsey?" Brandon finished cleaning the grill. "There is a new John Carpenter movie at the cinema, how about coming with me to watch it?"

"What's it about?" Lindsey asked, stalling.

"Vampires." He licked his lips. "You know, sexy vampire babes and he-man types battle it out. It's supposed to be really good."

Lindsey was positive that 'really good' translated into 'really bloody' in Brandon's mind. He seemed so immature when he was only a few years younger. Compared to Tag – well, comparing Brandon to Tag was ridiculous. Brandon was out classed.

"I don't think so," Lindsey said shaking her head. "I've got too much work to do. Sorry."

"Come on, Lindsey, you need a break." Brandon dropped his voice to croon seductively. "Let your hair down and live a little."

"Sorry, Brandon."

"Ah, girl, you don't know what you are missing," he said, still in that low tone. "See you tomorrow."

Shawn gave Lindsey an unreadable look as he followed Brandon out the door.

Lindsey gathered up her purse and her moneybag. She waited until they were both gone before she left. She didn't want to take the chance of being trapped in the parking lot alone with Brandon.

As she drove by her sister's house, Lindsey saw the boxes on the porch right off. Then she saw Heather sobbing into one of Rich's old uniform shirts, a dozen boxes stacked beside her. Lindsey sucked in a deep breath as she backed up her truck to pull in Heather's driveway.

She wasn't sure where Heather's personal demons came from, but they were tormenting her sister again.

"What's going on?" Lindsey guessed her brother-in-law's belongings were in the boxes.

"Would you take all this to the Goodwill for me?" Tears spilled from Heather's eyes, running down her face. "I know it has to be done, but I can't do it."

"Are you sure you want to do that?" Lindsey would rather see Heather hang on to the boxes, instead of berating her for getting rid of them.

"Yes," Heather's voice was sure. "It needs to go."

"Okay." Lindsey was tired but if this would help Heather let go of her husband, then she would do it. "Are you sure about this?"

"Lindsey." Heather had that set look again. "I'm going through a really rough time right now. I don't mean to take it out on you, really."

Lindsey paused, not sure how to respond, she settled for the truth.

"You really hurt my feelings," Lindsey said.

"I am sorry." Heather looked tired and sad, but her eyes were drier. "I was so afraid that you would fall for Brandon's line of crap. I should have known better. I spent all that time at the restaurant with him, he really got under my skin."

"I never meant to leave you there that long," Lindsey said. "But Dad was so worried about Mom. I couldn't tell him no."

"I didn't know that the restaurant was so much work. I thought – I don't know what I thought – but I couldn't do it." Heather dissolved into tears. "I'm really sorry."

"I – I forgive you," Lindsey said. "I'm sorry about the sackcloth and ashes crack." Lindsey hugged her sister, grateful to see the Heather that Lindsey loved once again.

"I've got to let go of Rich, or I'm not going to be able to get on with my life." She gestured to the boxes. "I'm trying, I'm really trying. But I can't take these into town. Will you, please?"

"Yeah." Lindsey wiped her eyes. "I'll take them in, as long as you are sure that you are ready."

"Thank you." Heather blew her nose. "I just wish it didn't hurt so bad to let Rich go." She started handing Lindsey boxes. But she didn't last very long; she faded back into the house, still clutching Rich's shirt.

Lindsey stopped a moment to wipe her stinging eyes; it tore her up to see her sister like this. She was grubby and tired, now she had another task to finish before she could rest.

"Need a hand?" Tag stood at the side of the truck. He was watching her with his head cocked to one side. Assessing her mood?

"Sure." Lindsey smiled. They hauled boxes until the porch was clear and the truck bed was full. Tag helped her secure the load with a cargo net. They looked at each other for a moment.

"I never thought she would do it." Lindsey waved at the boxes. "Not in a million years."

"I told you there was hope for her," he said. "You never know."

"Miracles happen?" Lindsey quipped wrinkling her nose at him. "Optimist!"

She got into the truck. She was tired but the trip back to town was the least she could do for her sister. With luck, she could be back in time for supper.

"Hey, you want some company?" Tag had his hand on the passenger door.

"Sure, hop in." She winced at her unfortunate choice of words. When was she going to get a handle on her mouth?

Luckily, Tag didn't notice. They chatted about the garden, the one safe topic they always came back to. As they drove up 31W, they started pointing out the new construction on either side of the road. He told her a little about growing up in E'town. After growing up an Army brat, Lindsey couldn't imagine living all those years in one place. Tag didn't seem to mind comparing lives.

They dropped the boxes off at the Goodwill store. On the way home, Lindsey stopped at Dairy Queen for ice cream, to reward them both for good behavior. She had to admit that she found Tag's company soothing, she could talk freely to him. Lindsey was feeling the strain of keeping secrets more and more as the days passed. They started to talk about Heather over blizzards, seated in the restaurant. Lindsey couldn't hide her resentment.

"I think you should cut her some slack," Tag said. "It hasn't been easy for me to lose my friends. I can't imagine what it would be like to lose a wife or a husband."

"I have cut her slack, five years of slack." Lindsey countered. "One minute she's a tyrant, a minute later she's crying like the world will end."

"She let go of his stuff today," Tag said. "Give her credit."

"It was all packed for the move or she would still have it all in the closets." Lindsey made a face.

"This doesn't sound like you." Tag raised his eyebrows as he looked at her. "Really, Lynn, why are you so angry?"

Lindsey thought about it for a second, decided that she could tell him how Heather had attacked her for going out with him.

"Sunday she was all over me for – going out to the movie with you." Lindsey looked down at her nearly empty ice cream cup.

"I didn't know," Tag said softly.

"I'm still mad at her. Heather's been driving me crazy for weeks. It was pretty strange, like she was jealous." Lindsey toyed with the cup, needing to know, but afraid to ask. Still, this was Tag, someone she could talk to about anything. "Is there something between the two of you?" Lindsey looked at him, her expression closed.

Tag looked down at the table. Their hands were only inches apart. He took Lindsey's hand in his.

"No," he said. "It's not Heather I want to spend time with, it's you." Tag rubbed his fingers across her knuckles and smiled. "People keep telling me that it's time I get on with my life."

"Who?"

Tag gave her a wry, almost embarrassed look. "It's a group of guys. Some of them are still in the hospital; others are getting intensive physical therapy. Others are out on their own, like I am. We get together once a week, for support. There is a councilor leading the group. When it started, I thought it was stupid. I was wrong. I feel better when I talk to them. We all have the same trouble adjusting to civilian life."

Lindsey smiled at the revelation. "Is that why you keep telling me to talk about my problems?"

"Yes." Tag smiled. "I never thought I'd use any of it."

"Did you tell them about me?" Lindsey was curious.

"They figured it out when I cut my hair." Tag was blushing. He dropped his gaze back to their hands.

Lindsey stifled the impulse to quiz him. He was already uncomfortable.

What would a room full of young men talk about while getting back into the civilian world? Would she ever like to be a fly on the wall for one of those sessions! She grinned, maybe not. The proverbial 'locker room' would be a tea party by comparison.

"I have learned a lot of things, not just from talking, but from listening too." He toyed with the cup, still evading her eyes.

"You are a great listener," Lindsey said. "It's uncanny some times."

"Thanks." Tag looked into her eyes and smiled. He was breathtakingly handsome when he smiled like that. The scar on his cheek gave him a rugged air, but his eyes, light blue, ringed with black, were soft when he looked at her. He rubbed his thumb across her knuckles in a gesture that could convey a great deal.

He was the first person who made her wish that she had more free time. He was the first man she'd known for years who was worth freeing up her time. How ironic that she would meet him now, when there was so much chaos in her life.

"I wish I had more free time," she said aloud. "Between the restaurant and the garden, I'm booked solid all day."

"Don't worry about the garden. Jim and I can handle it," Tag told her. "The work agrees with me. It gives me something else to think about."

They sat for a moment in companionable silence. Lindsey noticed just how relaxed he looked, confident and content. What more was there to want in a man: A shoulder to lean on, a friend to talk to, someone who was witty, caring and kind?

Tag's cell phone rang.

"It's Jim," he said looking at it with surprise. "Yo." He listened for a moment; his eyes half-lidded. His mouth pulled to one side in amusement.

"No, everything is good to go. There is a timer on the transplants." He looked at his watch. "I'll be back before then."

Tag closed his phone. He and Lindsey exchanged a look then burst out laughing. The Colonel hadn't fooled them, he was checking up on his daughter.

"I guess we'd better get back." Lindsey giggled under her breath as she picked up her empty ice cream container.

"Before he sends the police to bring you home," Tag snickered. "Fathers never trust me with their daughters."

"They know a wolf when they see one." Lindsey laughed.

"I've reformed," Tag protested. "Really."

Lindsey grinned and shook her head. "My father is never going to believe that."

Chapter 15

Brandon bounced into the restaurant, greeting Lindsey with a wink and a grin. "I see you have a head start this morning. What have we got today, anything exotic, some obscure vegetable from the wilderness?"

"Sorry, nothing exotic this morning," Lindsey said. "We have three kinds of beans, a yellow, a green and some white shell beans."

"You really need to get something interesting going on." Brandon had a malicious gleam in his eyes. "Throw some magic mushrooms in the stir-fry; or wacky-tobacky in the dressing. I want to see some of these stuffed shirts get high and get crazy!"

"Could you see some of these straight-laced lawyers strung out on 'shrooms?" Shawn laughed. "I'll bet some of them would be chasing their secretaries down the street in no time!"

Shawn pranced around while Brandon chased him. "No. Don't! Stop. Stop!"

"Yeah, yeah, keep it rated 'g' okay?" Lindsey chided them.

"I've got a better idea: Viagra in the coffee." Brandon thrust his hips forward. "Shwing! Pull the plug on all the posing and let the party start!" He grabbed a carrot from the counter.

"Put that back." Lindsey pointed to the carrot using her chef's knife like a finger. "No molesting the vegetables." She made a slicing motion with the knife.

"You need to buy a sense of humor." Brandon glared at Lindsey.

"This is not a playground," Lindsey said. "People come in and out of here from the city government. That kind of horseplay isn't professional."

"Give it a freaking break!" Brandon was too loud, the look in his eyes not quite sane.

"Do you *like* working here?" Lindsey lost her temper.

"What?" Brandon stepped forward, his dark eyes blazing. "Did I hear that right?"

"Yes, you heard me. Knock it off. Now." Lindsey was shaking inside, but she stood straight and used her father's whip-like voice. She hated confrontations, but she wasn't backing down. He needed to keep it professional or he could go home.

The tension between her and Brandon tightened. Lindsey didn't dare step back from him. She gripped the knife tighter, unsure. Brandon looked at her for a very long, tense minute before he broke eye contact.

"That's the thanks I get for all I've done for you?" He turned the tables on her. "You couldn't have made it without me the last few weeks. I can't believe how ungrateful you are."

"Hey!" Shawn made a face at Brandon. "I smell bacon."

Four people walked in the door, two of them officers in uniform. Brandon made a 'gag me' motion, rolled his eyes and went back to work.

Lindsey couldn't forget the confrontation, her stomach twisted for an hour. Long after the rush started, she was wary of Brandon. Brandon was scratching his arms and twitching his shoulders. A tense snarl was never far from his lips.

Was this what Tag had meant about tweaking? Good God, what was next?

Lindsey was grateful that business had picked up and the register was right. She let them go early. She wanted them long gone before the locksmith arrived. She had him re-key all the locks. She no longer underestimated Brandon or Mychou's cunning. She even had her doubts about Shawn. The bill was steep, but the locksmith assured her that no ordinary master key would open her locks again.

When Lindsey got home, there were three envelopes in the mailbox, each from a separate vendor. Lindsey resisted the urge to leave them. Instead she carried everything to the house. She knew that Tag had been in her house because the screen door latch didn't stick.

In a burst of humor she thought of him as the Fix-it fairy – everywhere he went things were fixed behind him. Tag McTaggart, her personal Tinkerbell in a tool belt. She nearly giggled aloud at the mental image of Tag with fairy wings sticking out of his tank top, and a long screwdriver as a magic wand, then pulled a straight face. Her twisted sense of humor would get her in trouble some day.

Tag was working on the loose ceiling panel, a bottle of glue in one hand. He was dripping sweat in spite of the air conditioning. The damp tank top clung to his upper body, outlining his shoulders and chest. All traces of a farmer's tan line was gone. The work had worn any softness away. He was hard-muscled and golden tanned. His short hair bleached blonde and not the faintest trace of beard shadowed his sculpted jaw line.

With his arms over his head, the shirt was too short to cover his middrift. The view of his flat belly with the trail of golden hair that vanished into his jeans was positively yummy. Lindsey licked her lips then forced herself to look away.

"Hi." Tag was concentrating on the task at hand. "How did it go today?"

"Busy, today." Lindsey tried to keep her eyes off him. She didn't want to get caught drooling. He would tease her unmercifully – if he caught her.

"The locksmith came out to change the locks. I won't have any more surprise visitors in the morning." The envelopes burned her hand, so she set them down. There was no telling what was in those invoices. She didn't want to face this alone.

"I think I have the invoices from the last few weeks," she said.

Tag immediately stopped working on the ceiling panel. He set the glue bottle down, wiped his hands on a towel, and walked out to the kitchen. Lindsey drank in the sight of him.

"Have you seen them yet?"

"No." Lindsey shook her head. "God only knows what is waiting for me." She sighed, rubbing her forehead. That blasted headache was back. "I've taken his key, and changed the locks, but this is going to be proof if he's screwing me over.

"You've been working hard." The cabinet doors were back up, and the sink wasn't dripping. "It's a big improvement." The little things he did for her really warmed her heart. He made the worst time of her entire life bearable. She gestured to the repaired kitchen. "You've done a lot for me. Thank you."

"You're welcome." He cocked his head at her to remind her that the bad news was waiting. He pointed to the envelopes. "You're stalling."

"I know. I just need a couple more seconds to breathe, really. Could you put the tea kettle on? There's a box of tea on the counter, blue box with a dragon on it." She sat at the table. "I have a feeling I'm going to need something to quiet my nerves."

"Got any whiskey?" He shot back. "Something stronger than tea may be in order."

"There is bourbon at Heather's house." She picked up the first envelope.

He didn't offer to get the bourbon. She heard him running water behind her. She opened the first envelope, taking out several folded sheets of paper. She heard the microwave chirp; he wasn't going to wait for the teakettle. She closed her eyes for a moment, praying for strength. Then she unfolded the papers. She worked down the orders line by line, finding the extras amongst the regular items. A few things stood out right away. The most telling had been marked "cash" and "pickup."

"Good grief," she said. "Four cases of sirloin steak; who is he feeding? At least he paid cash for that. Where is he getting the money from?" She went to the next page. "I paid for these: two cases of hamburgers, hash browns, sausage, and bacon. There were never more than two or three breakfast customers but all that food is gone. A couple hundred bucks down the drain."

"What else?"

"Looks like he tried to buy some liquor, too," Lindsey said, shuffling pages. "We don't have a license for it. Thank God for small favors." She flipped back to the previous invoices. "Well, six invoices, almost six hundred dollars." She rubbed her forehead, one vendor down. The microwave chirped again. She heard him moving around behind her, very glad for his company.

"The supply company." She sighed again, dreading what she would find.

Tag placed a cup on the table then sat in the chair next to her. Very sweet of him, she thought for a second, before she opened the second envelope.

There were eight invoices. Again, there were the usual items mixed in with things that her restaurant would not have ordered, sometimes the extras were by themselves, marked 'cash' and 'pickup.'

"This one has ... what the hell? Why would anybody buy a case of cold medicine?"

"He has a hell of a cold?" Tag replied, though there was no humor in his voice.

"Very funny."

"Either that or he's making crystal meth." Tag tsked under his breath, moving closer so he could see the entry on the invoice. "That's the right brand."

Lindsey swore as she dragged her hand through her hair. She looked over at Tag, but he only shrugged.

"I wish I had been wrong about him." Tag gave her shoulder a pat.

"Yeah, you were right." Lindsey flipped through the other invoices. "He ordered two cases, only got one. That was May 19th?" She looked up at

Tag. "He'd only been working for me for a couple weeks! Oh shit, he was screwing me over from day one!"

She thought about the first interview, the way Brandon had flirted with her. Had he come to the job interview with this in mind, or had he taken advantage the minute her back was turned? Whichever, the snake had taken advantage of her trust!

"Batteries, towels added to the usual paper supplies, more batteries and a case of drain cleaner." She set the second down. "This is another case of drain cleaner. I was back for this one. It's marked returned." Lindsey handed the invoices to Tag. Her hands shook and her stomach churned. She could barely breathe. "I don't know what to do."

"You need a lawyer!" Tag handed the invoices back to her. "Look at the signatures." Tag pointed to the date. May 19th, the invoice that had the cold medicine was signed with Heather's looped 'H' and wavy line signature.

"Sweet suffering Pete," Lindsey whispered. She flipped to the next invoice, also signed by Heather. The date was about the time that Heather had been running the restaurant.

"Heather signed for all this?"

"Look at these," Tag said. The rest were signed with what looked like Lindsey's own signature. "I'm not up on civilian law, but this looks bad to me. This guy can't be more than a step or two ahead of the DEA. For all you know he's under surveillance, which means they are watching you too." Tag took her hand, looked into her face. "The DEA could shut the restaurant down for months while you try to get this untangled."

"I can't afford to close for a week, let alone for months." Lindsey felt her neck muscles lock up as the tension headache crawled up her spine. What could she do? Could she go to the police? Would they believe her? If they didn't, what would happen, could she go to jail?

"Oh God, I can't take any more." Lindsey closed her eyes then laid her head on her crossed arms.

"Are you okay?" Tag rubbed her hand. "Your hand is ice cold."

Lindsey just shook her head. Her ears were ringing and she was trying to keep from crying. She'd been such a trusting fool! She'd let Brandon sweet-talk her into giving him the account information. Now look what he'd done!

"The human body can only take so much stress." Tag's voice was compassionate. He gave her a one-armed hug. "I think you hit your limit."

His compassion was the last straw.

"Just freaking shoot me." Her self-control broke. Lindsey started to cry.

"Oh hell, I knew this was coming." Tag tugged at her. "Come here." His voice was patient, Lindsey blindly came to his open arms. He settled her on his lap, hugging her tight. "Go on, cry." She cried until she became aware of him less as a shoulder to cry on and more as a very large, strong man. He handed her a napkin.

"I'm so glad you're here." Lindsey sniffed, blotting her eyes.

"I'm here," Tag said stroking her hair.

"You've got to think I'm a coward...."

"Shhh." He covered her lips. "The absence of fear is stupidity, not courage."

"I'm pathetic." Lindsey's eyes were still leaking tears.

"A basket case," he agreed.

"You're not supposed to agree with me." Lindsey stopped crying; it was almost funny.

"Girls don't come with owner's manuals," Tag chided in a dry voice. "A guy just has to muddle through." He shifted for a moment, then gave her the tea mug off the table. "Drink this, it's still hot."

Lindsey had to sit up to drink the tea. He must have dumped sugar in the mug. Her tea was very sweet. The tea helped calm her shaking hands, the shock and the fear were still there, but she was facing it. She found another napkin on the table, wiped her face, blew her nose and felt human.

"Should I get up?" She couldn't decide how she felt about being in his lap. Could she be embarrassed and intrigued at the same time?

"Not if you're going to fall over." Tag tested her cheek with his free hand. "You've got your color back. Stay put awhile."

"Thank you." Lindsey kissed him, a chaste kiss. To her surprise, Tag cupped her face. He kissed her slowly, the brush of his lips firm and gentle. When he broke away from her lips, she made a soft sound of protest.

"Hmm." The questioning touch of his lips against hers was deliberate and restrained. When he stopped, her hand slid up his arm to the back of his neck, keeping him close. His lips were so close she could feel him smile, before he gave her a kiss that made her tingle to her fingertips. Then softness became teasing, her breath quickened. He broke away from her lips, she whimpered in protest.

"Ah, you liked that, did you?" he said against her cheek.

Lindsey nodded slightly, breathing deep, not trusting her voice. They kissed again, both lost in the pleasure of it. Somehow she shifted her weight wrong, she felt the jolt of pain hit him. He broke away from her lips.

The moment hung suspended between them: fragile.

She hid her insecurity behind veiled eyes, waiting for him to make the next move in this delicate dance. Tag was just as still as she, frozen with indecision, where a moment before there had been certainty.

When his hand left her cheek, Lindsey realized that he was going to stop. The thought left her bereft for a breath. She looked into his solemn eyes.

"Don't stop," she whispered.

"You are so beautiful, so vulnerable." He traced her cheekbone with the pad of his thumb. "You have enough problems; you don't need to tackle mine, too. You're not made of steel."

"What am I *supposed* to be made of?" She asked, frustrated.

"Sugar and spice and everything nice." The quirky half smile came back. "That's what you're made of, little girl."

"You think I'm a mess." She threw his words from Saturday back at him.

He hushed her with his fingers against her lips.

"Don't twist my words." Tag's blue eyes were dark and sad. "You are the one person who gets me out of myself. When I'm with you, I forget about Sergeant McTaggart and Iraq. All that shit no longer matters." He stroked her hair, smiling at her. "That's pretty cool."

"Then why stop?"

"One night stands have lost their appeal for me," he quipped, but his smile faded. He looked down for a moment, then back into her eyes.

"You have no idea how screwed up I am." His face was bleak. "For the longest time I couldn't even look in a damn mirror. Shaving in the morning used to really suck, so I quit shaving or looking into mirrors." He played with her hair. "Until you made me think about it, again."

"I'm sorry about that," she said rubbing his shaven cheek.

"Don't be, I looked like hell." Tag smiled at her.

She protested, but he stopped her again.

"Lynn, you're so stressed you're not thinking straight. Be reasonable, please?"

She kissed his cheek, making a silent promise that she would find a way to make him forget for good. She slid off his lap, retreating to the bathroom, where she could sponge her face with cold water. She was weak in the knees, still scared silly on one hand, and painfully aroused on the other.

These conflicting emotions were exhausting.

She needed to talk to a lawyer. She had to find out what she could do without being arrested or sued.

She sighed, knowing that she would have to face him. She shivered again, remembering that tender moment with every nerve of her body. When this was over she vowed she would do more than just kiss him! That wicked thought let her flash a smile at her reflection in the mirror before she went back to the kitchen table.

"We need a plan of action," she said. "I can't let this go on."

"Get a lawyer." Tag was sitting down at the table. "It's the only way."

"The expense is going to break me." Lindsey sighed. "But I can't go to my parents for help with this. I'll just have to cope."

"Don't tell me that you are planning to keep this from your father?" Tag shook his head. "That isn't right."

"Dad doesn't need to know, until after I talk to a lawyer." Lindsey shook her head. Heather had been right, back when Lindsey fired Mychou. She couldn't hide behind their father, like a child scared of the boogieman. The restaurant was her responsibility.

"It's bad enough he doesn't know that you have problems with your employees, now you're going to keep legal problems secret?"

"I can't go whining to my father like a child every time I have a problem." Lindsey wasn't going to let Tag talk her into it. "It's only for a few more days."

"Lynn, this is a bad idea," Tag warned her. "He's going to be furious if he finds out about this later."

"This is my problem. I'll handle it." Lindsey let her frustration out.

"Bullshit, Lynn. I thought you and your family were all partners in this? You can't hide the fact that the whole business is in danger! They have a right to know." Tag got up from the table. "How dishonest is that?"

"I'll handle it first, then I'll tell them."

"Your pride and your ego will get you into more trouble than you can handle." Tag walked to the door. He stood looking at her for a moment, one hand on the doorknob, the doorway open behind him. "When you are ready to be reasonable, let me know."

"Good night," Lindsey said coldly.

"Good night, Lynn." Tag tipped one finger at his eyebrow in a mock salute.

Lindsey watched him leave. She was furious with him. Tag, of all people, should understand why she needed to prove she could handle it. These last few weeks had taught her not to rely on her family or anyone.

She'd just gotten proof that someone she trusted had screwed her over. Why should she trust Tag? Tag had no right to tell her what to do. It wasn't any of his business. A few, very hot, kisses could not change that.

Lindsey sighed. She would find a lawyer. Until then she would go on pretending that nothing was wrong. If there was one thing that she could learn from Brandon, it was how to keep secrets.

Chapter 16

Lindsey reached the garden after a restless night. She was no longer sure of herself, but she was going to keep to her plan. Tag came over to where she was cleaning out baskets.

"How are you doing this morning?" Tag's eyes searched hers.

Was he looking for her to tell him that he was right and she was wrong? That wasn't going to happen. She needed to hold her ground or he would walk over her, too.

"I'm fine." Lindsey smiled, but there was a ring of insincerity to her voice. "I'm sorry about yesterday."

"So am I." Tag made an aborted gesture, as if he were going to touch her. "I can't tell you what to do. I can only make suggestions."

"I know that you mean well…"

"I'll butt out." Tag shrugged. "Just remember that I'm here for you. Okay?"

"I will."

They pinched the basil and cilantro. Heather washed and packed the leaves. Travis ran back and forth carrying baskets. The work went fast. Lindsey was soon in her truck driving up 31W.

Why did she feel like something precious was lost to her?

She should be concentrating on what to do about Brandon, not stewing over how she'd managed to get so close to Tag one minute then alienate him the next. She was flipping emotions again, angry with Brandon and lusting after Tag. At this rate, she was going to go stark raving mad. She blotted it from her mind. There was work to do. She needed to focus on the day, and not think about what a lying fink she had hired.

Brandon and Mychou were waiting outside, pacing and smoking. Lindsey greeted them cheerfully. Mychou was wearing an expensive thick gold chain necklace with delicate filigree earrings that Lindsey had never seen before. How she could afford jewelry when she couldn't afford to fix her car?

Brandon helped Lindsey unload the coolers from her truck; he was wearing his whites, they looked starched and pressed. Once inside Mychou started cleaning the back counter. Brandon sharpened his knives with quick even strokes.

Lindsey set a pot of water to boil before she dumped baskets of basil tips into cold water. Lindsey put parsley, cilantro, garlic and basil into the food processor with olive oil. The whole kitchen took on the sweet smell of basil. Then she toasted pecans, spilling them in the processor next, following that with Parmesan cheese. She ground it all together, as whole-wheat pasta boiled in the pot. When the pasta was ready, she tossed it with the pesto. The mingled odors became a dusky siren song that brought everyone to the kitchen.

Grinning, Lindsey passed the pasta around for everyone to taste. Shawn and Brandon each ate a bowl. Mychou nibbled a few bites. Lindsey meditated on the flavors, thinking what vegetables she could sauté.

"Too bad the asparagus is gone." Brandon remarked.

"The baby yellow beans will be great with carrots and snap peas," Lindsey assured him. "It will go out the door as fast as we can cook it."

The phone started to ring with orders: the rush was on. Lindsey gave her station in the kitchen to Brandon so she could ring up tickets.

Lindsey cleared the counter – waited on customers. Most of her customers worked on the square for the city government. The regular customers brought the tickets and their money to her, exchanging a word or two, many asking about her mother or her sister. They had been coming in nearly every day since she opened. Lindsey and the restaurant were a part of the town-square.

There were several tickets for coffee only; she didn't know these customers. They came and went quickly. But there did seem to be quite a few of them. Lindsey saw them and wondered, why come in and not eat?

It was hard to keep her mind on her work. She kept flashing back to last night; the memory of kissing Tag was electric. The mixture of strength in his arms as he had held her and tenderness in his kisses still made her tingle all over. She ignored the reason she'd been in his arms in the first place.

At the end of the day, Mychou's grandmother dropped off the children. Lindsey surreptitiously checked the condition of the girl's clothing. Today the child wore a brand new dress, and her ears were pierced. Delicate gold hoops hung from her tiny ears. Lindsey winced for the child's sake.

Once her employees were gone, Lindsey looked through the yellow pages. She needed a lawyer, but she didn't want to call Mychou's lawyer by mistake.

"What was that idiot's name?" She tapped the pad with her pen. She thought his name was Burns, as in 'burns in hell.'

She went through the attorney section. No lawyer named Burns, not alone, or in a partnership. Well, maybe he was in Louisville. She got out the yellow pages, went over the list of names. Burns and Someone, no listing, Someone and Burns? Burns had no listing in either book.

It made no sense at all. Who had she spoken to? Had she been scammed? Why make such a fuss over a waitress job? Waitresses came and went out of restaurants; they made tips and wages. They were taxed a set amount on their wages to cover their tips.

Mychou always had a pocket full of money, tips from customers who bought only coffee. Biting her lip, Lindsey thought very hard. Had she seen Mychou do anything suspicious? The only thing suspicious was Mychou's inability to ring up a ticket without screwing it up.

Something was going on, but she had yet to spot it.

There was no doubt in Lindsey's mind, she needed a lawyer, a good lawyer. It was going to cost her a fortune. She would have to get a loan after all. Damn, damn, damn! She was in deep trouble.

She took a long breath then started making phone calls. Unwilling to reveal the extent of her problems she was quickly frustrated. She was already in a tricky situation; she had to use all her tact to get the information she needed without spilling her problems to some gossipy secretary.

One by one she called the lawyers in the phone book. Most handled only divorce cases; quite a few were injury lawyers. Still she spent a couple of hours, tap-dancing around secretaries as she asked her careful questions. Twice she talked to the lawyers themselves, but she wasn't satisfied with their answers.

It was getting late; she would try firms in Louisville tomorrow. Lindsey locked up the restaurant, driving back to Sonora and home.

Her mind churned as she drove.

Keeping silent and keeping secrets, where was it all going to end? She had secrets from her employees, her sister, her father and her mother. The one person she'd felt free to talk to was Tag.

Lindsey sighed. Kissing him had set her on fire. Had he felt it too? Lindsey rubbed her forehead, remembering those kisses made her heart beat faster. Would their fragile bond survive their difference of opinion?

Now what? Should she tell her father everything? Was Tag right? Could her father take the additional strain of knowing that the restaurant was doing badly, thanks to two dishonest employees?

Her thoughts circled back to Tag. What emotional scars went with the physical? Which were deeper? Lindsey heaved a sigh, if she hadn't been such a wreck last night, would she have let him get so close?

She'd needed a friend. He *had* been there for her, until she'd decided to leave her father out of the loop.

Tag had told her right up front that he didn't want a one-night-stand or to take advantage of her when she was vulnerable. He'd said that he wanted to be part of the solution. She wanted him to be part of the solution. On that, they agreed. How in hell were they going to manage such a tall order with things so screwed up?

Her experience with men was limited to casual dating and Tommy. When the relationship with Tommy ended, her hope for marriage and a family had gone with it. The pain of failure was too great. Going to culinary school was a safe way out. Now at thirty, she worked sixteen-hour days, seven days a week.

Shouldn't there be more to life than work?

She envied Mychou's darling daughter, but that didn't mean she was ready to add the responsibility of children. She shuddered to think of the horrendous changes that a child would make to her life. Which brought another problem to light: she wasn't on birth control. That needed to change soon!

The sweltering humidity smothered her as she stepped out of the truck. She heard the lawn mower in the back yard, her eyes following the sound. Tag was mowing lawn, wearing camouflage BDU pants and dark sunglasses.

He had taken off his shirt.

The sight of him brought a little growl from her throat. Sunlight reflected off his sweaty skin, outlining the muscle structure with light and shadow. There were several black lines on his upper left pectoral muscle, some kind of tattoo.

She licked her lips and swallowed, her throat was as dry as a desert.

In the house, she poured two glasses of iced tea then walked out again. She stepped into his line of sight. He flashed a smile then cut the mower engine. She handed him the glass, careful not to look at the network of burn scars on the left side of his body.

"Take a break?" She asked with a smile. He reached for the t-shirt hanging from the handle of the lawn mower, hesitated then slung it over his left shoulder. Was he shielding the scars from her sight? They walked over to the porch, sitting on the steps, sipping sweet tea.

"How did it go?" Tag asked, sounding casual. He propped his sunglasses on the top of his head so she could see his eyes.

Such kind eyes, she thought. "I called every lawyer in town, no luck," she sighed. "I'm going to try Louisville law firms tomorrow. I don't know what else to do."

"You're making progress."

"It doesn't feel like it."

There were numbers branded into his right shoulder, white scars against his tan.

"What are those?" Lindsey traced the numbers with a fingertip.

"My unit." Tag's voice was hoarse. He took a drink of tea. When he lifted his glass to drink, the shirt fell off his left shoulder. The tattoo on his chest was a list of five names. Three had the same date beside them.

It was a list of the fallen.

"Your men?" She should stop looking, stop touching him, but the map of his military career, written on his body, was irresistible.

Tag nodded and swallowed.

"I'm sorry." She looked into his face. "Is this okay with you?"

He looked away. For a moment she saw only his strong profile, handsome and vulnerable, the combination drew her like a magnet. She pressed her cheek against his shoulder, until he let out a deep breath. He shifted a little towards her. He watched her, his expression wary.

"It's okay," Tag assented aloud. There were slash mark scars down his arm, from a bullet maybe? Old scars like jagged cuts down his back. The burns across his stomach, splattered like paint, were still a little pink. He flinched when she traced them, her hand jerked back.

"Did I hurt you?" She looked up, alarmed.

"It tickles." His smile was strained.

"How bad were you hurt?"

"My foot was gone, nothing they could do about that. My right leg was broken." Thus exposed he was wary of her, but he was truthful. "There are more burns." He gestured across his abdomen, down his legs, areas hidden by pants. "The physical is only half of it. I'm a mess."

Lindsey shook her head. Inwardly appalled, she tried not to show it. "Don't tell me that it doesn't matter."

"It explains a lot." She meant his shyness.

"Yeah, I'll bet it does."

"Tag." She caught his wrist so he didn't pull away. She needed him to understand she wasn't offering him pity. "What I meant and how you choose to take it are two different things."

"Are they?" His blue eyes were cold and hostile, he was practically growling.

"Yes." Okay, she would make her point unmistakable. She dropped her eyes to his bare chest, followed the sweep of light gold hair trailing down his abdomen and back up. With a fingertip, she traced a line from sharp collarbone to the swell of his biceps. In spite of everything he was damn fine. He had broad shoulders and defined pecks, with a fine sheen of sweat on his tanned skin, like oil.

The admiration on her face was genuine.

"You are a good looking man. You could have anything you want out of life. Or anyone." The look on his face, so vulnerable at that moment, twisted her heart. The memory of his kisses shot to the base of her spine. She wanted more, much more, than a few kisses.

What would it take to get the message across?

Absolute honesty might do it.

"After being so badly hurt, it would take great trust in someone, to have sex the first time." Her voice, husky with lust, betrayed her. She couldn't help the way her lips curved, or hide the heat as she looked into his eyes.

"One night stands have lost all their appeal." He repeated the same feeble joke from last night.

"I would like you to trust me that much." She swallowed. "One day."

That bold statement hung on the air between them. Unconsciously Lindsey licked her dry lips. He sucked in a breath as his expression changed from wary, to surprised, to hungry.

Message received, she thought with breathless anticipation. Oh, now he was the man who had kissed her with such tenderness the night before. She leaned a little closer, hoping he would meet her halfway.

"It's not that simple." Tag's face became serious and sad. "You have no idea...."

The dinner bell rang.

The mood shattered at the sound, they both jumped. Lindsey looked towards the house. Heather was watching them.

It was like getting hit with a bucket of ice water. Lindsey was unable to resist the impulse to pull away.

"Heather?"

"Yes." Lindsey affirmed, her eyes darting to him.

"Think we ought to wave?" he grinned at Lindsey, wolfishly.

"God, no!" Lindsey was aghast. "I should get cleaned up." She moved away.

"Hey, don't let her run you off." He grabbed her hand. "Just because she's around doesn't mean we can't..." he floundered "... talk."

As if these intimate moments were light conversations.

"You deserve to have a life."

"Tag, you give good advice." Lindsey shook her head exasperated. "Listen to yourself!"

They looked at each other for a moment. Tag was still holding her hand. He rubbed his thumb across her knuckles, a gesture that communicated his need for her understanding.

"Yeah," he admitted. "It's so much easier to say it than to do it."

Lindsey squeezed his hand.

"Ah, hell," Tag swore. "You blow me away." He released the grip on her hand. He looked at her with his soul in his eyes. "I'm not sure I like being so ... naked ... with you."

"I don't think it would be so bad," Lindsey teased, giving him a wink. It was time to back off. "Drink up. I've got to change clothes. We still have work to do."

He drained his iced tea, put the glass in her hand. The look he gave her was centered where he'd been unbalanced a moment before.

Damn Heather for interrupting them, why couldn't she leave them alone?

There was plenty of work for them to do after supper. They worked with Jim and Travis, getting more raised beds ready for lettuce and later succession crops of beans and cabbage. They started talking about the hot summer months coming up.

"County water for a garden of this size is going to be really expensive," Tag said. "We are going to need another source of water, a stream or a pond, or something."

"We get more than enough water in the early summer and fall," Jim said. "If we could store it in a cistern for later use, it would help a lot."

"Use the barn roof to collect the water." Tag looked over at the barn. "We could measure it, get the square footage, I could calculate the size of the cistern from there."

"That sounds like a big investment," Lindsey said, wondering what something like that would cost, as opposed to the water bill. She followed as they drifted over to the old barn.

"A one-time investment that would pay for itself in a couple of years," Jim said. "It would all depend on how it was constructed. I don't want something that's going to freeze solid in the winter."

"It wouldn't freeze if you put it underground." Tag shaded his eyes as he looked at the barn roof. "Is the barn thirty by forty? I can calculate the how many gallons you can catch in a one inch rain. That will get us an idea of how big the cistern would need to be.

"How far is it from the barn to the farthest part of the garden?" Tag stopped and turned to Lindsey. "Lynn, can you get me something to write on? I need to get this down on paper."

Lindsey got a notebook from her house while Tag and her father measured the barn with a tape. She marveled at how well they worked together. They bent over the notebook talking about square feet, pitch and different types of tanks.

Lindsey couldn't follow the conversation. She didn't feel that she needed to. It had been years since she'd seen her father so intent, so focused. He and Tag appeared to be delighted with the challenge. She felt funny watching them. Not left out, because she was going to benefit from the project but this was *their* challenge. She was willing to let them enjoy themselves.

"How old is the house?" Tag asked. "Maybe there was a cistern or a well at one time?"

"I'll ask Heather," Jim said, taking the notebook. "If there was one, it was probably covered up or filled in long ago." The two men walked off, still talking about cisterns and wells, pacing off the distance from barn to house.

Lindsey didn't join them. Her mind replayed the conversation on the porch. She was drawn to Tag by emotions so strong they scared her. He had so much emotional baggage to overcome. Could she give him what he needed while she was working these long hours? She could talk to Tag later. Right now, she had plenty of work to do. Her employees and the government wanted money.

She caught up with taxes and payroll that evening. Her eyes strayed to her cell phone, but it remained stubbornly silent. She picked it up around nine, sending the text message herself 'rup?'

Tag called a moment later.

"Hey," he said in a lazy voice. "I didn't expect you to be awake."

"I'm still up." Lindsey was drinking her third mug of tea. "I – want to talk about this afternoon."

"Yeah?" Tag's voice lost its lazy drawl. "Are you sure?"

"Yes," Lindsey lied. Maybe this was a bad idea. "You keep telling me that I don't know what's going on with you. I want you to tell me."

"Truth or dare?" He sounded snide.

"No games. Just tell me." Lindsey dropped her voice, coaxing. "We can talk about my problems, why can't we talk about yours? Why do you shut down? I want to know what's going on with you."

"You don't want to know."

"I do." Lindsey voice was firm but her heart was breaking.

"I've had twenty surgeries, including ten skin grafts. I spent a year in Walter Reed hospital. I was on suicide watch the whole time. When I came home to my mother's house, I got drunk and stayed drunk. I was a real ass. I overdosed on pills and booze twice. I don't remember if it was on purpose or by accident." He continued in a flat tone. "The second time I overdosed I ended up in a rubber room, wearing a 'love-me' jacket. The doctor told me to stop drinking or she would throw away the key.

"My mother wouldn't let me come back, so I got this apartment. That may have saved my life. I had to get off my ass. A few weeks ago, I went cold turkey off the pills because I can't function on all that crap. Then I started working with your father.

"Once I stopped taking the pills, the nightmares came back." The edge in his voice wasn't the Tag she knew. "I still have therapy sessions once a week. I don't mind the group, but I hate the one-on-one counseling. That warm-fuzzy crap makes me want to puke."

Lindsey grinned, no doubt about it: he wasn't the 'warm and fuzzy' type.

"Does that tell you enough? There's lots more." He seemed to be working himself into a rage. "How deep do you want to get into my screwed up life?"

"I didn't mean to upset you."

"I'm sorry." Tag sighed, the rage drained from his voice. "Your father saved my sanity by asking for my help. He's the only person who asked me for help. He asks me if I can handle it, most of the time I can. Everybody else treats me, well, like a cripple or a bomb about to go off. I hate that. I'm not a nut case."

"Trust goes both ways."

"Oh, hell." His voice dropped to become soft and tender. "I don't want to be secretive, but it's hard to talk about it. You are – so…"

"What?"

"You are so smart, and so damn fine." There was a touch of desperation in his voice. "I am such a mess, I – don't deserve you."

"That isn't flattering," Lindsey said. "It sounds like self-pity."

Tag was silent for a moment.

"Maybe," he admitted with a sigh. "I'm really tired, it creeps up on me at night."

"Then get some sleep. I'll see you tomorrow." Lindsey put her mug in the sink.

"Goodnight."

"'Night."

Lindsey looked at her phone for a long moment before she put it away. She'd asked, he'd told her. Too bad it didn't make her feel any better. He had suffered. He had been crazy enough to overdose. Yet he was the one person that she could turn to when her life was in shambles. What did that say about her, about him?

Maybe he was right, they didn't have a future together.

There were more customers coming in who did not eat. Men and women, some were well dressed, all of them had a gaunt look to their faces. They sat at the table closest to the door, drinking coffee and putting packet after packet of sugar in the cups. They never stayed long.

Lindsey had just noticed this, a day or so ago, now there were more people. It was strange, sinister. It seemed too much of a coincidence that the same people would be in and out all week. Lindsey's mind was full of alarm bells that would not stop.

Did they make some mysterious connection with Brandon and buy drugs from him later that day? She saw nothing suspicious, nothing out of the ordinary.

When business was over for the day, Lindsey called more law firms, asking careful questions. She crossed more names off her list.

There had to be lawyers who did more than just divorces and personal injuries, but she couldn't find them. She wished that she had the courage to ask 'my employees are dealing drugs, what do I do?' But what would they think? Wouldn't someone just pass her information to the police?

Instead, she asked if the firm ever represented a business owner in a case against a dishonest employee? The answers didn't reassure her a bit.

It had rained all afternoon; Tag was gone before she got home.

That night instead of a text message, Tag called at nine.

"Hi," Lindsey said. She was already in bed; the stress had caught up with her.

"I owe you an apology for yesterday, I was really tired." Tag's voice was low, without the edge of anger from last night. "I was up most of the night before. The nightmares have never stopped." He dropped his voice even farther. "They will never stop."

"It's okay," Lindsey said. "I understand."

"How could you?" Tag asked, his voice sharp.

"Remember who my father is?" Lindsey came back in the same tone. "Don't you think he came home from Vietnam with nightmares and paranoia? There wasn't any treatment for him. They didn't even have a name for it. I was just a little kid, but I remember. We weren't allowed near him when he was sleeping. I remember him waking up screaming. It went on for years."

"Yeah, Jim and I talk a lot." He sighed. "I'm not the only one."

"So, we've settled that." Lindsey took a deep breath. "I accept your apology."

"Hey, I didn't call to be a jerk. I want to know if you'd like to get away for awhile?" Tag's voice was lighter. "How about we take tomorrow off? Go have some fun?"

"What's fun?" Lindsey asked dryly. "I forget."

"All the better reason to do it," his voice dropped in tone and timbre, coaxing. "Can you get away tomorrow?"

"Where to?" Lindsey asked, her lips were curving into a smile. He could send chills down her back with just his voice.

"How about I make it a surprise?" He was teasing now.

"Okay." Lindsey yawned. "What time?"

"How about eight o'clock?"

"Too early," she protested. "I need some sleep."

"Ten o'clock?"

"That will give me a couple extra hours of sleep."

"I'll be there," he said. "Good night."

"Good night." Lindsey looked at her phone. She'd done it again: Agreed to go anywhere he wanted to take her without hesitation or reservation.

It felt good to be able to trust someone.

Chapter 17

Saturday morning there was a knock on her door. Lindsey stumbled to answer it, dressed only in her nightgown, to look through the glass at – Tag. With a groan, she opened the door.

"Good morning." He grinned wickedly at her disarray.

"You're early." She considered closing the door in his face. He didn't have to give her *that* grin; her nightgown was opaque. At least he was looking her in the face.

"Yeah, I am." There was mischief in his eyes. He presented her a red rose with a flourish. Lindsey took the rose and held it to her nose. Deep, deep red, full bloom with crystal droplets of dew on it, the rose was richly scented. It was one of Heather's Mr. Lincoln roses, from the bush by the driveway.

"Heather will kill you if she catches you taking her roses." Lindsey smiled at him from over the rose.

"It's for a good cause."

Lindsey rolled her eyes at him, but let him in the house. She put the rose in water. Then she smelled coffee. "Okay, I'm up and you're here, is that coffee?"

"Yes." He held out a paper cup for her.

"What time is it?" She took the cup from him, sipping it experimentally. Cream, no sugar, he had remembered. The coffee was hot and smooth, from Lindsey's favorite place, Arnold's coffee shop.

"Nine o'clock."

He'd given her an extra hour of sleep. That was almost enough.

"I need a shower." She shooed him back out the door. "Wait there."

"What, you don't trust me?" He tried a hangdog look, but his laughing eyes ruined it.

She wrinkled her nose at him.

"Out." She shook her head. She took in the fact that he was dressed in a polo shirt and good jeans. They were going somewhere respectable. She'd better dress for it. The shower and the coffee woke her up. Lindsey dressed in a tank top, walking shorts, good tennis shoes and enough make up to fit in anywhere. When she let him back in, his eyes were appreciative; his face lit up with a smile.

"You look nice. Time wise that was fast – for a woman." Tag shook his coffee cup. "I haven't finished my coffee yet."

Lindsey charitably let the 'for a woman' crack pass without comment. "What's on the agenda?"

"Breakfast." He looked smug, up to something, she guessed.

"Am I going to have to cook?"

"Nope, just get in the car." Tag opened the door for her.

"What's that, redneck foreplay?" She quipped.

"Don't get me started on redneck jokes, I know them all." Tag followed her out the door. The white Mustang with the blue racing stripes looked newly washed and waxed. Lindsey could still smell the leather cleaner when she sat in the car.

They traded redneck jokes on the way to E'town. They quoted blue-collar comedy during breakfast. Then he drove them to Six Flags for a morning of roller coasters and arcade games. They ate lunch on Bardstown road late in the afternoon. When Tag suggested a movie, Lindsey raised her hand in surrender.

"Enough," she smiled as she said it. "Coffee, maybe, but I'm done for the day."

"Too bad." He took it well. "Coffee it is." They found a coffee shop on Bardstown road and sat on the veranda. Lindsey was enjoying the day very much, she couldn't recall ever having ridden a roller coaster as an adult. Tag looked as relaxed and content as she felt. It was easy to forget everything else and live in the moment.

"So tell me where the idea for the farm came from."

"Oh, I was in culinary school and we had a course called 'Slow Food: fresh and local' it was all about how to find and showcase food grown locally. The course concentrated on fruit, strawberries and raspberries, food that doesn't ship well. We watched a series of videos showing farms in California where they grew organic fruit specifically for the restaurants.

"It was all very idyllic looking. The chefs and the farmers sat down and planned the menus along with the planting and delivery schedules for organic milk, meat and cheese, free- range chickens and berries. It was something that I'd never seen before."

"Organic has always sounded like a gimmick to me," Tag said. "I mean, food is food, why does it matter how it is grown?"

"I used to think like that. While I worked in Louisville I never cooked, I ate whatever was handy. I gained weight and felt sick most of the time. When I started eating better quality food at the college, I felt better. At the college I learned organic food doesn't just taste better, it has a higher nutritional value as well." Lindsey cocked her head at him. "Don't tell me that you can't taste the difference."

"I don't know ..." Tag pretended to think about it, just to tease. "Yeah, organic does taste better."

"Better than Army food?" Lindsey prodded him playfully.

"Hands down – no contest." Tag grinned. "But we aren't just growing common vegetables organically, we are growing those heirloom varieties. I watched Jim pour over a dozen catalogs in order to find those tomatoes. They are rare varieties, so they are going to taste different."

"Exactly," Lindsey said, pleased he was getting it. "I can't get decent tomatoes. We limp along using commercially farmed hybrid tomatoes until ours are ready. The tomatoes I get are shipped green from California or Mexico. They never really ripen. Now there are genetically engineered tomatoes with genes spliced into them to make them hardier. Any more, you don't know if it's really a tomato or if it's some Frankenstein cross between a tomato and a fish."

"Cross a tomato and a fish? Come on," Tag scoffed. "You are exaggerating."

"Don't be so sure, genetically engineered food is everywhere. Ever heard of canola oil? It is made from genetically engineered rapeseed." Lindsey was leaning forward, talking with her hands. "You don't know what you are eating, unless you grow it yourself."

"The FDA controls all that." Tag shook his head. "I can't imagine the government allowing anything weird to get into the food supply. You are mixing food with politics."

"Think about farm policies. The government pays farmers to not grow certain things. Milk, corn, soybeans – all have price supports, all controlled by the government. This is the twenty-first century, choosing what you eat is a political act."

"How did a nice normal military family produce a radical tree-hugger like you?" Tag teased. "The next thing you are going to tell me is that we need a woman president."

"Why not?" Lindsey shot back.

"You're cute when you're all riled up." He grinned at her.

"I think you're changing the subject because you are afraid to talk politics with me." Lindsey challenged him.

"Got it in one, I don't care about politics." Tag held his hands up in mock surrender. "A smart soldier knows when to stand down."

"Did you learn that in basic training?" Lindsey giggled.

"No, I learned that from my mother, the night she clocked my father with a frying pan," Tag told her. "Knocked him out cold."

"Oh my God." Lindsey covered her mouth with one hand. "Why did she do that?"

"He was a jerk." Tag seemed pleased to have distracted her. "It made a big impression. My sisters still talk about it. I think they use that as an example to keep their husbands in line."

"Did they fight like that very often?"

"It was the only fight I ever saw them have. We were gone before he got up." Tag recalled. He chucked her under the chin. "I guess we had better start back."

They took their time getting back to the car. Too soon, Tag was driving down I-65. They were holding hands. A powerful magnetism had woven between them long before they pulled into her driveway.

"This has been a great day," Lindsey said, stalling for time, a few more minutes to spend with him. "I haven't ridden a roller coaster since high school."

"I'm an adrenaline junkie," he admitted. "I ride them every chance I get." He turned the car off, still holding her hand.

Was he waiting for her to make the next move?

Lindsey didn't want to end the day just yet, she could invite him in, or – could she? Maybe it wasn't a good idea. She'd taken enough flak from Heather last time.

No, Heather would have to get over it.

Lindsey ran her hands behind Tag's neck, bringing him closer so she could kiss him. She was hungry for his kiss.

This time, when he broke the kiss, he rubbed his mouth against her jaw, eased her head back; exposed her throat. Then he grazed her throat with his teeth. Lindsey felt an electric shock through her system, her hand knotted in his hair, she sucked in a breath. A throaty chuckle escaped him.

He bit her playfully. The second shock made her toes curl; she gasped aloud.

"Damn," he muttered. "You're so sensitive."

Lindsey hoped he'd do it again, but he kissed her lips instead. This kiss spiced with just a hint of his teeth against her lips. He pulled her hard against his chest. Lindsey shuddered, unable to catch her breath. His hands shook as he ran them across her back.

"Woman, you are so beautiful." His voice was ragged. "I don't want to stop kissing you." Tag was still. "Damn it."

"Necking in the car is for kids," Lindsey said.

Tag released her body, trailed his fingers down her arms until he caught her hands. He brought her left hand to his lips, kissing the back. His eyes were dark, very calm, and determined.

"You're right," Tag said. "Let's get out of here." He released her hand to start the car.

"Tag, wait." Lindsey was light-headed, yet this sudden change in plans alarmed her. She laid her hand over his hand on the shift. "I – I need some clarification here."

"Okay. What do you need to know?"

"Where are you taking me?"

"Let's go back to my apartment, in town." Tag eyes flicked to the house. Lindsey turned to look: her sister hurried back behind the house. Heather had spied on them, again. "I want to be able to kiss you without an audience."

"Ah hell." She felt ashamed that her family life was so complicated.

"Ignore her." He took her hand again. "What I had in mind was –" his eyes crinkled at the corners, "— a little necking. How about it?"

"Okay." Lindsey bit her lip, every nerve in her body tingled. At that moment, she wanted very much to be alone with him. On the drive to E'town, she cooled off enough to wonder if this was a good idea or a bad one. When he pulled into his apartment complex, she doubted the decision.

When Tag opened the door to his apartment, Lindsey stopped at the door.

"Won't you step into my parlor?" He teased her for her hesitation.

"Said the spider to the fly," Lindsey finished the nursery rhyme.

"There are no locks on the doors." Tag gestured for her to come inside.

"I don't know," Lindsey made a joke of it. Kissing him in the car was one thing, but being alone with him *here* was a little scary. "Maybe you're the big bad wolf in disguise?"

"Hardly." Tag grinned, settled her at the dining table, and brought her a beer and a glass. "I think you need to have a beer and relax."

"Okay." Lindsey poured her beer into the glass. "I like wine better. White is better to drink."

"I'll remember," he promised as he drank his beer from the bottle. "But don't expect too much. I'm not that civilized."

"I didn't have to ask for a glass." Lindsey smiled at him. "Maybe you are a wolf in sheep's clothing."

"Baaa," he bleated at her, making her giggle. "I'm gonna keep my sheep suit on."

"Is that a line from another song?"

"It is, would you like to hear it?" Tag asked.

"Sure." Lindsey agreed, glad for the distraction.

"Hold that thought," he said. "I'll be back in a minute." He walked down the hall.

Lindsey looked around; Tag's apartment was sparsely furnished. There was a caramel suede couch, with an over-stuffed chair, slate tiled coffee table, and an entertainment center. Army pictures covered most of one wall, photographs of various places he'd been, and a map of some place she didn't recognize. There was a photo of him in full dress uniform.

Lindsey smiled. He looked about twenty years old and so serious. Fate may not have been kind, but she thought he was better looking now. She sat on the couch, kicking off her tennis shoes as she waited.

When Tag came back, he sat next to her. He played the song on an MP3 player. It was a silly song. The big bad wolf singing to Little Red Riding Hood. After a few minutes she was relaxed again, her apprehension forgotten. Tag sensed it; he brushed her hair away from her face then kissed her gently.

"Come here." Tag's tone was firm, he pulled her onto his lap and settled her against his chest. He eased the clip from her hair. Dark waves slithered to her shoulders like a fall of silk. "That's better."

After a day in the sun, Tag smelled faintly of musk. Lindsey buried her face in his throat just to breathe the male scent. His face pressed to her hair, the embrace was soul satisfying. Lindsey had time to feel his heart beat, to settle into his shoulder, to exhale all the tension she'd been holding onto for days. Eventually they kissed again long, slow and delicious.

Lindsey filled her hands with the breadth of his chest. She ran her hands over the hard muscles on his shoulders. She trailed her fingers over the ripple of his biceps. He was so strong, yet so gentle with her; she was drunk on sensation in seconds.

Tag found the sensitive spot under her ear, used his lips and his teeth to make Lindsey gasp and shiver with pleasure. The soft sound made him aggressive, he closed his teeth too hard, pinching her.

"Hey." Lindsey twitched away, cuffing his shoulder. "Play nice."

Playfully, Tag growled at her.

"Down boy." Lindsey giggled. "Not so rough."

He growled and nipped at her as she giggled some more. Lindsey caught his face with her hands, bringing his face up so she could kiss him. His mouth was made for kissing. She held him still so she could savor the faint taste of malt and salt. Lindsey slid her mouth off his lips to follow the line of his jaw. The faint trace of salt on his skin was overlaid with something else, something sweet. Lindsey was tempted to lick his throat until she figured out what it was.

Instead, she nipped his earlobe, to pay him back for the nips to her.

"Who's the one with the teeth now?" Tag laughed, a husky sound, but he grasped her shoulders to hold her back. "Settle down for a minute.

"The other day, you said you wanted me to trust you, remember?" Tag looked into her eyes as he spoke, his voice was low.

Lindsey remembered very well, it seemed pretty outrageous now. They had talked about sex, about the trust he would need in the woman he took to his bed.

"Yes," her voice was husky.

"I want you – to trust me." There was humor and something hungry in his eyes. He stroked her hair, his touch gentle; there was a telltale tremor in his hands.

"Tag?" What did he mean?

"You are so – freaking – sensitive." He rested his forehead against hers then breathed his desire against her mouth. "I want to run my hands over your soft skin." His free hand trailed down her ribs, down her hip, down the bare flesh of her thigh to her knee, and back up. It was a teasing touch, that promised much more.

"Will you let me touch you?"

Lindsey closed her eyes. She was starving for contact. It had been so very long since a man touched her. Was he feeling that tactile hunger too? The ball was in her court. It was strange and exciting that he *asked* her. The hair on her arms stood on end; she felt butterflies in her stomach. She nuzzled him under the ear, finding a hollow where she could whisper "Yes," though she shivered with anxiety even as she consented.

"You won't regret it," Tag promised as he eased her backwards against the arm of the couch. He gave her soft kisses until she relaxed. Then he began the assault on her senses by running just the tips of his fingers on her throat and her shoulders. He followed the curve of her arms, light and teasing. Then he ran the open palm of his hand over her bare thigh, down her leg to her calf.

Everywhere he touched, her skin tingled. Lindsey became hypersensitive under his slow exploration. It seemed to go on forever. It was no longer possible for her to be still. She ran her fingers through his hair, down the swell of his shoulder, to the flat plane of his shoulder blade pulling him closer. Lindsey found that she was hungry to touch him; starving to feel his warm skin under her hands. She started to take his shirt off.

"Hey." Tag resisted her for a moment. "Fair is fair you know." He warned before he ducked out of the shirt.

Lindsey looked into his eyes and smiled. He slipped his hands under her shirt. She let him take it off. She was sitting on his lap, wearing just her bra and shorts. She looked down, at the tattoo on his chest, ran her fingers across it.

Tag chucked her under the chin. "Do you know how beautiful you are?" He studied her as if to imprint her face onto his heart, forever. "Your hair has streaks of mahogany and red. You have tawny colored eyes."

Lindsey blushed.

"You are so beautiful." He kissed her, a long deep kiss. She hardly noticed when he unfastened her bra. Lindsey let it fall to the floor and went back for another kiss. One that left her with her arms around his neck and her body limp in his arms.

The games escalated until there was no more restraint. She writhed under the touch of his hands, the press of his mouth. She sat up, straddling him, rubbing against him in unmistakable invitation. His teeth closed on her neck, sending a shock down her spine that had her moaning. He took a second and third bite as she wantonly tormented his swollen flesh.

"Tag don't tease me anymore." Lindsey pleaded. Common sense be-damned, she was on fire! She hooked her fingers in the waistband of his jeans and tugged at the snap.

"Hey – hey, play nice." Tag pulled her hands away, keeping his jeans in place. "Not this time," he said shaking his head. "Trust me, Lynn?"

Lindsey was drunk on endorphin and instinct. The shadows in his eyes were too serious to suit her. She tickled his ribs, made him laugh. They wrestled playfully as Lindsey tested her strength against his. They slid off the couch.

Was he strong enough to make her stop? Tag was much stronger; he held her wrists, pinning Lindsey underneath him. Their bodies rubbed exquisitely together.

It would have been perfect except they were both still half-dressed. Lindsey used her legs to lock his body to hers.

"Got'cha," her voice was soft and husky.

Tag released her wrists to take his weight on one arm while running the other hand over her thigh. Lindsey gasped as his firm touch trailed slowly from thigh to calf.

"Tag, you're driving me crazy." Lindsey didn't mind feeding his ego. She swept one hand from his shoulder to his hip, an urgent caress against his hot skin. "Don't tease me anymore."

"Your skin is so soft, so sensitive," he murmured in her ear before sliding down to explore her breasts. "You're so damn responsive."

Lindsey moaned as Tag found places where his touch would arch her back like a bow. She was panting, her body locked to his, begging for more.

"Yes," Tag hissed. "Oh yes, just let it happen." He licked her collarbone before he levered himself over her. Lindsey hooked her heels over his thighs. They let friction and pressure work for them both, even through the clothes that covered their lower bodies.

Her nails dug deep into his shoulders, demanding more, demanding release. Lindsey was tensed like an over-wound spring. She arched her back, each breath a sharp exclamation of pleasure as Tag rubbed against her. Lindsey shattered, shrieking aloud, short and sharp, ripping her nails down his side. Only an instant later, Tag caught his breath, convulsing against her in release.

When Lindsey opened her eyes, Tag was draped across her. His breathing was as ragged as hers. He stirred, winced, planting a kiss on her neck, before releasing his crushing grip on her wrist.

"I think I'm bleeding." He shifted his weight off her to check. Three red slashes, in places beaded with blood, bisected the scars from his left shoulder to his waist.

"I'm so sorry." Lindsey apologized sincerely.

"Just a little necking." Tag laughed. "Freaking dangerous." He laughed again, then buried his face in her shoulder, shuddering; his tears ran down her skin.

Lindsey wrapped her arms around him, rubbed her cheek against his hair. She didn't understand his tears. She held him while he shuddered, torn by some inner wounds that she would never understand. There were tears in her eyes. She touched him very gently, stroked his shoulder. But she didn't try to stop him from weeping.

He was so strong, so proud. What had the war done to him? Her heart burned with hatred for the blind, selfish government that had sent him to Iraq to be broken, sent home and discarded. It should be a crime.

It was certainly a sin.

"Are you all right?" she asked when he stopped trembling.

"I'm a basket case." He wiped his eyes, did not look at her.

"Why?"

"I thought – this part of my life was over. Thank God, I was wrong." Tag shifted onto his side, pulled her tight to his chest.

Lindsey hugged him tight, her eyes closed, languid.

"I've had this hang up since the Humvee was blown up. I wasn't sure about –" he took a deep breath. "I didn't know if I was going to be able to enjoy making love to a woman."

"Well?" Lindsey tipped her head then batted her eyelashes at him. It made him smile. He reached out to touch her face.

"Yes, I did."

"So, where did you get that idea?"

"A guy knows when there is something wrong." He didn't go into detail. "The nurses too, they get this look of pity in their eyes. I've lived with that for the last two years, not knowing."

"What did the doctors say?" She ran her hand up his arm, just to touch him. "Surely you asked them."

"I asked," he said. "What I got for answers was long conversations about nerve damage, needing time to heal." Bitterness was thick in his voice. "The usual crap: 'you're young,' 'give it time.' 'Some medications have these side effects.' Never a straight answer."

"I never expected to have a woman in my arms again." Tag rubbed his face against her hair. "Getting off while pleasing you was more than I hoped for." They stayed like that for a long time, until Lindsey had to get up to use the bathroom.

The bathroom mirror revealed a red mark at the junction of neck and right shoulder. She couldn't recall when or how it happened. Hopefully it would be gone in the morning, otherwise she'd have to wear button down shirts to work until it faded.

She didn't want Brandon to see that mark. As many times as she'd turned Brandon down, he'd surely give her a world of flak. She didn't want any crap from Brandon, or anyone else.

Bitterly, she reflected that she couldn't have a date or make-out with a man without having to worry what somebody was going to say about it. Not that it was anybody else's business what she did or with whom. It was a toss up who would give her more grief, her sister or her employees.

Lindsey heard Tag in the bedroom. She used a washcloth to wipe stickiness from her shoulder. Damn, he was so vulnerable, in so much pain. What had happened to him? She didn't know, and was afraid to ask. The last thing she wanted to do was re-open his emotional wounds.

There was no doubt in her mind that she wanted him, wanted to be there for him as he was for her. Was she strong enough? There were too many 'what ifs' she couldn't answer. What if he'd made love to her; the way she had begged him? She wasn't on birth control; what if she got pregnant? What if he wasn't able to keep it together, emotionally? Could he hurt her without meaning to?

Oh boy, her life was already complicated and getting weirder by the moment. This had 'high maintenance' written all over it.

She found her tank top and bra on the floor, dressed matter-of-factly as he walked back into the living room. He came over to her; so close she could feel the warmth of his bare chest. She looked into his blue eyes, saw peace and contentment. She leaned into him, lifting her face to him; he kissed her tenderly. Somehow, she'd find the strength to see it through.

She wanted this man with all her heart.

Lindsey was tired, she'd been at the restaurant since ten o'clock, cleaning and toying with a couple recipes. She roasted several heads of garlic; the pungent smell made her hungry. She squeezed three large cloves into a small bowl, mashed them and added a touch of butter, olive oil and salt. She slathered it on a split hoagie roll with basil, salami and cheese then toasted the whole thing.

At the first bite, her eyes started to water. This wasn't mild elephant garlic. This was one of her father's super strong heirlooms! The sandwich was delicious, but the aftertaste! There wasn't any fresh parsley for her to chew to cut the taste. Well, she could tough it out until she got home.

Her cell phone rang about four thirty.

"Hey, where are you?" Tag's low voice sent a pleasurable chill down her back.

"At the restaurant, cleaning," Lindsey replied. "What are you doing?

"I'm at my mother's for Sunday dinner. I'm not far away." There was a pause. "Can I come by?"

"I'm a filthy mess."

"What a switch, I'm all cleaned up, for once."

"You're a brave man. Come on down."

She finished up in a couple of minutes. The restaurant looked good, but she felt tired and filthy. Wanting to see him warred with her common sense. She stank of sweat and disinfectant; her breath must reek from the dratted garlic. She checked by breathing on her hand.

Oh god, it was poisonous! She looked in vain for chewing gum or a breath mint; *something* to get the garlic off her breath.

When Tag arrived, Lindsey was already at the door. She ducked him when he tried to hug her. The expression on his face changed from pleased to anxious.

"What's wrong?" There was hurt in his eyes.

"I'm covered in dirt and disinfectant." Lindsey squirmed, it was her breath she was really worried about. "It's embarrassing for you to see me like this."

"Oh, really?" Tag stiffened. "Is that the real reason?"

"Of course it is." Lindsey snipped, then winced. Damn, she hadn't meant it like that. Now there was doubt in his eyes.

"I'm not fit to be seen in public." Lindsey was tired, in no mood to go anywhere but home. "How about we drive to Freeman Lake? Find a tree to sit under?" She locked up the restaurant.

They drove to the lake, in separate cars, where they got out and walked to a picnic table under some trees. They sat side by side on the table, looking out toward the water. He reached for her, to bring her closer.

"Please don't." Lindsey moved away before she even thought about it.

She'd hurt his feelings. She could see it in the hunch of his shoulders, the nervous way he pulled his watch. Tag took a deep breath; let it out slowly. When he met her eyes she saw his raw emotions, the worry, the fear and the need all wrapped up in one package, along with the strength she depended on, and the tenderness that made her blood sing.

"What's going on?" Tag asked. Then he saw the smudge mark on her neck. "I'm sorry, did I do that?"

"Is it still there?" Lindsey had forgotten about the mark, she tried to look at it.

"Is that why you're angry with me?"

"I'm not angry with you." Lindsey looked down. She felt like a vain little fool.

"Why are you holding me at arm's length?"

"It's not you." Lindsey bit her lip. She felt her cheeks get hot. "I don't know how you can stand to sit next to me." Lindsey burst out, as she threw her hands in the air. "I smell so bad I can't stand myself."

"You see me every day after a full day working in the sun." Tag shook his head. "What difference does it make?" Then he took her hand, looked into her eyes. "Why can't I kiss you?"

"I've got garlic on my breath." She blushed furiously. "I ate three cloves of Dad's super hot garlic at lunch."

"Three cloves, eh?" With a sudden pounce, Tag pulled Lindsey to him. He was so close she could feel his breath on her cheek. Lindsey closed her eyes and turned her head. She should have known he wouldn't take her word for it.

"You *are* pretty rank." He teased. "I've smelled worse, just not here in the States. Think about five guys crammed together in a Humvee for thirty days without a shower. That's rank!"

"Let me go." Lindsey giggled in spite of herself. "You can't possibly want to kiss me." He was never serious about anything.

"I've got breath mints in the car." He grinned at her discomfort. "If you ask me nicely I'll unlock the car for you."

"Please?"

With a grin, Tag used the key fob to unlock the car doors. Lindsey jumped off the table. Tag locked the door just as she reached the car.

"Tag!" Lindsey turned and glared. "I swear, if you don't let me in the car, I'll come back there and breathe on you."

He threw back his head and laughed, unlocking the door. The mints were on the console as promised. Only three were left. Lindsey ate all three mints on the way back to the table, one for each clove of garlic, praying that would be enough.

"I swear you enjoy tormenting me!"

"I grew up tormenting three sisters." Tag grinned. "You get the benefit of my years of experience."

"Huh." Lindsey sat at the other end of the table.

"Come back here." Tag patted a spot next to him. "You owe me, for scaring me like that."

"I didn't mean to." Lindsey was contrite, she wondered how long it would be before he let her live this down. She scooted a little closer, careful of possible splinters. She'd already destroyed her dignity once today. A splinter in her tush would be the last straw.

"Don't make me come after you." He warned.

Lindsey giggled then launched herself off the table. "Try it!" She darted behind the tree, remembered that he was handicapped but he caught her anyway. He pulled her close as she shrieked with laughter. Then they landed in a heap in the grass. Tag was on top, nearly squashing her.

"Got you now!"

"I give up!" Lindsey panted. "You're crushing the life out of me."

Tag gave her enough room to roll on her back, then pinned her. He gave her a hard kiss that took the last of her breath away. She was clinging to his neck before it was over, her body molded to his.

"Do I still taste like garlic?"

"I don't know." Tag kissed her again, teasing her lips before he plundered her mouth. They kissed for a very long time, before he let her go. "Nope, not a bit."

Lindsey sighed, her arms locked around his neck. "I didn't mean to worry you."

"Not your fault, I'm paranoid."

"Because of your ex?" Lindsey asked. "You said once that she came to see you at Walter Reed."

"She did." Tag shifted his weight off her, onto his side. "She thought she could handle it when they changed the bandages. She ran out of the room screaming." His voice was bitter, his expression pained. "I was doped to the gills. I hardly knew what happened at the time. The nurses told me about it later."

"Some people know just where to stick the knife." Lindsey agreed, as she ran her fingers through his sun-streaked hair. "Tommy was like that. He did every rotten thing to me that he could think of."

"That bad?"

"You name it, he did it, wiped out my work files, subscribed me to every sick mailing list he could find, got me into trouble for surfing porn sites. The whole works."

"How did he rationalize that?"

"Well." Lindsey gave him a tight smile. "I've never told anyone about this."

"I have a Top Secret clearance. You're secrets are safe with me."

"I broke his nose."

"What?" Tag sat up, releasing her. "This I want to hear."

"Well, it goes back to nine-eleven when I came home."

"You said he was smoking crack and in bed with a girl."

"Not exactly." Lindsey took a deep breath. "He was on the couch with a guy."

"No lie?" Tag's eyebrows went up; he snickered.

Lindsey dusted off her hands. She wanted to stop holding onto her miserable secrets. "My brother-in-law was dead, and Tommy was screwing this guy." Lindsey shook her head. "I was so stressed, I lost my mind."

"You punched him in the nose?" Tag chuckled. "I'd like to see that."

"It was a lamp." Lindsey bit her lip. This wasn't funny, but she wanted to get it out and get it over with, even if he cracked some sick joke over it.

"What happened?" Tag cocked his head at her waiting for the rest.

"We were shouting at each other. Then his buddy came up behind me. He grabbed my arms." Lindsey looked down. "They tried to rape me."

Tag lifted her chin to look into her eyes. "Did they?"

"No." Lindsey took a deep breath. "Dad taught me some really dirty tricks. I used them all. I tossed his buddy into a glass coffee table. It broke, cut him up. I hit Tommy in the face with a lamp. There was blood all over the place." Lindsey shrugged. "I was gone before the cops got there."

"I hope I never run into that jerk." Tag gathered her against his chest. "He had it coming."

"I know that trust doesn't come easy," Lindsey said. "Not for either of us."

"What a messed up pair we are."

"My life is one huge snafu," she agreed. "No end in sight." Lindsey shrugged; she sat back, taking his hand. "We're working through it, surely that counts in our favor?"

In the early hours of the morning it happened again, he felt the heat, and smelled the dust. They were in a convoy to Baghdad; he was driving the Humvee. There were four guys with him, singing silly rap songs and pounding on the body of the Humvee. He started to panic; the car heading the other way held three guys chanting in shrill, frightened voices.

The world heaved as the Humvee flipped over and over. Fire everywhere. He was pinned under the Humvee. He and it were on fire. He thrashed and screamed as it rained glass, blood, body parts, hot fluid and burning metal bits that flared red hot, burnt his body and cut him to shreds.

He sat up in bed, panting, the room still echoed with his shout. The pain shot up his leg. His foot was on fire. The damn foot wasn't even there and it still hurt like hell. He rolled over, nearly sick with the horror: This was going to go on for the rest of his life, the nightmares, the pain and the memories. He cursed viciously, every foul thing he could think of until the pain dulled to a bearable level.

There were half a dozen different types of pain pills in the bathroom. He'd tried them all without success. With and without bourbon, he thought wryly. He didn't keep bourbon here. He felt he'd spent enough time in the bottle.

He didn't have to stay here, pretending to sleep. There was plenty of work for him to do. Jim might be up. He was an early riser himself.

Maybe for the same reason.

Chapter 18

Lindsey went out to the garden first thing. Tag, Heather and her father were already outside; the four of them picked beans, lettuce and radishes. Jim was teasing Tag about something military and obscure. Lindsey enjoyed the banter and 'in jokes', it was comforting to see her father and Tag getting along so well.

Heather was humming under her breath, picking beans, down the next row. Lindsey joined her sister, cautious of Heather's uncertain moods.

"Good morning," Heather said with a smile. "We've got a bunch of beans today."

"They look great, don't they?" Lindsey said running her fingers through a basket of green and yellow beans.

"How are you going to use them?"

"Sautéed with carrots and mushrooms. I'll put a little pesto in for seasoning."

"They look a lot better than last year." Heather finished her basket. "Let me get you another basket." Heather got up, carrying the full basket down the row.

Lindsey looked after her, curious. Who was that person in her sister's body? She looked around, but didn't see any plants with huge pods on them.

At the restaurant Lindsey brought out the baskets of baby beans. She trimmed the ends, chopped them in half, sweeping the pieces into a bowl. When Brandon came in, she had him julienne carrots into matchsticks.

"Hey," Brandon said, "what are we doing with these?"

"These are going into a stir-fry," Lindsey said. She glanced at the carrots piled in front of him. "Make sure the carrots are all cut the same."

"This thing has lost its edge again." Brandon picked up the knife sharpener. "I hate a dull knife."

"Make it quick." Lindsey could barely keep herself from rolling her eyes. Brandon seemed hypnotized by the sharpening process. "We have to get all this cooked before the orders some in."

"I can't do anything with a dull knife."

Lindsey looked away. She scanned the dining area to see what Mychou was up to. She couldn't see her. Shawn was stacking soda in the vault.

"Where's Mychou?"

"I think she went out to smoke." Brandon set down the knife. "I need to go burn one myself." He reached in his pocket, pulled out a cigarette and lit it.

"Outside with that," Lindsey reminded him.

"Sure." Brandon cut her with his eyes. "Mom." He snickered under his breath as he walked outside.

Just before he walked out, Lindsey saw a cloud of smoke roll towards the ceiling. She shook her head, loosening her blouse to scratch an itchy spot on her neck.

Shawn snickered from behind her. Lindsey quickly straightened her blouse. The smirk on his face told her that he'd seen the mark on her neck. Damn it! She didn't think her nerves were up to taking any teasing from him or Brandon.

The damn mark had better fade quickly.

That evening Tag and Lindsey worked alone side by side, and talked about her problems with her employees. Their relationship had changed. There was a quiet understanding between them that was rich with undertones.

They were under the pergola. The wisteria was dropping the last few flower petals. They were sharing a peaceful moment as the sun set behind the garden. Tag leaned on a support, with one arm around Lindsey's waist. She stood with her back against his chest, leaning on him. Her father cleared his throat behind them.

"What is going on here?"

They both froze. Tag released the pressure from her waist, gave her the option to move away. Lindsey peeked around Tag's shoulder, smiled at her father, but pointedly didn't move away from Tag's loose embrace.

"Dad, what's up?"

The look on her father's face tipped her off. He wasn't looking at Lindsey; he was looking at Tag with undisguised fury.

"Get your hands off my daughter." Jim was white-lipped with anger. He advanced on them, until he was only a few feet away.

"I'm not hurting her." Tag said in a quiet voice. He was tense and very still.

"Dad?" Lindsey was bewildered; her father hadn't done this in years. "Dad are you okay?" Why had seeing the two of them together set him off? Was all the stress on her father making him see things from Vietnam?

"Lindsey, get away from him." Jim took a menacing step forward.

"Dad, what's wrong?" Lindsey moved between Tag and her father. She had to appease her father before he exploded.

"McTaggart!" Jim took a step forward, locking eyes with Tag. The tension escalated another notch. He said something in a different language to Tag.

"Go, Lynn." Tag gently pushed her aside.

Lindsey felt a rising panic. What had happened in Vietnam that could set her father off, thirty years later? She wanted to scream for her mother and run into the house. She was so scared she couldn't move, she could barely breathe.

"I would never hurt Lindsey." Tag held out his empty hands. "You know that."

How Tag could nonchalantly face a man who had been a Green Beret?

"Please, Dad, don't hurt him." She'd seen what her father had done to Rich. She struggled to keep from crying.

"I set the hoses on the tomatoes to run four hours starting at 10 o'clock." Tag's voice was calm, the words ordinary. "Will that be long enough?"

Jim's eye flicked from Lindsey to Tag and back. His fist stayed clenched at his sides, though he didn't advance on Tag.

"The squash will need watered tomorrow." Tag continued to report on the progress of the garden. "They are flowering right on schedule."

Jim looked around, blinking as if confused, his clenched fists opened slowly. He shifted backwards slightly, no longer aggressive. He turned, hesitated for a moment before walking back into the house.

Tag and Lindsey exhaled their tension, taking a couple of deep breaths.

"Oh, hell." Weak in the knees, Lindsey grabbed Tag's arm for support.

"So that's what it's like to be on the other side of a flash back."

"Oh, no, please." Lindsey groaned. "You can't make a joke of this."

"He didn't kick my ass. I guess he likes me." There was a cocky tilt to Tag's head. The sheen of sweat on his face told the real story: he was talking smack.

"Lynn, he doesn't have a problem with us. He was surprised, that's all."

Lindsey sighed, leaning on him. Tag hugged her. Deeply shaken, Lindsey walked with him to his truck.

"I wish I knew what set him off," Lindsey sighed. "What happened over there?"

"You don't want to know." Tag tipped her head back to kiss her. The usual humor was not in his face. He looked unnerved. His kiss was brief and hard. "Old soldiers don't like surprises."

"But –"

"It's going to be okay. Trust me."

Tuesday Lindsey got up early to help pick beans. A cheerful Heather joined them, stayed on task and didn't find anything to complain about. Travis galloped up and down the rows, ferrying baskets while the adults picked.

When it was all over, the produce rinsed and packed in coolers, Lindsey and Tag had a moment to sit on the tailgate of the truck and drink coffee. Tag was quieter than normal, looking out over the garden with a solemn expression. He was toying with the band of his watch.

"Everything all right?" Lindsey wondered if he was thinking about the night before. She was still worried about her father. He seemed tired and out of sorts.

"Can we go somewhere tomorrow?" Tag turned to her. "I'd like to have a couple of hours alone with you." The unspoken message sent and received was 'somewhere where Jim wasn't going to find them.'

"What have you got in mind?"

"Let's go out to dinner," he suggested. "Where would you like to go?"

"It's a long drive here and back to town."

"How about I pick you up at the restaurant?"

"After a hard day of cooking?" Lindsey wrinkled her nose. "I'd need a shower."

"Bring a change of clothes." Mischief lit his eyes. "I've got a shower at my place."

"No peeking!" Lindsey teased.

"Spoilsport."

Lindsey got to the restaurant, had the coolers inside when Brandon and Mychou came in. The tense, almost mechanical way they moved set Lindsey's teeth on edge.

"Good morning," Lindsey ventured.

"What's on the menu today?" Brandon bared his teeth in a parody of a smile. Brandon's clothes were clean, and he had shaved, but he looked haggard and drawn to Lindsey.

"More bean stir-fry." Lindsey kept her voice light.

"Better get started." He talked with his jaw clenched, in a voice that was rushed while his words were clipped. The first thing he did was pick up his knife and sharpen it. He twitched his shoulders, repeatedly, as though his back itched, then scratched his jaw.

"Mychou, can you wash lettuce for me?" Lindsey looked up, she did a double take.

"Sure." Mychou was a mess, deep lines cut her face, her hair looked dirty, and her makeup was smudged under her eyes, like a bruise. It was the first time that Lindsey had seen her look less than perfectly groomed.

"Is everything all right?" Lindsey asked before she could stop herself.

"I was up all night with the baby," she said. "He had colic." Periodically, she would smooth her hair back with a dripping hand. Her blouse was soon water spotted. She didn't seem to notice.

Brandon wasn't on task. Lindsey had to bring him back from sharpening his chef's knife.

Shawn dragged in, bleary-eyed. His chocolate complexion had a gray cast to it. He gulped down several cups of coffee as soon as he came in the door. He didn't speak to Lindsey or Mychou for most of the day. Instead, he stayed in the kitchen, washing dishes and glowering at everyone with bloodshot eyes.

Mychou continued to scratch the spot behind her ear with her pen. Soon she had a raw spot that opened into a bleeding wound over the course of the afternoon. The customers were staring.

Lindsey kept smiling, waiting on the counter and chatting with customers. She wanted to scream or better yet, run from the restaurant.

By the time they closed, Mychou had blood all over her neck. She'd dug a dime-sized sore behind her ear. Lindsey conquered her revulsion to take her to the woman's room and show her the mess. Mychou blotted up the blood, but she developed a twitch to her hand, like an aborted impulse to scratch at the sore.

Fortunately, both Brandon and Mychou were able to get their cleaning chores done. In fact, Brandon kept cleaning the grill even after she told him it was fine. Shawn collapsed in a chair, looking like death warmed over.

Lindsey watched them, horrified at the changes a few days had made in them. She didn't know what to do. She was grateful to get them the hell out of her restaurant.

That evening Eleanor sat under the pergola while Jim, Tag, Lindsey and Heather worked in the old garden, weeding and watering. Lindsey took a quick bathroom break. When she came back outside she paused, watched her sister for a moment, then asked her mother:

"What's with Heather?" Lindsey noticed her mother's expression was smug. "Is that an alien in my sister's body?"

"I got her to see the doctor about those mood swings of hers." Eleanor smiled at her youngest daughter. "The doctor said that she's held onto Rich for so long and so hard that she's gotten stuck in the anger stage of grief. She's been taking it out on all of us." Eleanor shook her head. "The long and the short of it is that he prescribed anti-depressants. He said Heather would snap out of it."

"So how long has she been on them?"

"Only a week, but the difference is dramatic." Eleanor smiled. "I tried to talk her into getting counseling, but the therapists on Post are swamped with boys coming back from the war." She shook her head. "God knows those boys need all the help they can get."

"You and Tag seem to have hit it off." Eleanor slanted Lindsey a glance.

"He fits in pretty well around here."

"Your father says he's done quite a bit of work over at your place." Eleanor wasn't too proud to interrogate her daughter. "It seems you are spending a lot of time with him."

"It's all very casual, last Saturday we went to 'Six Flags Park,' to ride roller coasters." Lindsey couldn't help but smile. There was nothing casual about what happened back at his apartment, but *that* wasn't anyone's business.

"Oh, really?" Eleanor arched her eyebrows. "I seem to have heard that someone was snuggling under the wisteria the other day."

"There was that." Lindsey blushed.

"Hmm, the all important third date looms," Eleanor said, slyly. "When is that?"

"We're going to a movie tomorrow," Lindsey said becoming acutely uncomfortable at the direction of the conversation. There were times, like now, that her mother's open-mindedness was embarrassing. There was no privacy when you lived next door to your parents, Lindsey reflected.

"I've seen how his eyes follow you." Eleanor's eyes twinkled. "Are you coming home tomorrow night?"

"Mom! Not so loud." Lindsey darted a glance at the garden. She hoped no one heard that but her. Lindsey's voice dropped. "It's not that simple."

"Oh?" Eleanor shot a speculative glance at Tag. "Was he hurt *that* bad?"

"Mother please!" Lindsey rolled her eyes. "I don't want talk about it."

Eleanor sat back in her chair, her expression thoughtful.

"Don't you dare ask him!" Lindsey knew that look all too well.

"I wouldn't dream of it." Eleanor lifted her chin, giving the impression she was looking down her nose at her daughter. "I'll ask your father."

"I'm serious, Mother!" Lindsey groaned. "You can't have him vetted like a racehorse."

"Too bad," Eleanor said with a straight face.

Lindsey giggled in spite of herself. She could picture her mother looking Tag over and checking his teeth.

"He cleaned up better than I expected. He's a handsome man, soft-spoken, intelligent. Your father likes him quite a lot." Eleanor dropped the teasing tone. "Tag is quite a step up from Tommy. But then, I've always had a soft spot for military men."

Lindsey made a non-committal noise.

"They make good husbands for the most part. When they think they are running the show." She slanted a sly look towards her husband. Eleanor chuckled, reminiscing. "I was a flower child in those days. Your grandfather was horrible to all my boyfriends. He was terrified I'd marry some drugged-up dropout. I brought a couple home over the years, just to mess with his mind."

"Fathers are really crazy when it comes to their daughters. You have to work around that. Sometimes you need a big brick." She grinned maliciously. "Dad was relieved when I brought your father home, in uniform, fresh out of Officer's Training. He never objected to our being married."

"Unlike Dad. He was always opposed to Heather and Rich." Lindsey sighed.

"Your father didn't approve of the age difference." Eleanor sighed. "Ten years is a lot when the girl is only nineteen."

"I thought he was going to kill Rich that night." Their father had caught the two necking, pulled Rich from the car and beaten him senseless. It had taken four men to pull their father off Rich.

"One of his own staff, necking with his daughter." Eleanor shook her head. "He threatened to have Rich court marshaled, right up until the wedding." Eleanor tsked under her breath.

"Do you think that was why Rich and Heather didn't get along?" Lindsey remembered the stormy relationship very well. She had always wondered if Rich had married Heather out of love or fear of his father-in-law.

"If they had loved each other, it wouldn't have mattered. But I don't think Rich ever really took off his uniform," Eleanor said sadly. "Heather's so stubborn, always wants her own way. She won't admit that she made a mistake. Guilt does strange things to people."

The two women were silent. Lindsey worried about her father's reaction to finding her with Tag. Had the friendship between the two men suffered because she'd snuggled with Tag on the patio? Would a scene like that happen again?

"Lindsey," her father called from the garden. "We need all hands out here."

"Better go," Eleanor said with a smile.

The lunch rush was half over when Tag came in. Lindsey poured him a cup of coffee. Shawn was clearing the counter. She needed to ring up a customer, but she watched Shawn and Tag out of the corner of her eye.

"Well, look at what the cat dragged in," Shawn said to Tag in a mocking voice. "Tag McTaggart."

"Hey. Long time, no see," Tag greeted Shawn with raised eyebrows. "You're working here?"

"A man needs to have a job," Shawn replied tersely.

"That's true." Tag gave Shawn a searching look. "How's your mom and your son doing?"

The question seemed to aggravate Shawn. He carelessly tossed dishes into the dishpan, wiped up the counter with a scowl on his face.

"You waiting for somebody or are you here to interrogate me?" Shawn's tone was belligerent. He cocked his head at Tag, his expression closed and hostile.

Tag bristled, his face set and his eyes narrowed.

The two men squared-off like growling dogs posturing before one or the other took the first bite. Lindsey bit her lip, wondering what bad blood lay between them.

"I'm waiting for Lindsey."

Tag's answer made Shawn flick a glance over his shoulder, at Lindsey. He grabbed the dishpan then stalked back to the kitchen.

What the hell? Why had Tag set Shawn off?

She didn't have time to think about it; eight more customers walked in the door. The rush finally slowed to a trickle. Brandon didn't seem to notice that Tag was hanging around. He kept checking his cell phone. Shawn stayed in the kitchen, as far from Tag as he could get. Eventually all the cleanup work was finished, and her employees left. She was alone with Tag, finally.

"This is a lot of work," he said, as she locked the door behind them.

"This is a typical day." Lindsey shrugged. "Did my father say anything?"

"No." The quirky smile was back. "But your mother said something that made him laugh. I'm glad I didn't hear it."

They drove both vehicles to his apartment building. She followed him inside his apartment.

"You want something to drink?" Tag asked when she sat down at the table. "I don't have any wine."

"Sweet tea or soda is fine," Lindsey said.

"I've got sweet tea." He poured her a tall glass of iced tea. He showed her the master bath, off his bedroom.

She looked around at typical masculine furnishings in rustic pine, four-poster bed and dresser. There was a set of metal crutches in the corner. The room was sparely furnished; to Lindsey's relief it contained nothing cheesy, no mirrored ceiling, pinup girls or anything that put up a red flag.

The bathroom had handrails on the wall, in the tub and the separate shower, reminders that he wasn't as strong and fit as he appeared. It was too easy to not notice, to forget that he was disabled.

She cleaned up, put on a sundress and heels for the first time in ages. When she looked in the mirror, she noted her tan lines didn't match the dress, not much she could do about it. She applied makeup with a light hand. Let her dark hair down from the clip, but pulled it back. It was the final critical scrutiny in the mirror when she noticed just how worn out she looked.

Holy shit, she thought, I look over-worked and under fed. No wonder he's dragging me away from work in the middle of the week. I need time to relax.

"I deserve this," she said aloud. "And I'm taking it."

Tag complimented her when she walked into the living room. Lindsey was able to smile and be a woman on a date. They found an early movie, a comedy. Had a late dinner, Chinese food at a little place they both liked. They ordered dinner, comparing favorite dishes from various restaurants.

When the food arrived, Tag changed the topic of conversation.

"How long has Shawn been working for you?"

"About a month." Lindsey picked up her chopsticks, looking for water chestnuts in her chow-mien. "I needed someone to bus tables. Rose told me he needed a job. Why?"

"I didn't know he was still in town." Tag wasn't paying any attention to his meal.

"Did you know him well?" Lindsey popped a bit of water chestnut in her mouth.

"I thought I did." Tag looked down. "He was my best friend in high school." His mouth twisted. "His son is named after me."

"I'm sorry." Lindsey put one hand over her mouth. She reached across the table to him with the other. After a brief hesitation, Tag took her hand.

"People change." Tag eyes had that haunted look again.

"Rose said he was going to college."

"It seems strange that he would still be in college after all these years."

"Things happen." Lindsey thought about it. "Rose said she had great plans for him."

"I'll say." Tag snorted. "Shawn was supposed to go to law school."

"No lie?" Lindsey set down her chopsticks. "Then why is he working for me?"

"That's what I'd like to know," Tag said. "I never looked him up when I got back in town. I figured he was a big shot lawyer. He seemed pretty bitter."

"Honestly, anything could have happened to him. Rose quit because she said she needed to be home to keep her grandson out of a gang. It seems like half of Rose's family is in and out of jail and rehab."

"The girls, Dee and Rachel, were sent to prison when I was in high school. They had been honor students; top of their classes, then all of the sudden they were in jail on drug charges. I don't think either Shawn or his mother ever got over the shock of that."

"That's rough," Lindsey said. "You would think he'd have learned something."

"Shawn was really upset about his sisters," Tag said. "That's why he wanted to go to law school, to help them. I don't get why he never finished." He picked up his silverware and attacked his dinner.

"I have to keep on him, or he sneaks off with Mychou. I don't know what he sees in her. I hear she's married to a drug dealer. She has two little kids. Her grandmother watches them while she works."

"That's what I'm talking about." Tag shook his head. "I can't imagine him involved with drugs or dealers. I could see him as a lawyer, a cop or anything else except busing tables in a restaurant.

"It's something that I never thought about," he said finally. "I guess that I'm not the only one whose life has completely derailed."

"No, you're not the only one," Lindsey said thinking about her life with Tommy. How her parents had lost their house in Phoenix, and how her brother-in-law had died. "Shit happens to everybody."

Their eyes met over the table.

"We can play 'one-up' in the tragedy game. But in all honesty, Heather and Rich win hands down."

They were both silent for a moment. They finished the meal, speaking of less serious topics. Then Tag drove Lindsey back to his apartment parking lot. Tag walked her to her truck. They kissed goodnight. Lindsey leaned into his embrace for a long moment, savoring his touch.

"Lindsey." Tag stopped her from getting into the truck. "Listen, I've been thinking about your employees. That girl, your cook, they're tweaking really bad."

"I know, it's awful," Lindsey said.

"You shouldn't trust Shawn. I don't know who he is any more."

"I have an appointment with a lawyer on Monday," Lindsey assured him. "As soon as I have help, I will get rid of all of them."

"I want you to promise me something." Tag brushed a lock of hair from her face. His expression was troubled.

"What?"

"If things get out of hand, if you get the least bit scared, I want you to call me, or text me an SOS, promise?"

"Nothing is going to happen." Lindsey protested but he hushed her.

"Promise me." Tag brushed her lips with his fingertips. "You will call me."

Lindsey shook her head.

"This is important to me," he said, pulling her closer. "I want you to promise."

He was using the magnetism between them, leaning closer until his mouth was just above her lips.

"Promise?" He feathered a kiss against her lips.

"Cheater." Lindsey smiled.

"All's fair…" Tag murmured against her lips.

Lindsey knew the quote: 'All's fair in love and war.' Was he saying that he loved her? Lindsey's heart sank when she should have felt overjoyed. She had no time to give, just stolen moments like this in a life fouled up beyond all redemption. He deserved better.

"I want you to know that you can count on me, anywhere, anytime, for anything," Tag murmured in her ear before he trailed kisses down the soft skin of her throat. He closed his teeth on that certain spot, leaving Lindsey gasping softly, melting in his arms.

As Tag felt her relax, he murmured in a low voice. "Promise me?"

"Okay," Lindsey said softly.

"That's better." Tag smiled. "Now I want to hear you say it."

"Tag," Lindsey protested. "It really isn't necessary. Nothing is going to happen."

"Say it." Tag brushed his lips against her ear.

"I promise," Lindsey murmured. "If I suddenly turn into a brainless chicken –" She gasped as he nipped her throat. "– Lose all my common sense. I will call you or send a text message. So you can get my whole family upset over nothing."

"Damn, do you have to fight me every inch of the way?" Tag caught her earlobe in his teeth. "Stay safe for me," he breathed softly in her ear. "When this is over, really over, I'm going to make you mine."

It should have sounded corny, but he made it sound delicious.

"Unless you change your mind," Lindsey teased, but struck a nerve.

"Touché," he admitted. "It's taken some time to get here."

Lindsey shivered at the steadiness in his eyes, a glint of blue in the darkness. He brushed a tendril of hair from her face. The tenderness in his touch was eloquent.

"Get in the truck," he said with a faint smile. "You have a long day tomorrow." He gave her a hug, holding her tight. "The only thing I might change my mind about is waiting."

Lindsey giggled.

They had a big raid planned, a house-to-house search for "persons of interest." Everything was planned, down to the last detail. Nothing went right from the moment they entered the kill zone. The door guy kicked down the first door, and was met with hostile fire. He staggered backwards, dead before he hit the ground.

Sniper fire blocked them from the vehicles. Tag stifled the impulse to dive for cover. He had to get his men out of the kill zone. His night-vision picked up shadows, flickers of moving heat. He fired off a few shots, got his men behind him and barked their orders.

They moved out, a few at a time, he watched their backs, keeping the door blocked with covering fire. As he turned to go he caught a bullet to his armored vest, it slammed him into a wall. Shrapnel from another shot laid his face open. Blood filled his mouth. He spat out the blood; the pain was staggering.

He ran, hearing shouts behind him and shots in front of him. He bled but he couldn't drop his weapon to put pressure on the wound. Someone shouted his name. A soldier darted back to help him. They almost got to the

Humvees when the soldier dropped, shot in the head. Tag took a bullet in the arm, he shouted to his men for help. The nearest Humvee exploded in a blinding flash of light. The concussion blew him backwards.

He woke up, searing pain shooting down his leg to the toe that wasn't there, but was now on fire. He rolled over, clutching the stump of his leg, trying to tell the nerves that the damn foot was gone.

He groaned, remembering fear and the screams of his men. The orders had come from above, but he was the one in charge. He had led them to their deaths.

He had felt a savage joy when his men had branded their unit numbers into his shoulder. The smell of his burning flesh should have been a warning to him. At the time, it had eased the pain in his soul. Weeks later, when he had their names tattooed over his heart, the endless bee-sting of a tattoo needle had brought him peace.

No matter what, they were with him. He cursed and wept, mourning the fallen yet again. They had not suffered. They had died quickly.

He continued to suffer.

It was fitting.

He had failed them.

Chapter 19

Lindsey enjoyed the morning in the garden with her father and Tag. Heather cooked them breakfast. Eleanor was up and around on her walker. It seemed as if the garden was exploding with beans and lettuce. The tomatoes and squash were in flower.

The gray sky promised rain. The wind had picked up and the air was cool. They got everything washed and in coolers before the first drops of rain fell.

"It is supposed to rain all day," Tag said as they sat down to breakfast.

"The forecast is for thunder showers this afternoon," Jim agreed. "We need the rain."

"Cisterns would be handy right now."

"I'll settle for getting the rain barrels filled."

"My flowers are in terrible shape," Heather said. "The deer have eaten my Mr. Lincoln roses and my daylilies."

Lindsey pulled a straight face. Tag hid his grin behind the coffee cup. They exchanged a guilty look, but didn't comment. Luckily, for them, Heather didn't see the exchange.

It wasn't raining in E'town. Shawn was waiting for Lindsey in front of the restaurant. Lindsey didn't have long to wonder about why he was there.

"Good morning," Lindsey greeted him.

"Morning." Shawn smiled. It wasn't a pleasant smile. He was showing his teeth in a 'cat-that-ate-the-canary' smirk.

"Would you help me with the coolers?" She asked as she lowered the tailgate. Lindsey wondered why he was so early. She didn't have long to wait.

"Sure." Shawn sauntered over to the back of the truck. "Why are you running with Tag McTaggart?" Shawn asked with avid curiosity in his eyes.

"He's a friend." Lindsey was tempted to tell him to mind his own business. "He's been helping my father on the farm for the last month or so."

"A friend? Don't pull my chain. I saw the mark on your neck." Shawn snorted. "He hasn't changed a bit. Love 'em and leave 'em with a smile."

Blushing, Lindsey barely stopped herself from covering her neck with her hand. The mark was gone. She'd checked the mirror that morning.

"Have you talked to him?" She was tempted to blurt out the extent of Tag's injuries. But it wasn't for her to say. "Did you see how he is covered with scars? He didn't get those sitting at home."

"I'm sure he's more than happy to show them off." Shawn grinned. "Clueless women like you fall for a sad story every time. One scratch and he's a hero." Shawn lowered his voice. "I'm sure Brandon would like to know that you're secretly seeing Captain America. What do you think? Should I tell him about that little love bite?"

"You had better watch your mouth if you want to keep your job." The threat was out of her mouth before she thought.

"Oh yeah? Consider this my week's notice." Shawn said with a cocky look on his face. "I got better things to do."

"You never should have left law school." Lindsey snapped.

"Law school?" Shawn sneered. "Did Tag tell you I went to law school?"

"What happened, did you flunk out?" Lindsey attacked. "Couldn't take it?"

The door swung open, Brandon and Mychou came in.

"Mr. 'I-wanna-be-tough-guy' sold you a line of crap. He's a lying loser."

"He's got a lot more going for him than you ever will."

"The only thing Tag ever had going for him was that he could bull shit a woman into believing anything." Shawn had a malicious gleam in his eyes.

"Are you selling tickets to this fight?" Brandon asked. There was a noticeable twitch to his face. As he walked passed, Lindsey smelled old sweat and something acrid. Brandon was wearing the same clothes from the day before.

"No, we don't need to sell tickets. This little spat is over." Lindsey gave Shawn a raking glance. When she turned, she was face to face with Mychou.

Mychou was skeletal, dehydrated. The sore behind her ear was open and raw like she'd been picking at it. She pulled compulsively at a lock of hair from her bangs, a couple of hairs stuck to her fingers.

Lindsey grimaced. When would this nightmare end?

They got the restaurant opened, all the work done very quickly. Brandon and Mychou worked feverishly at their tasks, twitching and scratching. Mychou blotted behind her ear with the base of her thumb. There were bloodstains on her tickets. Lindsey was loath to touch them, wanting to scream every time Mychou touched food. The set look to Mychou's face and her ticking eyelids warned Lindsey against mentioning anything.

Good God, it was only Wednesday!

The afternoon continued with tension thick in the air. Lindsey felt like she was walking on eggshells. Just as things were winding down, Lindsey thought she saw Brandon take something out of his pocket and put it into a take-out order. Mychou brought in another couple of orders.

"I'm out of freaking clamshells. Mychou, get me some."

"Get them yourself." Mychou face twitched into a scowl.

Brandon snarled then stalked off to the storeroom. He left three Styrofoam clamshells on the counter when he went into the storeroom for more. Lindsey opened the nearest, hissing with fury as she spotted a plastic wrapped package with the sandwich.

"I've got you now," Lindsey growled, reaching for her cell phone to get a picture. She got the first one, as she folded the second clamshell top back, a black hand caught her wrist. She glared at Shawn, palming the cell phone, praying he hadn't seen it.

"Don't touch that." Shawn spoke softly, with menace in his voice. "If you're smart, you'll forget you saw it."

She pulled her hand back, he squeezed harder. Tag was right; Shawn was dangerous!

"Lindsey, I'm telling you forget that!" Shawn towered over her, threat in every line of his face.

She jerked her hand again, furious and frightened.

"Hear me? Don't say a word!" Shawn was crushing her wrist.

Lindsey nodded, terrified of what would happen if she cried out, surrounded by enemies, in her own restaurant. They heard the telltale squeak from the vault's hinges. He released her bruised wrist.

She turned away, back to the prep counter. She was terrified to the point of nausea. Was there something she could do? Mychou came in the kitchen, collected the clamshells, brushing past Lindsey as if she weren't there.

Shawn left the kitchen to bus tables. Lindsey had to keep her cool. She had the proof she needed that Brandon was dealing drugs out of her restaurant. She couldn't let this opportunity go by! Lindsey stepped outside, pulling her cell phone from her pocket. She dialed the police department.

"This is Lindsey Bennett, I own 'Let's Do Lunch,' I need help." She said quietly to the 911 operator. "One of my employees is selling drugs in my restaurant. I need to get them out of here. Now. Can you help me?"

"Yes," the operator said. "But I need more information before I send out a car."

Lindsey told her everything she knew, or guessed. When the short conversation finished she sent a text message to Tag: "SOS, come now."

Lindsey walked back to her station behind the counter,

Had it been just last night that he'd made her promise? Now she needed to wait for help to arrive. She hoped that this wasn't a false alarm. She hoped that this would truly be the end of the nightmare. The minutes ticked away. She kept busy, made herself stay focused, instead of looking out the window.

Two police cars parked in front of the restaurant, then an SUV pulled up, and four men with "DEA" on their jackets got out. What was the DEA doing here? Lindsey looked for Tag's truck, but there was no sign of him. She glanced at her watch; he should have been here by now. Two officers walked into the restaurant. One stayed by the door, the other walked up to the counter.

"Miss Bennett?"

"Yes." Lindsey leaned close, aware that Brandon was watching out of the corner of his eye. "My cook put white powder wrapped in plastic in a box. It's on that table." She pointed to the table nearest the door.

The officer turned and gestured to the table by the door.

"Would you two stand up?" The officer by the door asked the men at the table.

The two men got up from the table. One threw his coffee in the officer's face. The other man ran for the back door, knocking into tables, scattering cups that shattered on the floor. Half the people in the restaurant ducked against the wall or under their tables. The officers scrambled after the two fleeing men, who ducked in the kitchen. Customers bolting outside were stopped by the DEA agents.

A hand clamped in Lindsey's hair.

"I'm going to kill you for this," Brandon snarled in her ear. He yanked her over to the end of the counter. "Clear out, or I'll cut her throat!"

The rest of the customers in the restaurant fled. Two men in DEA jackets came inside. It was a standoff. Shawn was closest, between them and two men at the door. Mychou was behind him, flattened against the vault. Lindsey held her breath, staying very still as the knife gave her throat a burning kiss.

"Brandon, put down the knife." Shawn held up his empty hands. "You can get a better deal if you let her go." He stepped away from the cramped maze of tables. Moving very slowly, he pulled a badge from under his shirt.

"I'm DEA, dude. Make this easy for everybody. Let her go."

"You freaking narc!" Brandon shouted. "Get out of my way!"

"Put the knife down!" Shawn closed in on them. Brandon shoved Lindsey against Shawn, and lunged forward, slicing Shawn across the stomach. Shawn twisted away, Brandon kicked him, knocking him into a table, face first. Shawn groaned. His blood splattered the floor.

Brandon yanked Lindsey against his body like a shield.

"Mychou, get my keys. We are out of here."

"No." Mychou huddled by the vault, her eyes wide and staring, her hands clenched in her disheveled hair. Her sunken eyes darted from Shawn to Brandon. Shawn was still alive. He groaned, moving slightly, clutching the wound in his midriff.

"Are you with me or not?" Brandon demanded.

"I got kids," she whimpered, a convulsive movement brought her hand from her head and a handful of hair with it.

"You won't have them long," Brandon threatened. "I'll see to that."

Mychou kept shaking her head.

"Your funeral," he snarled. Then he gave Lindsey a shake. "Come on, bitch, you got a lot to answer for." He brandished the knife at the two DEA agents who blocked his path. "Anybody else want some of this?"

The agents held their guns pointed down. They stepped backwards as Brandon advanced, neither spoke aloud but they had hard expressions on their faces that promised violence.

"Get back! I'll cut her throat!" Brandon backed out the door; there was twenty or thirty feet to the parking lot behind the restaurant. Lindsey saw Shawn push himself up as Brandon twisted her around again.

It was raining. There were four sheriff's cars blocking the square, lights flashing, no sirens. It was quiet enough to be eerie. People pressed against the huge glass windows of the government offices, watching. Everyone outside was soaked, Lindsey started to shiver, her teeth chattering with cold and fear.

"Let me go," she pleaded. "Please let me go."

Lindsey held onto Brandon's arm with both hands, his whole body shook with tension and rage. He'd been sharpening this knife for weeks! Lindsey could feel the sharp edge graze her throat, the burning kiss as its razor edge sliced skin. There was blood streaming from the shallow cut. She could smell it, could feel the stickiness soaking her white coat.

Surrounded by police, sheriff, and DEA officers, all with guns drawn and leveled. Lindsey looked in vain for Tag. She'd never been so frightened. She didn't know what to do. She should do something, but what? Even with all her strength, she couldn't get the knife from her throat.

"Look at them, too scared to move," Brandon gloated in her ear. "Not a full set of balls anywhere." Brandon dragged Lindsey toward the back parking lot. There were police cars blocking the alley behind it. Five policemen advanced, the senior police officer had his hands up, empty.

The clouds opened up in a sudden blast of cold rain.

"Nobody needs to get hurt here," he said to Brandon. "We can work this out."

"One step closer and I'll cut her throat." Brandon jerked her hair so hard it made her cry out. She fought to keep the knife away from her throat as Brandon wrenched her around.

"Clear the road, right now!" Brandon screamed at the officers behind them.

They could hear an officer on the radio ordering everyone back. Brandon turned around, slowly backing towards the car, trying to watch them all at once.

Time slowed.

The square was closed by squad cars with flashing lights. Tag swore, pulling his truck into a driveway and ditching it. He'd driven up from Sonora with no knowledge of what he was getting into. Now his worse case scenario was playing itself out before him.

Tag ran across the pavement, saw Brandon drag Lindsey from the restaurant. Brandon was using her as a shield against a body shot. A shot to the head would take him out. It was a dead easy shot with an M-16. He felt the heat of a desert sun, smelled dust and cordite. He reached for a weapon he did not possess.

The sky opened up. Cold rain gave Tag a sense of time and place. He was behind the crowd of officers as they followed Brandon to the parking lot.

"Tag." Shawn staggered out of the restaurant, blood slicked his clothing, a small dark handgun clutched in his hand. "He's got Lindsey."

Shawn fell to his knees, dropping his badge and the handgun.

Tag swooped to pick the gun up. The small caliber handgun slid into Tag's hand with cold familiarity. He chambered a shell as quietly as he could, thumbing the safety off. He would need to get closer. He ran to the brick arch that separated the square from the tiny parking lot.

There were five officers close to him. The oldest glanced his way then motioned the others to stay back. They acknowledged him with a single flickering glance. The senior officer stepped forward, the rest stayed out of the line of fire.

Good, they were going to let him kill the bastard.

Tag heard Lindsey pleading for Brandon to let her go.

"Nobody needs to get hurt here," the officer said. "We can work this out."

"One step closer I'll cut her throat."

The rain came down harder.

Lindsey gave a little shriek.

"Clear the road, right now."

Tag heard cars start; he crept closer to the edge. Brandon was holding Lindsey by the hair. Lindsey's throat was bleeding; blood and water soaked her white uniform.

It was the last straw.

He had the range.

Hot rage turned cold, blowing his uncertainties away. Tag stepped out from behind the arch. The small pistol was steady in his hand.

He had the choice between a shot to the head and a shot to the shoulder.

He looked into Brandon's eyes.

Brandon's mouth curved into a sneer that said 'you don't have the balls to shoot.'

It wasn't his job to negotiate with terrorists. Tag smiled, his job was to kill them.

He inhaled – and fired.

Brandon lurched backwards in a spray of blood and brain, taking Lindsey down with him.

Lindsey saw Tag come around the corner. She never heard the shot. Brandon jerked backwards, knocked her to the pavement. Hot blood and worse sprayed her, burning her skin, soaking her clothing. Brandon's body twitched under her. She screamed, shoving his arm away. The smell of blood followed her as she scrambled to get away.

The police moved forward, guns drawn. Lindsey ducked and ran to her right. Blinded by blood and rain, utterly panicked she ran right into Tag.

They lost their balance on the wet pavement, fell hard behind a parked car. Lindsey fought to get away, but Tag pressed her against his chest.

"Stay down." Tag blocked her from looking back. "Don't look!"

She didn't.

They scrambled across the sidewalk. He brought her to cover. They crouched in a doorway, out of the rain. He guarded her shivering body with his own.

"You all right?" He touched her throat; his hand came away bloody. "Shallow," he said with a sigh.

"Let me up!" Lindsey twisted, shoved against his chest with all her strength.

"Stay down." Tag held her down. Sirens suddenly screamed from all directions.

"Tag, you shot him!" Lindsey was near hysteria.

"What did you expect?" Tag's face was set, hard, his voice callous.

"Will you go to jail?" She tried to calm herself, tried to be like him.

"You're alive, that's all I care about." Tag dismissed killing Brandon like swatting a fly. He gathered Lindsey against his chest. "I couldn't let him hurt you."

"It's my fault," she murmured.

Tag set the gun down, took her face in his hands, looking straight into her eyes.

"No. It was him or you. Don't ever forget that." Tag looked up at the police officer walking towards them. He pushed the gun farther away from them.

"She all right?" It was the senior officer. He watched Tag carefully, his gun holstered at his side. He motioned for Tag to get up.

"Pretty much." Tag got up then helped Lindsey stand. "The cuts are shallow."

"That your gun?" The officer asked, pointing at the black pistol.

"No," Tag said. "It belongs to the DEA agent." He motioned back toward the restaurant where two DEA agents were picking Shawn up off the pavement.

The three of them walked to the restaurant. There was a small crowd gathering. Lindsey was shuddering, clinging to Tag as they stepped back into the pouring rain. The officer took her other arm, with their support she was able to go back inside her restaurant.

"How long were you in Iraq?"

"Thirty months." Tag added. "Sir."

"Don't sir me, boy, I was a non-com." The officer scowled at him.

Lindsey cowered against Tag, not sure if she was afraid for Tag or afraid of him. Between these two men, she felt small and helpless. Her teeth were chattering. She clamped her jaw shut.

Tag eased Lindsey into a chair, bloody water dripped off her clothes onto the floor. Tag whipped off his t-shirt. He folded it and gave it to Lindsey.

"Here, put this over the wound, press hard." He showed her the amount of pressure to use.

"You'd better come to the station when this is over." The officer's face was stone cold. He made no move to arrest Tag.

"I'll come," Tag said.

"Do that."

The officer glanced at the scene outside. Police and DEA officers swarmed like ants around the parking lot. An ambulance arrived, lights on, sirens silent. Mychou was being put into a van, with two other men.

"Lindsey, are you all right?" Shawn was sitting at one of the tables, clutching his stomach. Blood covered Shawn's hands and the front of his shirt. Two DEA agents supported him.

"Shawn!" Tag shifted. "Shit, are you okay?"

"He cut me in half, do I look okay?" Blood dripped from the wound at his side.

"He's still sucking air," one of the agents joked.

"Getting stabbed sucks." Shawn looked at the scars on Tag's arm and torso. "You look like raw meat."

"Iraq was hell." Tag shrugged.

"I didn't know I could bleed so much." Shawn tried to shake it off, turning to Lindsey. "Lindsey, I'm sorry. I couldn't tell you why I was here." He was gray with shock. "I told them you had nothing to do with the drugs."

"Brandon was selling drugs," Lindsey said softly to Tag. "Right under my nose.'

"It was both of them," Shawn said. 'They put dope in sugar packets so Mychou could pass the drugs unnoticed and the money would look like tips. They didn't get away, did they?"

"The police have Mychou." Lindsey glanced at Tag. "Brandon is dead."

"Dead?" Shawn looked shocked. "You killed him?"

"What did you think I was going to do with the gun?"

"Shit man, I never thought you would kill him."

"What do you think I've been doing in Iraq?" Tag demanded. "You think I lost my leg playing paintball?" He indicated the scars on his body. "I was fighting insurgents and running real missions while you and your amateur squad of idiots were pretending to be soldiers. This is the most screwed up operation I've ever seen."

"Why don't you come out some time and show us how it's supposed to be done?" Shawn challenged then groaned. "Jesus this hurts."

"Hey." Lindsey tugged on Tag's arm. "Critique it later."

"I'm sorry." Shawn's eyes were glazing from shock. "It wasn't supposed to go down this way. We planned to take down Brandon at his apartment on Saturday."

Lindsey sucked in a breath, almost a sob.

Tag turned to Lindsey. "It wasn't your fault," he said, the anger was now alarm. Tag put his arm around Lindsey, held her close. She hid her face against his chest.

"Don't waste any guilt over Brandon," Shawn said. "He was trying to pin the whole thing on you and Heather. He was forging your signatures to get the chemicals."

Tag and Lindsey exchanged a look.

"I knew that," Lindsey said. "But how did you find out?"

"I have sources," Shawn said with the ghost of a smile, then changed the subject. "You know Brandon was turning somersaults trying to get hooked up with Lindsey. He was so pissed when she shut him down." Shawn smiled at Tag. "I realized when you came in why Brandon was striking out. He couldn't compete."

"Save the bullshit for the nurses," Tag growled.

"Your ride is here," the officer said to Shawn, as two ambulances pulled up. Two EMT's helped Shawn into an ambulance. Another EMT came over to check Lindsey out. She pronounced Lindsey in shock, and wrapped gauze round her throat to stop the bleeding. The EMT and Tag got her wrapped in a thin blanket, just as the police came back to ask questions. Lindsey felt numb. She answered all the questions mechanically.

The senior police officer came back.

"There is a TV truck on the way. I want her out of here." The officer motioned Tag to get going. "Take her home. She doesn't need to be part of the circus. A squad car will follow you. You can come back to the station later."

"Sounds good to me, I'll get my truck." Tag walked out of the restaurant.

Was this the end of the nightmare? Lindsey closed her eyes.

Chapter 20

Tag came back after a couple of minutes. She let him lead her outside to his truck.

"You want to go to the ER?"

"No, just take me home."

A squad car followed them all the way to Sonora. Tag pulled into Heather's driveway, helped Lindsey out of the truck. Lindsey's family was on the porch, behind Jim, Heather, Eleanor and Travis waited.

"What happened?" Jim looked at Tag and the officer who had pulled in behind them.

"In a minute, Lindsey is in shock." Tag helped Lindsey out of the car. She was cold and shivering, her vision blurred. Tag handed Lindsey to her sister then stepped back.

Heather took in the blood, the bandages; Lindsey's frightened face, the way her teeth chattered and she shivered convulsively.

"I've got you," Heather said, putting one arm around Lindsey's shoulders.

Lindsey stopped by her father, laid a bloody hand on his arm.

"Don't leave him alone," she said softly. "He shot Brandon."

Her father slanted a glance at Tag, nodding.

Her hand left a bloodstain on his arm. Lindsey fought a wave of nausea.

"I need a shower."

"Right," Heather agreed, she went into the bathroom with Lindsey; helped wash the blood from her hair. Lindsey got out of the shower only when the water ran cold. She dried off, slipping into a sweat suit of

Heather's. She wrapped her hair in a towel, not wanting to touch it. Even after five washings, she was afraid it wasn't clean.

Eleanor was in the kitchen making sweet tea. Lindsey didn't see her father or Tag, but she could hear them. Lindsey peeked around the corner; they were on the front porch, still talking to the police officer. She retreated to the safety of Heather's bedroom. She sat on Heather's bed, shivering. In a while her father came to check on her. He handed her a tall glass of tea that smelled of bourbon.

"Here." Jim's voice was very gentle. "Drink up."

"Is Tag all right?" she asked as she sipped from the glass. The bourbon burned all the way down; Lindsey made a face. She'd be falling down drunk if she drank the whole glass. Well, being sedated sounded good right now.

"As long as you're okay, he'll be fine." Her father looked at Lindsey. He understood Tag better than she did, because they were alike in so many ways. Her father had served two tours in Vietnam as Tag has served in Iraq. Her father had killed men, too. "He did the right thing today. You need to be clear on that, for his sake."

Lindsey nodded. Tag had saved her from a horrible death.

"I'm going to take Tag back to E'town. Do you want me to check on the restaurant?"

"Yes, I have keys – somewhere. Just lock everything up."

Jim sent Travis to find her keys before he and Tag went back to the police station. Lindsey lay down. Travis stayed with her while Heather started supper. Travis lay at the foot of the bed; they had the television on.

Lindsey was back in the arms of her family but her feelings were all over the place. She had set this horrible disaster off when she called the police. She was alive only because Tag had killed Brandon. Lindsey let herself mourn for Brandon, he'd been goofy and fun to work with, a cunning thief who had used her to make drugs, and the crazed addict who would have killed her without hesitation.

How could one person be all those things, all those people? She was sorry that she had hired him, sorry that she hadn't fired him at the first sign of trouble. More than sorry of the way it ended: with Brandon's gloating voice in her ear, his blood and brains splattered all over her like some foul paint.

It *was* her fault. Scalding water would not wash the guilt from her soul.

Yet she was glad – glad to be alive, glad Brandon was dead; glad Tag had shot him. She knew Brandon would have killed her, the minute she stopped being useful. He would have cut her throat, left her to die in the street.

It was the stuff of a lifetime of nightmares.

The glass of bourbon and tea left her drowsy. She passed a couple hours between sleeping and waking, as she waited for Tag and her father to return home. Lindsey was bleary from the bourbon and half-asleep when the news came on.

"Hey, Aunt Lindsey, look at this," Travis said pointing to the TV. "It's your restaurant."

"We are live in downtown Elizabethtown." The reporter, a woman, was standing outside Lindsey's restaurant. "This peaceful community has been shocked by what a witness described as 'a drug bust gone bad.' Police officers were called to this tiny restaurant only a few hours ago, responding to a report alleging drugs had been sold inside. When they arrived, two men fled; a third man, who may have worked at the restaurant, took the owner, Lindsey Bennett hostage. Lucy Taylor was there when it happened."

They cut to the reporter and a young blond woman, one of the customers. "Well, I come here for lunch almost every day. Today the police came in, real quiet, just strolled in. That's when these two guys at the first table bolted for the back door." The woman was breathless with excitement. "I heard the bus boy holler out."

"They took the bus boy out on a stretcher." The witness shuddered. "It looked like he'd been shot, poor guy."

"Then what happened?"

"Well, Ms. Lindsey has this cook, Brandon his name was, who would have thought he was a doper? Anyway, Brandon comes out from behind the counter and grabs Ms. Lindsey. He dragged her out of her own restaurant by the hair. He had a big old butcher knife to her throat and he was just a screaming at the cops 'I'll cut her throat, I'll cut her throat'"

"Then what happened?" The reporter asked.

"I ducked under the table," Lucy said. "I couldn't look no more. I was too scared, I prayed for Ms. Lindsey. Then I heard a gunshot."

"According to another witness Brandon Pendleton forced Ms. Bennett out of the restaurant where he was surrounded by the police." The reporter toned down her enthusiasm for the next part.

"In a fortunate turn of events, a bystander assisted the police in successfully neutralizing Pendleton, freeing Ms. Bennett."

"We asked Officer Dalton to identify the man." The picture cut to the senior police officer.

"Can you tell us who saved Ms. Bennett?"

"Sergeant McTaggart, I believe he'd just come home from his second tour in Iraq. He had the training and experience needed to get Ms. Bennett free unharmed." Officer Dalton's face was set in grim, hard lines.

"Do you know what chance had brought Sergeant McTaggart to the restaurant today?" The reporter asked.

"I believe he came in for lunch." The officer's grim face lightened slightly. "I've eaten here a time or two, myself."

The picture cut back to the reporter.

"A witness who prefers to be nameless told us that it was due to the Sergeant's quick thinking and highly skilled marksmanship that Ms. Bennett was able to escape with only minor injuries." She became solemn. "Unfortunately, Brandon Pendleton was pronounced dead at the scene." The screen was filled with a clip of blood on the pavement.

"A number of people are being held for questioning, both in the hostage situation and as suspects, in a methamphetamine manufacturing ring." The reporter seemed pleased with herself. "This is Mary Murphy reporting to you from Elizabethtown, Kentucky. Back to you, Bob."

Travis hit the mute button. "I guess that makes you famous, doesn't it?"

"More like infamous," Lindsey said. "It's the worst kind of publicity."

"Was that true, Aunt Lindsey? Did your cook hurt you?" Travis sat up.

"Yes." Lindsey nodded. "That's where I got the cuts on my throat."

"Did Tag shoot him?" Travis asked, his eyes as wide as saucers, his voice awed.

Lindsey wanted to lie to him, deny everything. Common sense made her tell the truth.

"Brandon said he was going to kill me. He had a knife at my throat. I believed him, the police believed him, Tag believed him too."

Brandon had been a clown and a pain in the rump, but he shouldn't have died like that. It was the drugs of course. The meth made him crazy. Her eyes filled with tears. Travis scooted across the bed to hug her.

"You were all bloody when you came home, was that his blood on you?"

"A lot of it." Lindsey did not want to have this conversation with her nephew. She heard the phone ring in the other room. "I can't tell you anything else or your Momma will beat me like a snake, understand?"

"Momma can't blame you for what was on TV." Travis grinned. "I'll ask Tag when he comes back."

Lindsey rolled her eyes.

"If he comes back," she told Travis. "He may go to jail because of me."

"Tag saved you." Travis was outraged. "They can't put him in jail!"

"The law isn't always fair." Lindsey heard the phone ring again. Could that be her father or Tag? Lindsey got up then peeked out the door.

"I'm sorry," Heather's voice was cold. "She isn't taking calls. I'm sure you understand. Good bye." She glared at the handset.

"Stupid reporters."

"It was on TV," Lindsey said, quietly coming out to the dining room. "Channel 11 was broadcasting live from the restaurant."

"Oh hell," Heather said. "I'm sorry Lindsey."

"Aunt Lindsey is famous." Travis followed Lindsey. "Will the TV people come here?"

The sisters exchanged a horrified look.

"I hope not," Lindsey said.

"I won't let them bother you." Heather vowed. "I'll run them off with a shotgun."

"They know about Tag too," Travis said. "They showed the blood on the sidewalk and everything."

"You saw that?" She walked over to Travis, her hands out to embrace him. "Oh, my God, baby. You shouldn't have seen that."

"I'm not a baby." Travis ducked her out-stretched hand. "Besides I saw Aunt Lindsey come home covered in blood. That was worse. It smelled bad."

Heather looked at her son and sighed; there wasn't much she could say.

The phone rang.

"What's going on?" Eleanor asked, coming out of her bedroom with her walker. "Who's on the phone?"

Heather held up her hand then answered the phone.

"Hello?" Heather rolled her eyes. "I'm sorry; she can't come to the phone." Heather listened for a moment. "She's okay, just shook up. I'll tell her. Goodbye." Heather turned back to them. "Neighbors, asking if you were all right. They mean well, but they just want to gossip." Heather looked at the answering machine.

"One thing I learned when Rich died, when the phone rings off the hook it's time to screen calls." She pressed a few buttons. "That should do it. We won't even hear the phone ring."

"What if Dad calls?" Lindsey asked.

"Have you got your cell?" Heather asked.

"Yes." Lindsey looked around for her purse. "I don't know."

"It was in your uniform," Heather said. "I think."

"I'll get it." Lindsey looked until she found it on the bathroom floor, next to the bucket where Lindsey's restaurant whites were soaking in bleach. The water was red. Lindsey shuddered. She would throw them away when Heather wasn't looking. She washed her hands twice before she left the bathroom.

Heather was in the dining room with Travis.

"That's disgusting." Lindsey shuddered. "I wonder how many people saw me like that?" Once again, her eyes filled with tears. "Damn, damn, damn, how could he be so stupid?"

Heather hugged Lindsey and let her cry.

"How can I be sorry he's dead and glad at the same time?" Lindsey sobbed. "I feel like I'm being torn in half."

"Feel what you feel." Heather let go of Lindsey. "You're my sister, I love you. I thought he was an arrogant prick." The answering machine kicked on. "I don't even want to be in the same room with that thing." Heather pointed at the phone. "Come on, Lindsey back to bed. Travis, check on your grandmother for me, please."

Lindsey downed the rest of the bourbon and tea. She curled up under the comforter, switching the channel so she wouldn't have to watch the news. She fell asleep. When she woke up, she went looking for her father and Tag. She found Heather in the living room.

"Aren't they back, yet?"

"Yes. They are on the patio, drinking bourbon," Heather said. "Dad's got Tag's car keys, he's not going anywhere. Dad said you'll stay here tonight, too." Heather's eyes glinted, a shadow of their father. "You can sleep in my room."

"Okay." Lindsey heard voices – her father, Tag, then her mother. Lindsey walked out the French doors to the patio, under the pergola.

"Why didn't you come to us with this?" Eleanor's voice was sharp. "This disaster could have been prevented."

"Hind sight is twenty-twenty." Tag shrugged. "I thought it would blow over."

"Blow over?" Eleanor shook her head. "Our daughter could have been killed."

"I know that, ma'am. I was there." Tag had his back against the wall. Lindsey couldn't see his face. Her father saw her come out of the house.

"Eleanor," Jim interrupted. "As much as I agree that someone should have come to us, I don't think Tag is to blame." He was looking at Lindsey. "Come out here, girl, you have some explaining to do."

Lindsey walked out to the patio, taking a seat at Tag's side.

"Why didn't you come to us?"

"I didn't have any proof until today," she said to her parents. "There was so much going on, with you, Mom, with Heather, then all the work in the garden." She slanted a glance at Tag. "I saw Brandon put drugs in a take-out box today. I think I have a picture on my cell."

Eleanor had her lips pressed together. Jim nodded, his hands steepled in front of his face. Lindsey concentrated on telling the story to her father's hands, not looking into his eyes. She had kept so much from him that she felt guilty for it.

"Shawn saw me with the box. He threatened me." Lindsey was talking with her hands. "I called the police then I sent a text message to Tag. I thought I could be rid of the bunch of them. I wasn't expecting – what happened."

"You didn't come to me," Jim said to Lindsey, his tone was regretful.

"You were worried about Mom." Lindsey's excuse for keeping secrets sounded feeble, foolish. Lindsey cringed inside. She had been wrong. "I'm sorry."

Jim shook his head. He turned to Tag. "You should have had more sense than to just run blindly into trouble."

"I didn't know what was going on, sir." Tag rattled the ice cubes in his glass. "The text on my cell phone said: 'SOS, come now.' The square was blocked off by DEA when I got there. I went looking for Lindsey."

"I need a refill. Honey, do you need a refill?" Jim indicated the bottle of bourbon, pouring more for Eleanor and himself. "Tag, how about it?"

Tag took another splash of bourbon, filling his glass with water.

"Lindsey?"

"I'm already half drunk," Lindsey admitted.

"This once won't hurt you," Jim said with just the touch of a smile.

In the relaxed atmosphere, Lindsey was able to tell the whole story. How Mychou's lawyer had blackmailed her into taking the woman back. She even told them about the invoices. Lindsey used the story as a peace offering. Her parents exchanged some pointed glances, but they listened.

Eventually, Heather served dinner, they all sat down at the table, but Lindsey couldn't eat. She went back to bed, then waited until evening to talk to Tag.

When the house was silent, she slipped out of her sister's bed into the living room. Tag lay on the couch, one arm across his face, the other at his side. Below the knee, the left leg of his jeans was empty. His artificial leg was by the couch.

Lindsey saw a man wounded by fate, permanently disabled in body, perhaps disabled in mind as well. He was a combat veteran, post traumatic stress disorder was a neat, tidy label for a host of problems. Problems that he would live with for the rest of his life.

She could no more erase the scars on his mind than she could erase the ones on his body.

She had seen the smile on his face as he shot Brandon. Lindsey shuddered. She never, ever wanted to have a gun pointed at her again.

What if Tag had missed?

What if he hadn't been there?

She brought her hand to her throat where the cuts still stung. Brandon would have killed her. Cut her throat like slaughtering a lamb. What a horrible way to die.

"Lynn?" Tag didn't move.

She could walk away.

"Is this it then?" He lay there, his arm over his face.

Lindsey hesitated, what did she want? Why had she come?

She had come to be with him.

"I'm here." She crossed the room to kneel by the couch, by his side.

"What now?" He asked in a low voice, his face still covered. "If it is over, tell me. Don't leave me hanging."

It was tempting to lie. Pretend she didn't understand. It was a fair question. Could she love him, having seen him kill a man before her eyes? He had done it to save her. It did not stop her from remembering the horror, a knife at her throat, and a bullet striking inches from her head.

"Talk to me." There was agony in his voice.

Lindsey licked her lips, not knowing how to put it into words. Fear was still a knot in her gut. "I don't know what to say."

"It was him or you." Tag shrugged. "He got what he deserved."

The fact that he kept his face hidden was irritating her. Why couldn't he face her?

"It can't be that easy," Lindsey said softly, her eyes stung.

"Easy?" Tag was silent for a moment.

Was he remembering? There had to be pain in his heart, somewhere. Was that what he was hiding: guilt, remorse? He'd drunk too much bourbon and had too much time to think.

"But it is," Tag said bitterly. "You know that now. I am a killer. Will you be afraid of me? Will I see fear when I look into your eyes? Lynn, I can't live like that."

"Stop talking like an idiot." Lindsey poked him.

He moved his arm, looked at her finally. There was anguish in his face, fear in his eyes. How many times had he been on the wrong side of a gun?

The absence of fear was stupidity, not courage. She was beginning to understand that, more than she liked. What was it about the deep hours of the night? She had felt it: surety was vanquished by doubt, confidence turned to fear.

"You know me better than that." Lindsey said, letting her voice drop. "I'm not some silly bimbo who's afraid of her own shadow. I was raised an Army brat. I'm not afraid of you."

"Why not?" It was almost a challenge.

"You are a soldier, like my father, like Rich." She struggled to put it into words. "I've lived my whole life around soldiers. I know, somewhat, what it means. You do what you have to do, even if it means killing someone. You did the right thing." Her father told her that she needed to be clear about that. "I'd be dead otherwise."

"Come here, Lynn." Tag sat up, opened his arms for her. She snuggled against him; felt him exhale his tension. He smelled faintly of bourbon, of sweat. If worry had a scent, he smelled of that too. For a long moment he held her, his cheek against her hair.

"Are you all right?"

"No, I'm – not," she said, giving him truth instead of white lies. Tears ran down her face, she shuddered and pressed harder against his broad chest.

"You are safe now." He stroked her hair. "Nobody is going to hurt you."

"Will you have to go to jail?" She asked in a small voice.

"No." His voice changed to soft and reassuring. "They were glad that you didn't get hurt."

"Why not?" Lindsey moved slightly, relaxing.

"In a hostage situation, all the rules change. When Brandon picked up the knife, he became fair game." The shadows were back in his face, but there was no regret. "I'll go to trial, the grand jury will dismiss it. That will be a couple months down the road. The important thing is that you are all right." He touched the bandage at her throat. "I went nuts when I saw you bleeding."

"I set the whole thing off, when I called the police." Lindsey sank back into guilt and misery.

"It wasn't your fault," he reminded her. "You needed to get them out of the restaurant. You did. That part is over." They were silent, 'when this is over' had been their magic phrase for the last few weeks. Yet it was far from over.

"What a mess." She sniffed. "I don't know – it was horrible." Lindsey took a deep breath. "What made you think of – how did you…" She didn't know how to phrase it. She looked up at him.

"If Shawn hadn't given me the gun, I would have taken one. I couldn't let him hurt you, not when I could take him out." He hugged her. "I could see the shot. I knew I could do it. I've done it before." Tag took a deep breath. "We were in so many firefights, in Falluja and Baghdad. We learned to make some tricky shots. It was that or die."

"I thought Shawn was one of them, until he tried to stop Brandon."

"DEA fits Shawn better than busboy." He stroked her hair. "It's a dangerous game."

"If the people who bought the drugs find out who Shawn really works for...." Lindsey said softly. "He wasn't arrested with Mychou He was taken to the hospital."

"Shawn is a grown man, he can handle it." Tag sighed. "I'm glad that you are safe."

"It's wrong to feel like this." Her voice dropped to a faint vibration. "I'm glad you shot him, I'm glad he's dead."

"It's okay to feel that way," he said. "You have to get through it."

"My father said he would have done the same thing." She clutched his shirt.

"Without hesitation." Tag nodded.

Lindsey relaxed; she was safe with Tag. She lay against his chest, listening to his heartbeat. Eventually he spoke again.

"What about the restaurant?" Tag asked. "Are you going to re-open it?"

"Open it, but not tomorrow. I need some time off."

"Time off sounds like a good idea," Tag agreed. "Let me know when you decide to go back, I'll come with you, if you like."

"Moron support?" Lindsey joked.

"Sure, I'm getting good at playing the supportive boyfriend." He sighed. "It's going to be all over the news."

"It was on Channel Eleven already." Lindsey shuddered. "You should have seen the news tonight. They made you look like Captain America."

"I can use the good press." He squeezed her a bit closer. "There will be hell to pay tomorrow."

"I'm going to lay low. Maybe I can duck the reporters."

"Lots of luck."

They were silent. There would be more reporters, more questions. The legal tangle would take months to straighten out. There was work to do at the restaurant; new employees she would have to hire and train. But right now, this moment, she was alive and Tag was here with her. Somehow, they would muddle through.

Eventually Lindsey left him. She drank the last of the bourbon and tea so she could get to sleep. In the morning when she awoke Tag was gone.

Chapter 21

Heather drove Lindsey to the restaurant the next afternoon. It was wonderful to have her sister 'back'.

The fire department scoured the parking lot, so no trace of that part of the tragedy remained. Fortunately, the restaurant felt just as familiar as it had for the last two years. Lindsey felt no lingering fear, but sorrow cut deep. They poured bleach water on the bloodstains, cleared the tables, threw away spoiled food, made a list of what needed to be done. Lindsey decided to repaint. A fresh coat of paint in a new color would brighten the place up.

The answering machine was blinking furiously. Lindsey looked at it once.

"What do I do?" Lindsey asked.

"Delete them all," Heather said ruthlessly. "Listening to them will drive you nuts."

There was a knock at the door. Heather swore.

"Hide in the bathroom. I'll send them away." It was the beverage delivery, so Heather took the order and paid the invoice.

"This is stupid," Lindsey said, as she came out of the bathroom. "I can't live this way."

"So pick one reporter, talk to them and tell the rest to go away." Heather grinned. "It worked for me."

"I'll have to think about that." Lindsey didn't want to talk about it. She just wanted to forget it ever happened. She changed the subject. "Are you coming back to work?"

Heather stashed the receipt under the coin drawer. "Actually, I wasn't planning on it." She took a deep breath. "I've been talking to a support group on the Internet, other women who lost their husbands while they were on active duty."

"Really?" Lindsey was intrigued.

"I'm thinking about going back to school. There is a nursing program, a teacher's program and an office management program here at the college. I'm not sure which one I'll end up taking. Nursing is a good paying job." Heather swept her hand over her hair. "I think it's time for me to get on with my life."

"That seems to be going around." Lindsey smiled.

"What about you and Tag?" Heather asked then looked down at the floor. "I was wrong about him."

"I don't know." Lindsey shook her head. "It's too soon to tell."

Saturday morning, Tag showed up at her door. He was dressed for work in old jeans and ratty t-shirt. Still the sight of him cheered her up. He handed her a cup of her favorite coffee.

"I came to help out. What needs done?"

"The restaurant needs painted."

"I'm up for it," Tag said.

"I'll get my purse. We can go now, if you don't mind."

"I'll drive." They got in his truck.

"Where have you been?" Lindsey asked.

"At the hospital," Tag said with a sour expression. "They were 'concerned' about me." He emphasized the word with a slight curl to his lip. "Somebody told them I was playing Rambo on Main Street."

Lindsey winced.

"I'm on a short leash." He snorted.

"It can't be too bad, they turned you loose," Lindsey teased.

"I proved that I can play well with others." Tag rolled his eyes.

At the restaurant, Lindsey mopped the floor with bleach water, just to be sure it was completely clean. Tag prepared the walls. They painted the walls light yellow. Around one o'clock, she set down the paint bucket. It was time for some lunch.

"Take a break," Lindsey called. "I'll feed us."

"Good idea." Tag set the roller down, wiped off his hands as he followed her to the kitchen. Lindsey poked around the coolers, set Tag washing vegetables while she chopped up the filling. She whipped up two omelets, set two places at the counter, served up everything just the way she wanted it.

But she just stared at her food.

"Are you okay?"

"Brandon cooked the last omelet that I ate." Lindsey rubbed her forehead. "I'm not sure how I can feel two conflicting emotions at the same time." She looked at him, her face heavy with sadness. "It's giving me a headache."

"It's the bleach," Tag joked. "Enough disinfectant in the air to choke an elephant." He attacked his omelet. "This would be perfect with home fries." Tag slid a glance at her. "A huge heaping plate fried in butter, doused in ketchup and ranch dressing."

"Heart attack food." Lindsey smiled. "You'd drop dead of a coronary the next time you lifted anything heavier than a soda."

Tag lifted his soda then clutched his chest, rolled his eyes, slumping over his plate. He spoiled the performance by grinning at her.

"First class Oscar material." She giggled. "We'll fly you to Hollywood as soon as you finish painting."

Tag straightened up; his blue eyes sparkled with mischief. The quirk to his smile and the scar on his cheek made him devilishly handsome. He turned back to his omelet.

"Not bad. You should try it."

Lindsey watched him eat, tried the omelet and found she was very hungry.

"I'm getting tired of feeling conflicted," Lindsey said. "Just once, I want to be positive about something. I feel like I'm acting all the time." She savored the omelet. "Maybe I'll join you in Hollywood, I could use a vacation."

"I've been to Hollywood, it's full of tall, skinny blondes." Tag winked. "I'm partial to petite brunettes."

Lindsey blushed in spite of herself.

"Flattery will get you everywhere, eventually."

"Yeah?" Tag grinned. "How about an outdoor concert at Freeman Lake? I've got tickets."

"A concert?"

"With fireworks."

"Sure, when?"

"A week from today, six to eleven." He watched her reaction. "It's a picnic, on the grass down by the lake; a blanket under the stars with a couple of thousand other people."

"Cozy," she remarked with a smile. "If we get this done, I'll be able to go."

"That a deal or a dare?" Tag asked.

"Both." Lindsey laughed. "We still have hours of work to do yet."

They finished eating when there was a knock at the door.

"Well, open the door!" Rose waved, smiling.

"Hey!" Lindsey opened the door. "It's great to see you." She gave Rose a hug. "Come in, come in."

Rose put her hand on her hips and regarded Tag as one would an errant child.

"Give me some sugar, boy, or you are in a heap of trouble."

Tag laughed and gave Rose a hug and kiss on the cheek.

"Rose, it is good to see you," he said.

"Oh, you are sight for sore eyes." She inspected the scar on his face, then the ones on his arms, shaking her head and tsk – tsking. "Lord you are lucky to be alive, son."

"Yeah." Tag nodded, stepping back to stand next to Lindsey.

"You didn't call me when you got back in town," Rose scolded. "I had to hear it from Shawn." She looked around. "Where is he?" She stepped outside and beckoned. "He got out of the hospital today, I'm bringing him home."

Lindsey flicked a glance at Tag, raising an eyebrow. Tag shrugged, but he had lost the delighted smile he'd given Rose. Shawn came in, leaning on a twelve-year-old boy who looked exactly like Shawn except his skin was caramel-colored, not milk-chocolate. Shawn nodded to Lindsey then sat on a stool by the counter. Rose slid into a booth. Lindsey brought iced tea for everyone. Tag stood by the counter, his arms crossed over his chest, his eyes hooded, his face expressionless.

"Good to see you, Lindsey." Shawn smiled ruefully as he pressed his hand to his stomach.

"I figured you would be here." Shawn said to Tag.

"Where she goes, I go." Tag shrugged.

Rose cleared her throat then looked from Tag to Shawn's son.

"This is your namesake, Kevin, meet Kevin." The boy looked at Tag a moment before he stepped up to shake hands.

"Call me Tag." Tag smiled as they shook hands. "That way nobody gets confused."

"He got all the looks, didn't he?" Tag looked at Shawn.

"Of course he's good looking, he looks just like me." Shawn gave Tag a big grin. That broke the ice. They both relaxed.

"What are you doing working for DEA?" Tag asked. "I thought you were going to be a hot-shot lawyer and make the big money."

"When Kevin's mother got arrested, I thought my world had come to an end." Shawn shook his head. "She's been in and out of jail for the last ten years. I'm after her dealers and the big fish, the suppliers."

"Brandon was a small fish, but I met some of his people along the way. It might be worth getting stabbed over." He gave Lindsey a wry half smile.

"I see you are keeping better company these days." Rose flicked a look at Tag. "You've got a good one this time. Don't screw it up."

"I don't intend to." Tag laughed and turned red, he put his arm around Lindsey's shoulders and pulled her close.

"The place looks better." Rose gave Lindsey a thoughtful look. "Nice paint job."

"We've been busy. It was a mess." Lindsey smiled a little sadly. She brushed a lock of hair back from her face, wincing a little when she brushed one of the cuts on her neck. Rose noticed the gesture.

"The Lord was looking out for you." Rose shook her head. "Nasty, ugly business." No one spoke for a moment. "I would imagine that you are looking for help again."

"Unfortunately." Lindsey shrugged. "In all honesty, if I could do it all myself, I wouldn't hire a soul. I'm a lousy judge of character."

"Well, I may be able to help you out." Rose acted like she had just been given a cue. "I know a young couple who just came up from Texas. They are from New Orleans, lost everything in Katrina. The church has put them up for a few days, but they both need jobs."

"I don't know." Lindsey shook her head. "I'd have to talk to them."

"Good idea." Rose gave young Kevin a nudge. "Go get Sam and Vicky for me."

Lindsey gave Rose a questioning look.

"Well, I have this big old house, it's just the three of us." Rose smiled at Lindsey. "Lindsey, I can vouch for these two. They are good kids."

Sam was a thin young black man. He smiled at Lindsey and Tag but looked to Rose for direction. Vickie's toffee-colored skin had that glowing vitality that women get when they are pregnant. She had a round belly, seemed to be mid-way through her pregnancy.

"Sam, Vickie, this is Lindsey," Rose introduced them. "That scamp with the big grin is Tag."

"I'm pleased to meet you," Sam said, shaking hands. "Rose has been kind enough to help us out." He hugged his wife. "We've only been here for a few weeks."

"Sam's family owned a restaurant just outside of New Orleans," Rose told them. "He's been looking for a job."

"Was it Cajun food?" Lindsey asked, intrigued. "Gumbo and crawdads?" She saw Rose and Tag exchange a satisfied look. "There isn't much call for that around here."

"Don't forget the barbecue." Sam smiled, showing white teeth against his dark skin. "It was just a little place, but we did real well."

"This place is really small," Vickie said, looking around. "Miss Rose says you do pretty good business."

"It's mostly carry out," Lindsey said.

"I was a waitress," Vickie said. "I worked for Sam's family." She looked down, almost a blush. "That was where we met."

"I know that you've been through some terrible times." Rose grasped Lindsey's hand. "Sometimes it works like that. But I think you, Sam and Vickie will do real well together, if you give them a chance."

Lindsey smiled then gave Rose a big hug. "Rose, you're an angel."

"No," Rose said with a twinkle in her eyes. "I'm no angel, but I've got connections."

Lindsey giggled, looking at the young couple. "Come on and have a seat. I'll get you some ice tea and we can talk about it."

Tag followed her behind the counter.

"Were you one of Rose's boys?" She asked as she got a couple of glasses off the shelf. Tag leaned back against the cooler, his half-smile changed to a broad grin.

"Yes," he admitted. "Shawn dragged me home with him so many times, I about lived with them. Rose called me 'tag-along' until it stuck."

"It looks like all my prayers have been answered."

"All of them?" Tag gave her a look that was pure hot lust.

"Almost." Lindsey returned the look.

There had been no time for them to be alone.

"We have to take care of that." He brought her close to give her a brief kiss. "Soon."

Chapter 22

The concert was in the evening, just as the heat of the day was fading. The lawn was full of people with folding chairs and tables, some cooking out, others chasing kids around. There were three guys that Tag knew from the hospital with their wives and children. Tag introduced Lindsey to everyone.

"Must be hot in those long pants," Nathan commented. Nathan was also an amputee; he was wearing shorts, walking with a cane. He seemed unconcerned about his metal prosthesis. He moved around slowly, but surely.

"You have no shame," Tag joked.

"I'm sick of that chair." Nathan pointed with his cane to a wheelchair folded against a tree. "I'm determined to lose the cane next." He slanted a glance at his wife, taking care of a toddler. "I'm getting ready to chase this rug rat. Gonna try my hand at being a father instead of a soldier."

They joined this family. Lindsey smiled and chatted from her seat while the afternoon turned into evening. When the music started, Tag sat down with a beer in his hand. Nathan offered one to Lindsey. She declined. They sat shoulder to shoulder listening to music and watching the fireworks. She reached for Tag's hand, felt the reassuring squeeze of his fingers.

Too soon it was over. Before the last of the grand finale fireworks faded from the sky, people were walking back to their cars.

"There is no sense trying to beat the crowd and the traffic on the way out," Tag said. "Let's take a walk down to the pier." So they walked, holding hands, while the crowd thinned out. The cars started up and the traffic jam got into full swing.

They sat on the edge of the pier not too far from the water. He slipped his arm around her. She laid her head against his shoulder. They listened to the car noises fade as the crickets picked up volume.

Lindsey sighed. There had been so much chaos, she wondered if the fallout end would ever end? They hadn't had the chance to do more than talk since everything had gone so wrong. That one exquisite night was a long way in the past.

"Hey." Tag's voice was soft. Lindsey looked up at him. He traced the line of her jaw with his fingers before he kissed her. She adored his restrained kisses more because she knew how much he held back. He ran gentle hands over her back and shoulders. Eager for his touch, she shivered under his trailing fingertips.

Tag left her lips to work his way down her throat. The way she hissed and shivered as he kissed the thin soft skin brought out the wolf in him. He closed his teeth over the juncture of neck and shoulder; she shuddered with pleasure. He traced the indentation of her jugular vein with the tip of his tongue, her back arched against him. A growl of amusement rumbled in his throat. He closed his teeth on her earlobe, just above her earring; his hot breath tickled.

"Tag, please," Lindsey protested. "Not here." Her voice was husky. "There are too many people here."

"Ah hell." He steadied. "You're right, I'm sorry." He drew back, stroking the free locks of hair from her face.

She pressed harder against his chest; she could feel his heart beat. The parking lot was nearly empty, the road was clear.

"Let's get out of here." He suggested. "My place is close." He shifted backwards until they were again looking into each other's eyes. "Will you stay with me tonight?" His voice was low, the tone hungry.

"I – I don't know," her voice cracked. Was she ready to take their relationship to the next phase? Could they go forward, passed the tragic events of last week when next week was going to be more of the same? "Maybe, when this is over."

"Lynn, it's never going to be over." Tag's expression was wry. "There will always be something. That's life."

Lindsey swallowed, looking over his shoulder at the houses across the water. She needed to collect her thoughts.

Trust.

There wasn't a pill that could make it happen. There was no Band-Aid for the bitter lessons handed out by people like Brandon and Tommy. Men who betrayed as a matter of course, as easily as they lived and breathed.

Was she over *her* battles?

"If the answer is 'no' I'll understand. Brandon will never be less dead, and I will always be the man who killed him." The hoarseness of his voice told her just how badly he needed her to accept the past and go forward.

Lindsey looked into his shadowed eyes. She touched his face, tracing the line of his jaw. He had such a strong face, yet his lips were soft as her fingers brushed across them. He was so dear to her, his touch melted her, his voice could soothe her after the most stressful day.

After all this chaos, was there going to be anything of herself left to give to him? He needed someone who could be there for him, always, and in all ways. He had suffered so much; he deserved to be loved. She wanted to love him, but would there be time?

"Talk to me, Lynn." Tag looked worried.

"I don't give a damn about Brandon."

"I thought he was your friend." He looked surprised.

"You were right about him." Lindsey shook her head. "He set me up from day one. The drugs changed him, drove him crazy. The longer I was around him, the more he scared me. I was terrified of him."

"You never told me." Tag asked. "Why not?"

"I didn't know what to do," Lindsey confessed. "I kept it a secret."

"There was plenty we could have done, if you would have told me. You could have trusted me." The set to his mouth and eyebrows spoke more vehemently than his voice.

"I'm sorry," Lindsey said, sincerely. "I never meant to – distrust you. At the time I was afraid to admit that things were so screwed up. I – it was stupid of me."

"I told you that your pride was going to get you into trouble." The growl in his voice told her that he was keeping his temper barely in check.

"You were right," Lindsey said sadly. "It almost got me killed."

"Got that in one." His eyes bored into hers. "Now what?"

"I'm sorry, that it came to – to – such a horrible…" Lindsey's voice fell, she hardly knew how to say it out loud. "It was my fault."

"No." Tag slid his hands to her shoulders, his anger gone. "It wasn't your fault. He could have surrendered at any point, but he didn't." He pulled her against his chest. "I couldn't let him hurt you."

Lindsey relaxed against him, so warm and comforting. The light touch of his hands as he held her close made her skin tingle; made her hyper-aware of him. Her senses were full of him, the slight musk undertone scent of his skin, the movement as he breathed. Lindsey felt all the tension drain from him. Yet there was conflict within her. Half of her wanted to lie down in the grass, pull him down with her, make love there and then.

The more rational half wanted to stay like this forever, motionless, safe. She couldn't have it both ways. She had to choose. It wasn't just *her* choice. It was his as well.

There was tension down her spine that his touch could not ease. Tag might think he was ready, but was he? Was she ready to take on his problems on top of her own?

"Little girl," he breathed in her ear. "Don't duck and run on me."

Lindsey sighed, released her arms from around his waist, looking up. Tag took a breath to speak again, but Lindsey brought her hand to his lips, hushed him with a fingertip. There was one risk she wasn't willing to take as silly as it seemed.

"There is something else," Lindsey said softly. "I'm not on the pill. There hasn't been time to see a doctor." Someday, she wanted his children, but this was not the time. "I can't risk getting pregnant, not now."

"That's why you are hesitating?" The corner of his mouth turned up.

"That's the only reason," Lindsey confessed.

"Fair enough. Come home with me." Tag moved forward to kiss her forehead. His voice was teasing and confident, the shadows were gone. "Everything we need is there: music, wine, and a nice big bed." He grinned. "Everything."

"Sounds like you had this planned," she murmured back.

"Every time we are alone you have this effect on me." He worked the clip out of her hair. "Why would tonight be any different?"

"Oh, good save." Lindsey shook her hair out, so it tumbled to her shoulders in a dark mass of silk. She let it fall across one eye, teasing him. The quirk to his lips and the lust in his eyes thrilled her.

"So?" Tag asked again.

"Okay," she agreed, with a shiver of anticipation.

They walked back to his car, the white Mustang visible in the darkness.

"Give me the keys," Lindsey said quietly, holding out her hand. "I didn't drink tonight."

Tag didn't hesitate; he laid the key in her hand. His apartment was only a few miles up the road. They walked in, hand in hand; he left the door open while he laid a long lingering kiss on her lips.

"This is your last chance to change your mind," Tag told her.

"I'm staying," Lindsey said with a smile.

Tag shut the door behind them. He took her hand, led her to his room. There were candles waiting. She caught the scent of sandalwood and cinnamon, the faint musk under-tone that was his alone.

Lindsey sat on the left side of the bed, waiting for him to come to her. He lit the candles, turning out the lights. Then he sat on the right side of the four-poster bed. For a moment, he just looked at her. Then he took her hand, rubbing his thumb against the back of her fingers. It was a familiar gesture.

He is unsure, Lindsey thought. We are back to trust. She smiled then very slowly took her top off; pleased to watch his eyes darken. As he came across the bed to her, she met him halfway. They kissed sitting up, touching and being touched.

Lindsey took his shirt off; Tag unhooked her bra. He ran his hand over her shoulders. Kissed her shoulder, her throat then teased her breasts, until Lindsey writhed against him. When she put her hands on his jeans, he hesitated.

"Get naked with me." She rubbed her breasts against his chest. "Come on, Tag."

"All right," he said as he let her take his jeans off.

Lindsey expected damaged skin, the scars of burns like a splash mark, from his hip to knee. Instead, she found the outline of a beautifully detailed tattoo. The coloring came up his leg like a wash, stopping a third of the way up his thigh, incomplete.

An armored angel held an American flag. Her armor was battered, her breeches torn; she was bloody, but unbowed. The outlines of streaming hair framed the angel's face: Lindsey's face.

"That is breathtaking." Lindsey's eyes misted, she swallowed the lump in her throat. This was not the time for her to start crying. She wanted to get the rest of his clothes off. She traced the feathers, stroking his thigh, gently tugging at his jeans.

"I don't know what to say."

"You're my angel," Tag said softly, then stroked her jaw with his thumb. They leaned together, kissing tenderly.

"You're hopelessly romantic." Lindsey laughed, shaking her head. That wasn't what she meant, but why get serious now? This was the time to be playful and passionate. She wanted more passion, less talk, but she couldn't resist one more joke.

"I thought you would bleed red, white and blue, but I never thought you would have the Flag tattooed on your tush. Doesn't that take patriotic over the top?"

Tag laughed, a joyful sound. "Maybe." He bent to remove the prosthesis.

Lindsey shed her walking shorts. She thought about the angel, wondered how long it had taken to get that large of a tattoo. Also, she wondered at the amount of pain the needles had given him. It had to hurt to have that much scar tissue tattooed over.

He came up behind her, kissed her neck. She arched against him, letting him run his hands over her. They were nude. Where before she'd sensed his hunger to touch, his kisses now spoke of starvation; of being too long alone, too long denied.

Raw need made his hands shake; he struggled for tenderness, but his touch was rough and demanding. Lindsey had expected the iron control to slip, but not this far, this fast. Tension, not tenderness, in his touch, made her shiver.

"Easy," she implored him, turning to face him. Lindsey's own hunger awakened as she gently traced the hard flesh of his shoulders; inhaled the musk-scent of pheromone-laced sweat as she licked the skin of his throat. She slid her hands against his hot, sweat-slick chest, feeling the ripple of muscle, the wiry hair.

He pressed his teeth against the point of her shoulder, tasting her skin in a sliding open-mouthed bite that made her nerves crackle like popping fireworks. When Tag closed his teeth just under her ear, the electric shock shot down her spine all the way to her curling toes. Lindsey moaned. He laced his fingers through hers, bent her backwards. He flexed against her, a ripple of muscle and dominant power that was overwhelming. He made her feel so small and fragile, it was frightening.

"No, Tag, please!" Breathless and trembling, she stopped him from laying her down and taking control.

"What's wrong, Lynn?" He released her hands, the moment of domination over as quickly as it had come. He looked down into her face with emotions she couldn't name in his heavy-lidded eyes. Tag cupped her face; his teeth grazed her lips. "Tell me, so I can make it right."

"Just not so fast. Okay?" She slid her hands over his slick skin; reveled in his strength, yet wary of it. He was so strong. Would he hurt her?

"I have an idea." Tag shifted, turning, drawing her down with him, on top of him. Until Lindsey lay on his belly like a cat, looking down at him. There was laughter in his eyes. He folded his arms behind his head, displaying the thick muscles of arm, chest and shoulder shamelessly. "Now I'm all yours."

For a moment she was surprised by his total surrender – surrender? Yes that's exactly what it was – total surrender. Then Lindsey slid her leg across his body, straddled his thighs. The control gave her a head rush.

"Be gentle." Tag snickered. "Or not." Candlelight outlined the planes of his face, danced across his chest. His heavy-lidded eyes were dark-blue in the dim light. The smug smile dared her to do what she wanted, whatever she wanted. "Lady's choice, girl. Any way you want me."

Desire flowed over her like a blush. She wanted to breathe the scent of his skin and taste him. She wanted to make him hard and hot; wanted to hear him gasp and groan as she did every sensual thing she could think of.

"You're too clever for your own good." She giggled at switching roles, savoring the freedom, the control he'd handed over to her. She ran her fingers through the hair on his chest, trailed down to his navel and back. She would have to move to do more than that. But she would savor this moment a bit longer.

"What's the matter, girl, never been on top before?" He teased her, tracing her thighs with the tips of his fingers, grinning wickedly. His hands slid to her breasts. He teased them lightly. "Do your worst. I can take it."

Lindsey explored Tag with her hands by candlelight; memorized the play of light and shadow, the hard line of bone and the firm texture of every muscle. She pressed her lips and her teeth against his throat. She gently kissed the names tattooed on his chest, the brand on his shoulder. She traced the width of his chest, the swell of his pecks, the flat slab of his stomach. Tasted his skin as she worked her way down the marvelous muscle structure that was the man she loved.

There was a fierce joy in having his strength and power under her control, to tease and please him. She delighted in every hiss and moan that she wrung from him. She found her way to his most sensitive flesh.

"Oh, girl, you're killing me." Tag moaned and arched, his hands clenched the blankets, crushed them in his fists. It excited her to make him mindless and groaning with pleasure. But Lindsey was careful not to take him too far. She didn't want to risk ruining it for them. She had to stop.

Where was the birth control he'd promised?

"Where are they?" She felt drunk and fuzzy headed with lust. If he didn't know what she meant, she was going to finish him off and to hell with it.

"Nightstand." His voice was hoarse. He waved in the general direction. "There, I think."

Lindsey giggled with triumph; he was in no shape to think. She released him long enough to find what she wanted. The drawer was full of all kinds of interesting things. She was going to have to get back to that, later.

There was an awkward moment when she took care of the birth control issue. She kissed him to get their loving restarted. When she was ready to bring them together, his hands urged and supported her.

"Be careful." Lindsey hissed against his mouth, awash with pleasure that bordered on pain. "It's been a long time." Her voice was breathy, feeling his hard flesh sliding against her soft slickness.

"Nobody ever complained before." He made a satisfied sound, slid his hands to her hips.

"Hush up." She slowly took possession of him.

"Your boyfriend wasn't much of a man, was he?"

"You talk too much." She locked her mouth over his to shut him up.

There was no more coherent speech for a very long time. They made love with a combination of tenderness and explosive passion that rivaled the fireworks at the lake. She learned how he tempered his strength, and gave control over to him willingly. His tenderness wrung her heart, until he had her shrieking with ecstasy. Over and over, they explored each other, from the depths of pleasure to the heights of ecstasy, until they were too exhausted for more.

Deep into the night, sleep found them, left them curled together, dreamless, sated and very much in love.

About the Author

Born on the south shore of Lake Erie, in the city of Ashtabula, Ohio, K. A. Jordan escaped from the Rust Belt to Kentucky in 1992. She writes and blogs from Jordan's Croft, where she lives with her husband, three horses, three dogs and two cats. When she's not writing novels she works as an IT specialist.

She holds a degree in Applied Science, rides American Quarter horses, gardens and can often be found on the back of her husband's Suzuki M109 motorcycle.

She says of her writing: "I write the stories that I want to read and can't find - complex characters, twisty plots and contemporary settings. There are no 'quivering bunnies', 'sniffing dogs' or 'ripped bodices' in any of my fiction, but you might find criminals, wounded heroes, mad artists and an occasional haunted motorcycle."

CPSIA information can be obtained at www.ICGtesting.com
Printed in the USA
LVOW08s1018270714

396232LV00007B/749/P